MOONSHOT

A SCALA TALENT & SPORTS MANAGEMENT NOVEL

NICOLE VIDAL

COPYRIGHT

TABLE OF CONTENTS

KEEP IN TOUCH WITH NV

Facebook (http://fb.me/NicoleVidalAuthor)

Instagram (http://instagram.com/nicolevidal_author)

Amazon (https://www.amazon.com/Nicole-Vidal/e/B082DJHPXP?ref_=dbs_p_ebk_r00_abau_000000)

My website (www.nicolevidal.com)

Pinterest (http://pinterest.com/NicoleVidal_Author)

Goodreads (https://www.goodreads.com/author/show/19827329.Nicole_Vidal)

CHAPTER ONE

COLBY

A chill runs through me as I climb the dugout steps despite the warm fall sun beating down. I'm at peace behind home plate on this freshly manicured field. For the first time since I was a young boy, I could fulfill my dream of winning a World Series. The hard work, discipline, and sacrifices I've made in my life might be worth it by the end of the day. Not true, there's one choice I regret. One decision I would take back in a single breath, a heartbeat.

When I realized my mistake, it was too late. She moved on. The blame falls squarely on me. I put the game before our relationship. Before her. Before us. My intention was to bounce around in the minors and then rekindle our relationship after I'd made it. Once I could give her the life she deserved. Sharing the last part with her would've been wise. Hindsight often lends clarity. I push the thought of her away—a feat I have never been particularly adept at—and refocus on today.

"Hey, old man, I thought I was the only early bird on the team." Cal Hatton interrupts my solitude.

He's in his third season in the big leagues. Starting a World Series at this stage in his career is a significant accomplishment and even more so when it's game seven. We have a great working relationship despite our age difference.

"You're a funny guy, Cal. My pregame ritual goes back to when I was in Little League. My pops took me to the field well before my teammates arrived. It solidified more when I could drive. What brings you here?"

Before he answers, I grip his shoulders in an older brother sort of way. "Shaking off some doubt before the biggest start of my career. We could win the whole damn thing!" He's rocking back and forth on his heels with excitement.

"We treat tonight like any other game. Follow my lead, don't ignore my pitch suggestions too often, and you'll blow them away."

He drops his head. "Thanks, man."

"Anytime. I'll meet you in the bullpen for warmups."

Cal raises his hand for a high five. I comply, and he takes off to prepare for the game. For the next ten minutes, I soak in the silence of the huge stadium and give myself an internal pep talk. *Twenty-seven outs stand between you and a World Series ring.* After a few deep, soothing breaths, I retreat to the clubhouse and dress for the game.

I join Cal in the bullpen. Less than an hour later, the national anthem echoes around me. Tonight, a country artist I happen to love sings the song with pride. As with each game before this one, I thank my teammates and coaches in my head and offer our little ritual. My ritual with the one that got away. True, she isn't here, but game day rituals are sacred. Some players follow the same order before batting, some refuse to wash their hats, and some abstain from sex the night before a game.

My ritual isn't crazy considering it started when I was younger, significantly younger. Before fall ball our sophomore year of high school, Julianne, who allows me and only me to call her Annie, gave me a chain with a catcher's mask dangling from it. From that day forward, I pressed a kiss to it before crouching behind home plate… every single game. Part of me hopes she has been watching over the years. The more realistic part reminds me I screwed up. Yet I still think of her… every single game. Hell, it's every single day when I wake up alone.

We're the home team and take the field first. I run through the signs for Cal. He immediately shakes me off. I frown, but line up where he wants me.

Strike one.

The crowd roars.

The batter steps back into the box. I call for a slider, and Cal nods tightly. He winds up and throws. The ball rotates on its way to the plate. I shift slightly closer to the batter.

The umpire growls, "Strike two."

Cal takes a circle around the mound and stands on the rubber. I drop my index finger, indicating fast ball, and set up on the inside corner. The ball sails toward me as if it's on a string. *Yes! We can win this!*

Swing and a miss. Strike three.

I throw the ball down the line to the third baseman and cast a look at Cal. "Let's go!"

The teams play scoreless baseball through six innings. Cal gives up one hit and a walk. The opposing pitcher allows five hits and two walks.

We take the field for the ninth inning with the top of the order set to hit. Cal successfully sends the leadoff batter back to the pine with his teammates.

"Strike three. You're out," rings behind me.

The second batter of the ninth skulks back to the dugout.

One more out. I run through the signs, and Cal shakes me off twice. *Come on, kid. We've made it this far.* While I wait, my pulse races. *Settle.* He agrees on a slider, which wouldn't be my choice, and it hits my glove for the first strike. Again, he shakes me off and throws a pitch against my suggestion. This time, it sails deep toward left field. It caroms off the padding in the corner. The crowd rises to their feet, the runner advances to third base, and I position myself to block the plate. The runner rounds third and is being waved home. The relay throw takes the perfect bounce. I secure the ball in my glove as the runner slides toward home.

Hold onto the ball. Hold onto the ball. We tumble backward, I feel a pop when my knee wrenches, and then I hear, "Out!"

The crowd erupts, and my teammates flood the field while Cal is helping me off the ground. *Fuck! My left knee is on fire.* Throbbing arcs of pain zip in my leg. I paste on my best smile and fight through the pain to celebrate with my teammates. After we receive our hats and T-shirts and the Commissioner's Trophy is presented to the team owners, we head into the locker room and celebrate more.

I have been standing mostly in one spot and accepting bro hugs and handshakes from my teammates.

"Somerset, let's go," Aaron Bishop, our athletic trainer, summons me. Aaron studied to be an athletic trainer while playing college baseball. He ruptured his Achilles tendon in his rookie season in the majors, then two years later, shredded his knee. Determining he wasn't going to be able to make it back to playing form, he joined the training staff in Florida.

This may be my only chance to enjoy winning a championship. I shake my head. "I need a few more minutes, please."

He acquiesces but doesn't move. Aaron is leaning against the door to the training room with his feet hip distance apart and arms crossed over his broad chest. He understands exactly what I'm about to go through… again. Well, another knee injury but on the other side.

As the guys clean up and leave, I reluctantly follow Aaron into the training room. Follow is a strong word. Hobble is more accurate. I can't put any weight on my left leg. When I tried earlier, it felt like arrows were being shot into my knee. Aaron helps me onto the table and rolls my pant leg up.

"Did it feel the same as last time?" he asks quietly.

"Worse, actually."

"Well, you're old now."

I scowl at him and then chuckle. I'm the oldest player on the roster. Overall, thirty-one isn't old. I started playing in the majors eight years ago. For baseball though, I've exceeded the average career by a few years, especially for a catcher.

He grins at me. "Anytime. Laughter will help you through the process. What's my motto?"

"Laughter is the best medicine after you've exhausted your training options," I mutter.

"Good. Let's ice this, and I'll find a brace for tonight. Then I'll see if I can get you in for an MRI in the morning."

"Thanks, Aaron."

"You're welcome. I know it isn't any consolation, but you won the game for the team."

My eyes flutter closed briefly, and I acknowledge him with a tight smile. I don't need an MRI or orthopedic surgeon to tell me my knee requires a full reconstruction. The test and office visit will merely confirm what my gut is screaming at me.

CHAPTER TWO

JULIANNE

Shortly into the new year, I'm giddy to have a get together with my siblings. We met late last year. It's been a whirlwind of texts, calls, and visits ever since. I was adopted when I was three by an older couple who was struggling to have children. My parents, Edmund and Caroline Silva, are amazing. My childhood was wonderful, but I longed for siblings.

Jordan, my younger brother, reached out to Blackthorne Security for personal protection for my niece, Reese. He chose the firm because it was recommended by his agent. He felt a bodyguard was necessary because his new team was closer to home than he would've liked. Alex was assigned to my niece. Soon after they met, Alex noted similarities with Jordan's early years to her boss's sister Jill's story. With a bit of digging by her foster brother Jake, who owns Blackthorne, we learned Jill is his sister and mine. In the span of one phone call, I went from an only child to having two siblings and two nieces.

I hurry out of the building and to my car. The drive isn't far, but traffic could impact me arriving on time. With modern country tunes blasting, I start the nearly one-hour drive to my brother's house. Surprisingly, the three of us have degrees in education, but Jordan is a star wide receiver in the NFL coming off a Super Bowl win.

A heaviness lands in my chest, not for Jordan but for Colby. My—he isn't mine anymore, not for a long time—high school sweetheart is coming off a win in the World Series. I'm happy for him achieving his dream. It cost him though. In the last play of the game, the runner injured Colby as he tried to score. It's a prerequisite for a catcher to block the plate. Colby's knee was seriously injured in the collision. The great news is his team won the game. On the flip side though, his knee may never be the same.

A normal fan wouldn't have access to those details, but since the injury, I broke my Chinese wall around Colby with our mutual best friends more than once to check on his progress. Yes, my bestie and his are married. Kind of like Colby and I were supposed to be by now. I push away the sadness and regret when I realize the ride has passed smoothly.

"Hi, Auntie! You're here!" Reese runs down the front steps with her arms wide open.

"Hi, sweetie! It's good to see you again."

Her arms collapse around me. Reese is a carbon copy of her father right down to the piercing blue eyes, a trait he and I share as well. "Moving here was the best ever. Dad met Mom, won the big game… again, and my family got really, really big!"

"It's pretty amazing, right?" When I learned about them, I was ecstatic. Unfortunately, the sentiment wasn't shared by my father.

She loops her arm around mine and leads me inside. Jordan and Jill are in the kitchen while Cruz, Jill's husband, hovers with his newborn daughter, Hallie, in his arms.

"Hi, everyone," I say before making my rounds greeting each of them.

"Hey, Jules." My siblings welcome me in unison.

"How can I help?"

Jill shakes her head. "We're set. You can get yourself a drink."

I circle the island and tug open the massive fridge. With a bottled water in hand, I take a seat at the dining table. Both my siblings are excellent cooks. A talent I don't possess. They set two serving dishes on the table. One is baked macaroni and cheese. I'm confident there is a secret ingredient or extra something in there and it'll taste amazing. The second dish is chicken with quinoa over kale with a spicy dressing.

We dig into the food, and silence befalls the table other than my newest niece cooing in Cruz's arms. Despite holding her, he expertly navigates eating his dinner. A sliver of jealousy slices through me. I thought I would be a mom by now. While I have dated a few guys in the past, none had longevity nor rose to the level of marriage. Well, Patrick proposed, but I knew it would never lead down the aisle. I drop my shoulders and polish off the food on my plate, silently ruminating on what could have been. Thankfully, no one notices or calls me on it.

Unwilling to stew in my thoughts any longer, I ask, "Care to share the reason for your invitation to dinner, Jordan?"

He glances over at Alex, who smiles back at him. "Would you like to tell our family?"

"Go ahead," she urges him as he wraps his arm around her shoulders.

"We picked a date and a location for our wedding," Jordan tells the group.

"Perfect. I'm there!" I animatedly announce.

"We didn't tell you when," Alex adds.

"Doesn't matter. I'll make it happen. As long as I can remember I wanted siblings, and now I have two plus a huge extended family. The more events I can attend the better."

Alex gives me a side hug in our seats. "We're getting married near the river at the Michelson's followed by a small reception here in late June. Then we're going to Columbia for our honeymoon." The Michelson's are part of my extended family. Technically, they are Alex's boss's parents. If I recall correctly, Alex is Columbian.

"What does small mean to you?" I wonder aloud.

Jordan tilts his head as if he's counting. "Family only, so about fifty people."

I laugh and rise to clear my plate. Reese joins me with hers. When I slide my dish into the dishwasher, Reese gushes about my ring.

"Auntie, your ring is pretty. Where did you get it?"

A pang of longing, missed opportunities, and a smidge of loss passes over me. My feelings have been stirred up since I broke down and asked about Colby. The last time I felt this way was after I saw him at our besties's wedding a few years ago. The ring she's referring to is two chevron accent rings soldered together to form what looks like a baseball diamond. He had the words "Moonshot" engraved inside. It was a phrase Colby and I used to repeat to each other… until we didn't. A moonshot is a lofty goal in layman's terms. In baseball, it's a long-distance, high-velocity home run. *What we hoped we would be… together for the rest of our lives.*

"Auntie?"

"Huh? Sorry, sweetie. It was a gift from someone special, a long time ago."

"Oh. Okay."

Thankfully, the rest of my family filters into the room, and I'm saved from divulging more to my precocious niece. We chat for another hour before Jill unveils a hot cocoa bar complete with warm chocolate chip cookies. How she kept them warm is a wonder.

Stuffed beyond belief with sweets and good memories, I work my way out the door nearly two hours later.

"Please text me when you get home," Cruz asks.

I'm not surprised, since he works at Blackthorne Security like Alex. Normally, she asks for the text though. "I will." Unfortunately, the drive isn't smooth. Reese's innocuous question has my mind spinning. *Why do I keep wearing the ring? We aren't together anymore. Haven't been for years.*

With a sigh, I call my bestie Lorelei via Bluetooth. "Hey, girl. You on your way home from dinner with your family?"

"Yeah. I still pinch myself sometimes to make sure they're real."

I see the smile on her face. Lorelei and I have been besties since kindergarten much like her husband, Jack, and Colby have been. We planned our double wedding in seventh grade. It fell apart for both couples for a while until Lor and Jack rekindled their romance after college and got hitched. Their wedding was the first time I'd seen Colby in five years. I nearly swallowed my tongue. Gone was the fit but lanky teenager. He was replaced by a finely honed wall of solid muscle. At least I imagined that to be the case beneath his expensive, perfectly tailored tuxedo.

"Are you in your head again?" Lorelei's voice breaks into my thoughts.

"Maybe. Sorry, I couldn't call you back before now."

"No worries. I need to give you a heads-up."

I wrinkle my nose. This can't be good. "About?"

"To be clear, you broke the wall first."

I close my eyes briefly before refocusing on the road. "Noted."

"Jack left for Florida this morning to meet with Colby's medical team."

"Okay. Good for Jack. What does that have to do with me?"

"Part of the proposed plan is for Colby to complete his rehab with Jack like he did earlier in his career."

Oh. Oh! "It's a different injury and the other knee. Isn't it?"

"Yeah. It's more significant than the previous one," she answers.

"Okay." My mind is spinning. After all these years he's coming home. Given our strained relationship, if you will, I don't know if he's been here since their wedding.

"Are you spiraling?"

"No, why would I? Colby and I are friendly exes. We were civil at your wedding. We will be when I see him next week." *Liar.*

"He thought you were engaged to Patrick at our wedding." She points out matter-of-factly.

I frown and pull into my garage. "What aren't you telling me?"

"Nope, not for me to share. Like I am for you, Jack is a vault for Colby. My husband and I still have hope the fearsome foursome will be happily married to one another, share a backyard, and flourish until we're old."

"I love your hopefulness, Lor, but I don't see it happening. He's had a different starlet on his arm in every event photograph. The fearsome foursome has been dead since Colby chose baseball over me." A wave of nostalgia and anger washes over me. I would take him back despite his choice to leave me and his current dating life. Wouldn't I? *Maybe. Probably. No.*

"How do you know who he's dating?"

Crap! Caught! I mentally chastise myself for spilling the fact I've been stalking him on the down-low since I returned Patrick's ring. "He's the darling of the league. Clean-cut with no tattoos, never been in trouble—

the kind of guy you put on a pedestal for younger athletes as an exceptional example. Plus, I love baseball, always have."

"I agree about your love of baseball. Checking the box scores is one thing. Scouring the sports page and gossip rags for a specific catcher all these years later is different. I'm sure it can only mean one thing."

"No. I'm not hung up on him." *Yes, you are. He's the man you measure everyone against despite him shattering your teenage heart.*

"Hmmm. Well, then let me set you up on a date with my coworker."

I transfer the call to my phone, close my car door, and step into my kitchen from the garage. "No thank you. I can find my own dates."

"When was your last night out with a man?" she inquires.

"Last month. Lor, I don't want you to fix me up. I appreciate the heads-up. Colby and I will be fine when we cross paths." While I chat with her, I send off a text to Cruz.

"Okay. Just doing my job as your bestie."

"I know. Coffee on the deck?" Every Saturday morning since I moved into my house, we meet in the middle of our yards for coffee. Our homes are on parallel streets, and our backyards abut one another. While we have fences on the sides, we don't in the middle.

"I'll be there. Not until nine, okay?"

"Sure." I end the call and wallow in my thoughts a bit more. Every word about Colby was a lie. A bald-faced, all caps LIE. Sort of. I'm sure we can be civil, but it won't be easy. Avoiding him in this picturesque small town will be a feat. Nothing has changed since high school.

Everyone knows everyone's business. I bet it only takes a few days before the old biddies come knocking and the reporters show up. I will be fine seeing him again. I don't have a choice. He may have been my first love, but we're barely acquaintances now. Rekindling a friendly relationship is all I can handle. Perhaps my brain should tell my pounding heart and attention-starved lady parts civil is on the table and nothing more.

CHAPTER THREE

COLBY

"Thanks for coming, Jack." I answer the door, and we bro hug. I'm able to move around my house on my own but at a much slower pace than before my injury. I may be one of the highest paid players in the league, but my home is modest by most standards. The only thing I splurged on was the private, gated waterfront community for my primary residence. With four bedrooms, a game room, and modern gym in the basement, I blend into the neighborhood. Hell, I'm rarely here during the season except to sleep.

"I appreciate your confidence in my skills."

"This injury is different. Worse. I'm old in baseball terms. I know a specialized physical therapy plan is required. If anyone can fix my knee, it's you." Within two weeks of my injury, I started pre-rehabilitation: a strength program to support my weak knee after surgery, created by Jack but executed by Aaron.

Jack wheels his bag into the kitchen and takes a seat at the island.

"Would you like coffee, water, or something else?" I offer.

"Water would be fine. When do we need to leave for the facility?"

"About thirty minutes. Why don't I show you to your accommodations?"

Jack chuckles. "You're so cheesy. I remember where the guest room is. I can do it myself."

I grab two waters from the drink fridge. Jack returns from the guest suite, and we walk to the deck until it's time for us to leave. We take the stairs… slowly down to my garage. While I didn't spend excessive money on my home, I opted for luxury vehicles. I have an Audi R8 Spyder, a McClaren Artura, as well as a practical Range Rover. Lastly and most importantly, I have my first car ever—a Honda Civic. My reason for keeping the car all these years is known only to me and one other person.

"I see you upgraded the Audi." Jack pulls me out of my thoughts.

"Yeah." We slide into the Rover and drive to the facility. I'm surprised when I arrive to find Madeleine and a petite brunette waiting to enter the conference room in the training facility.

"Morning, Madeleine. Thank you for coming. It's unexpected and unnecessary."

"Morning. I promised white-glove service when I took over for Stavros, and I never break my promises. I would like to introduce Anastasia Gentry. She's a junior agent with the firm." Madeleine Wilton Anderson has been my agent for the last six years. Before Stavros retired, he was my agent. I take Anastasia's extended hand and shake it. "Nice to meet you."

"Pleasure."

I continue, "This is Jack Harlow. He—" I shake my head. "—he fixed my knee the first time."

Jack greets them, and we're ushered into the room. We exchanged handshakes with the owner and the medical staff. The team doctor begins discussing my injury and the successful complete reconstruction of my knee a week ago. By complete, I mean three ligaments in my knee. According to my scans, my meniscus was already partially torn before Andy Hausman plowed into me, attempting to score. He didn't, but it certainly felt as if I was mowed down. I'm swimming in medical jargon when Jack speaks up. I've heard the words before and it's another reason I selected Jack for my therapist. He will tell me straight and explain the terms more clearly. Plus, having a friendly face when I torture myself is a definite bonus.

"Your timeline is overly optimistic." His words are pointed and laced with concern.

I shudder when I fully focus on the graphic on the whiteboard. The team doctor is indicating I could be back behind the plate in June. Four months? All my research and recall from earlier in my career indicates my recovery should take six at least. A timeline that short is for someone with perfect conditions and only one ligament requiring reconstruction, unlike my three.

Jack continues. "Standard guidelines suggest six months minimum for an everyday ACL rupture and reconstruction. Mr. Somerset's injury isn't standard nor is he twenty-years-old." He turns to look at me when the next sentence comes out of his mouth. "He'll be lucky to get behind the plate at all this upcoming season."

I drop my head and acknowledge his words. In my gut, I knew playing this season was a long shot of epic proportions with Jack's help. Hearing his words makes my stomach sink and my heart constrict. I'm terrified to ask the question... what if I can never play again?

The team doctor replies, "We have cutting-edge rehabilitation facilities in the area and the best therapists. We're confident we can get you playing by June."

I don't like the dig at Jack. Neither does he as he shifts in his chair.

"I haven't agreed to your treatment plan for my rehabilitation."

"Why wouldn't you?" The team owner, Stanford Wilson, joins the conversation. "Mr. Bishop can handle it like he did pre-surgery."

I turn my attention to Mr. Wilson. "Respectfully, sir, Aaron isn't a physical therapist." I swallow hard. "This organization has been my home for the last five years. I refuse to make a partial comeback. I won't get behind the plate until my knee is healed and my doctors state I can."

Mr. Wilson's response is immediate. "You're a stabilizing force behind the plate for our pitching staff. We need you to repeat as champions."

Only one person in my life would know the statistics on the number of times a World Series winner won back-to-back titles. *Annie.* "Sir, I don't have the exact statistics. However, I would estimate it's been about twenty years since a team won two consecutive titles. Additionally, a repeat isn't likely especially with the roster changes you'll be required to make in the offseason to stay below the luxury tax level."

Now it's Mr. Wilson's turn to squirm in his chair. Not sure if he's uncomfortable about me pushing for my own doctor or the fact I'm aware of the luxury tax predicament the team is in. "Precisely why we need you back as soon as possible. You will use our doctors," Mr. Wilson states emphatically.

"Excuse me?" I ask. I'm a number on a piece of paper until I can get behind the plate again. *Great.*

Madeleine, who is sitting on my right, sets her hand on my forearm. When I turn to look at her, the determination on her face is magnificent. "Mr. Wilson, I appreciate your position, but Mr. Somerset's contract allows him to select his doctor, treatment plan, and rehabilitation facilities. He isn't required to use the one recommended or provided by the team," Madeleine interjects.

I don't recall the provision in my contract, but I won't question her. When Stavros chose her as his successor, he knew what he was doing. It solidifies my decision to stay with her after Stavros retired further.

"Ms. Wilton, plea—"

She cuts off Mr. Wilson. "My name is Mrs. Anderson. I won't allow you to treat him in the same manner as D.J. Culliver. Your so-called medical experts rushed him back to the field, and D.J. paid the price, reinjuring his pitching elbow. Then he lost nearly two full seasons rather than one."

Mr. Wilson is stunned silent.

Dr. Brownstein speaks instead, "You're mistaken, Ms.... Mrs. Anderson."

"Don't insult me or my reputation, Philip. I will refrain from delineating facts to prove my statement correct." Madeleine jabs. "My client is here at your request and as a courtesy. He is not required, nor will he bow to your demands. Mr. Harlow is exceptionally qualified to handle Mr. Somerset's rehabilitation, and he has successfully rehabbed an injury with my client before. Have you done your due diligence, Dr. Brownstein? Was this meeting simply a farce to make my client believe you were considering allowing him to handle his own medical decisions?"

Staying with her as my agent was clearly the right choice.

Brownstein clears his throat. Mr. Wilson nods at him almost imperceptibly.

"Mr. Harlow, please provide a comprehensive treatment plan to my office by the close of business on Friday. My office requests at least monthly updates regarding Mr. Somerset's progress during his rehabilitation."

"I will have the plan to you by the end of the week, Dr. Brownstein," Jack replies.

"Good luck, Somerset. I hope you know what you're doing," Mr. Wilson states as he exits the room. Dr. Brownstein follows closely on his heels.

I wait for the door to completely close before asking, "How did you…?"

Madeleine smiles and her associate tilts her head in keen interest. "First, I do my homework. The owner and team doctors believe the agents don't talk. That is simply untrue. Culliver's agent is a good friend of mine and exceptional at his job. To the point I've tried to lure him to Scala more than once."

"Thank you, Madeleine," I manage. I'm still floored by the events of this meeting. Until today, I never felt like a slot on the roster. I suppose if you have no use for the team, then you're nothing more than wasted space.

"You're welcome. I'm heading back to DC in the morning. Would both of you like to fly with us on the Blackthorne jet? My husband prefers I travel private with his personally vetted pilots."

Inwardly, I chuckle. I've met her husband who co-owns Blackthorne Security. He is the epitome of an overprotective alpha male. "I can be ready by then. Please forward me the departure details," I reply.

"Excellent. Simon, my assistant, will be in touch." We shake hands, and Madeleine leaves with her associate.

The entire time I was speaking with Madeleine, Jack stared out the window toward the team medical facility.

"You good?" I ask.

He lifts his shoulders and drops them slowly. "Are you sure about this?"

"Absolutely. Not only have you fixed me before, but you won't let me slack, and you'll give it to me straight unlike Dr. Brownstein or his lackey

I would've passed me off too. You have my best interests at heart, and I trust you."

We bro hug. "Let's get out of here."

On the ride back to the house, my mind zips through details about packing and pausing things for my residence until Annie moves to the front of my mind. Honestly, she's always there. "Does she know?" I mumble.

Jack looks at my profile and then back to the road. "Lorelei plans to give her a heads-up, if she hasn't already."

"Thanks. I haven't made it easy on you straddling the line between us."

"Lor and I love you both. We want you to be happy, preferably together again. Maybe you have a shot, or maybe you don't. It isn't for me to decide."

His words shock me. "Wait. She didn't marry what's his name... Patrick?"

Jack pinches the bridge of his nose. "No, she didn't."

Surprise, elation, and a smidge of anger pulse through me. "Why didn't you tell me?"

Jack scowls at me. "I shouldn't have mentioned it now. You know why."

"Clearly, I don't."

"Dude, my wife and I have been between the two of you since our wedding. Jules begged Lorelei not to share. The same way you demanded

I not to share the starlets on your arm were setups by Madeleine, and you've been single and nearly celibate since before I married Lorelei."

I wipe my free hand down my denim-clad thigh. *She's not married.* A shot of excitement cascades from my head to my toes. *Perhaps, I'll have a chance to fix my mistake after all this time.* "Fair point. I'll find out in a few days if I have a shot, won't I?"

"Yup," he replies as I pull into the garage at my house.

I walk inside and immediately step into my office. With my laptop open, I draft a few emails and amend my schedules. I decrease my housekeeper to once a month and pause my newspaper delivery. A sliver of a memory passes over me. Every Sunday morning starting in seventh grade, Annie and I would meet at the park and work on the crossword puzzle until it was finished. I wonder if she still does it.

I smile and pack my clothes and personal items before ordering amazing takeout for dinner. With our Thai dinner spread on the tufted leather ottoman, I raise my beer in Jack's direction. "To my best friend and torturer to mold me back into playing shape. You've been there for me since grade school, and I'll never forget it."

Jack taps his glass against mine. "Same goes."

We polish off the food and watch a basketball game before turning in. The text from Simon Dumont, Madeleine's assistant, indicates our flight leaves at ten in the morning. I arrange for a car service to take us to the airport and flop onto my bed. I stare up at the ceiling and mull over Jack's words from earlier. If the situation were reversed, would I give me a chance? *Hell no.* I broke her heart, albeit with good intentions. Either way, I hurt her deeply, and I don't deserve a second chance. Yet, I want one. Desperately.

My mind drifts back to Jack and Lorelei's wedding. Due to my schedule, I arrived in the wee hours of the morning and crashed at the airport hotel. Once Jack and I were clad in sleek tuxedoes, we rode to the church in the center of town. The same church where I imagined I would marry Annie one day. Julianne took my breath away as she stood at the end of the aisle. Her emerald dress highlighted her body flawlessly. She was the most beautiful girl I'd ever seen in high school. I thanked my lucky stars each day I had with her. How she could be more stunning five years later was beyond my comprehension. It wasn't until after Jack and Lorelei were hitched and Annie graciously took my arm to walk out of the church did I notice the sparkling diamond on her left ring finger. Not my ring. Not the promise ring I gave her when we were together. In that moment, devastation coursed through me. I'd officially lost the woman of my dreams. I didn't know what to make of it until her fiancé gruffly introduced himself when we finished the receiving line, and he sought her out. It was obvious from our interaction he knew who I was, but crystal clear that Annie didn't mention our previous relationship. If she had, I would've expected a fiercer response to me escorting her down the aisle, regardless of my respectful manner.

Resigned I won't get any more answers down memory lane, I set an alarm and attempt to sleep. All I have is hope I can fight for a second chance with her, knowing full well I royally screwed up the first one.

CHAPTER FOUR

JULIANNE

Point Academy is a private high school near Wilmington. I have been the principal for seven years. We have a few high-profile students, but our endowment defrays about eighty percent of the cost of admission. It has been the week from hell. Numerous students have made stupid choices requiring multiple meetings with parents and the trustees. Additionally, my athletic director and baseball coach resigned to move across the country to care for his ailing mother. I have posted the positions and hope to have a replacement or two before the season starts. Otherwise, the boys will get the first female coach in league history whether it's me or the new athletic director.

The kicker is, despite my week, I scheduled myself a date this evening. Cancelling at this late stage isn't an option. Jimmy is a local guy. We went to elementary school together. He recently came back into town after working down south for the last few years. I rush out of the building and to my car. With any luck, I'll be able to stop home before we're set to meet.

Luck is not on my side. Traffic is bumper-to-bumper out of the city. I would like to take this as a sign allowing me to beg off my plans, but I won't. Pulling up the map, I find there's no chance I'm making it home in time for my date. I pull out my phone to text Jimmy and find one from him waiting for me.

James Bolden: I see you're stuck in traffic. Are you free tomorrow instead?

Concern shoots through me. How and why is he tracking me?

Me: I am not free tomorrow.

James Bolden: Rain check?

Not likely. Creepy. I shake off my weird feelings with some tunes blasting in my car. The trip, which typically takes forty minutes, lasts well over an hour. I toe off my shoes before stepping through the door and head straight for my wine rack. Rarely do I drink as soon as I arrive home from work. More accurately, I rarely drink. However, my brother-in-law Jake is a wine aficionado, and he has been teaching me about excellent vintages. His budget is significantly higher than mine, but I have a bottle of Mayacamas 2014 and Tablas Creek Vineyard Mourvèdre 2020. Either will work well to push away the concern about Jimmy and my terrible week.

With the bottle breathing on the island—something I wouldn't have done until I met Jake—I scoop up my shoes and climb the stairs to the master bedroom. My home is decidedly too large for me, but the location was perfect. The colonial is beautiful with a huge front porch and massive deck with a patio. The previous owner lived here for her entire life and was meticulous. I updated the wall colors and never looked back. The main level is mostly open concept. As you step over the threshold of the front entryway, the office is on your right and the dining area on the left. Past that, the remainder of the main floor is airy and spacious. The great room and kitchen are one large space. Lor and Jack moved into a house on a parallel street in line with mine a few years later. Another step closer to our childhood dreams… except.

The master bedroom is elegant and modern. The walls are gray with lavender undertones. The queen bed has an upholstered headboard and pinch-pleat duvet with violet accents and too many pillows. I strip off my clothes and deposit them into the hamper. While I tug on pajamas, movement outside my window catches my eye. Once I verify it's likely Lorelei, I return downstairs and take a heavy gulp of my wine. While I rummage through my fridge for dinner, there's a soft knock on the back door.

"Come in, Lor," I call out.

Yet she doesn't come in. I frown, close the fridge, and walk to the door, peering through the glass. *Sweet mercy!* Colby. He's hotter than the last time I saw him. He's a finely sculpted specimen of a man except for the knee brace. His hoodie can't hide his muscular frame. Gathering myself, I unlock and open the door.

His body monopolizes the entire frame, and the same familiar scent of him wafts toward me. "Hi, Annie." My name always sounded different falling from his lips especially since I only allow him to call me Annie. I've missed hearing it.

"Colby." You would think I would be embarrassed given my outfit, but I'm not. He's seen me in much, much worse than this. My pajamas are cute flannel ones with coffee cups on them.

His cobalt eyes meet mine. "I can go. I heard you invite Lorelei in."

"Of course not. Please come in." I step back to give him space to pass without getting too close to me. The slightest touch will mess with the shaky grasp I have on my emotions. Walking out of the church for our best friend's wedding with my arm looped around his was torture of the highest degree. The awareness and electricity zinging between us are two of the reasons I didn't marry Patrick. Nothing sexual or suggestive happened as we walked out of the church, but I knew… the tightening in my chest never happened with Patrick. Nor did the rush of desire from head to toe. If I'm being honest, the ache to find out if Colby and I could make it after the time apart tumbles forward. Even if I didn't end up with him, Patrick wasn't the one for me.

"Your home is gorgeous. Is it a mirror image of Jack's?" His words cut into my thoughts.

"Thank you. Yes, but my basement is finished, and theirs isn't. I've been here an extra few years. How are you feeling?"

"Jack hasn't gone full bore on me yet, but we're making progress with minimal to moderate soreness. I'll be cursing him out in no time. I'm sure being under his watchful eye all day every day is a perk of him being my best friend."

"Glad to hear it. You're staying with Lor and Jack?"

He grins at me. "Yeah. She didn't give you a heads-up?"

"No, she didn't. I'm sure it was by design."

He smiles. One that made my heart palpitate as a naïve teen still causes me to swoon just the same. "Tough day?" he asks, pointing to the open bottle and glass on the island.

"No, the whole week."

"Wanna share? I'm still an exceptional listener." The grin on his face melts what little resolve I had to spend the evening wallowing.

He is… at least he was a great sounding board. "Sure. Want a glass?"

"Shouldn't. I haven't eaten yet," he answers.

"Neither have I. I was planning on ordering takeout after failing to find acceptable food in my fridge. Want to join me?" *What are you thinking? Friends, just friends.*

"I would love to." He follows me into the kitchen.

I pull down a glass from the cabinet and set it beside the bottle. "Same faves from Golden Wok?" I ask, poised to dial.

"Yes."

I order our—there is no our—old entrees of choice and end the call. Colby has wandered over to the mantel.

"Who's the little girl? She looks remarkably like you."

"Funny story. She's my niece." Of all people, I don't need to rehash my adoption story with Colby. He knows every detail. It's comforting not to have to rehash my early childhood again.

He turns with the photo in his hand and furrowed brows. "Niece? Like found family niece?"

"No, literal niece. Near the end of last year, I learned I have a younger biological brother and sister."

"Amazing, Annie. How did you find out about them? Did you seek them out?"

"No." I take a deep breath and explain how I met my siblings.

"Wait. Jordan Devereaux is your brother?"

"Yes, he is."

"The little girl in the photo is his daughter, Reese. He's engaged to Alex," he states.

"Correct so far."

Colby continues, "Your sister, Jill, is married to Cruz, and they have an infant daughter."

"Exactly. Plus, there are about fifty more people who are related to them."

"How do your parents feel about your expanded family?"

I wrinkle my nose.

"I didn't mean to push. You don't have to share anymore. We can shift to your crappy week if you prefer."

"After all these years—"

Yes, he remembers my tells. "The time apart didn't cause my recollection of your tells to fade. I remember everything about you."

"Colby, I—"

The doorbell interrupts my words. I answer the door and accept our food. "Island or ottoman?"

"Your choice," he replies.

I set the bag on the island, and he walks gingerly into the kitchen. "Where is your silverware?"

"Sit. I'll get it."

"I want to help, Annie."

I exhale slowly and direct him to the drawer while I grab napkins. I appreciate the assistance and him asking for permission rather than searching. We take our seats and dig into the food.

A smile grows on his gorgeous face, a sly one I'm not sure I was meant to see. The longer he's in my space, the weaker my defenses become. Not sure they were all that sturdy to begin with. Lorelei has been strong for me from the day he left until I accepted Patrick's ring. Then she took up the fight again for me after I broke my engagement until his injury and I begged for information.

"Your memory is as good as mine." He lifts the shrimp egg roll I ordered for him.

"I suppose you're right."

"Tell me about your crappy week," he urges while savoring the first bite of his food.

"A few of my students made some bonehead choices, requiring me to hold meetings with their parents."

"What did they do?"

"A male and female, both juniors, were found nearly naked in the music room by the hall monitor."

He attempts to stifle a laugh and fails.

I pause in eating my chicken lo mein. "What's so funny?"

"Do you not recall us seeking out hidden areas or dark corners between classes to make out?"

My skin heats at the flash of a memory from our junior year when we ducked beneath the stairs between classes in high school. His kiss always left me wanting more, even then. *Would it now?*

"I'll take your reddening skin as a yes," he murmurs.

"Even so, I'm the principal. Their behavior needed to be addressed."

"Fair, but still funny. What else?"

"A freshman is struggling with his identity, and a few upper classmen are hazing him. I met with all the parents. Then, my athletic director resigned, and my date canceled after he saw I was stuck in traffic."

"He was tracking you? How?"

"I don't know. Traffic maps, maybe. It was creepy. I won't be rescheduling."

"Glad to hear it."

We eat in silence for a few minutes before I ask, "What about you?" The comfort of him in my home is contradictory. It's foreign but at the same time, the familiarity makes me warm and fuzzy. Not to mention the heat of him sitting beside me.

"Me?"

"How is your family?"

"They're fine. My parents moved to Texas, and Violet is a struggling actress in Los Angeles."

"Glad to hear it. That they're okay, not the struggling part. Although bumps are necessary, right?"

"Yeah, Violet's tough and resilient. I mean rejection isn't easy, especially if it's for your dream job. I won't let her be homeless. Her landlord calls me when she's two weeks behind, and I send him the money. If she pays, he holds onto it for the next time."

"That's sweet of you. To answer your question from earlier about my parents, I thought...." When I pause, he covers my hand with his. He's still in tune with me despite the intervening years. Familiarity and comfort radiate up my arm. Slowly, I pull it back and rise from the stool. *Just friends. It's what I can handle.* To mask my reaction, I refill my wine and lean against the granite countertop. Was I successful in hiding the goose bumps from his touch or my desire to lean into what he's offering? Doubtful. I forge ahead with my answer. "I thought they would be supportive. Mom is, but Dad is only to a certain degree. My parents have no interest in meeting my siblings, regardless of the fact I didn't seek them out."

"I'm sorry."

"Me too." I take a heavy sip of my wine with the glass in my left hand and stare briefly at the ceiling. My attempt to quell the increasing confusion fails.

"Can I ask you something?"

"I reserve the right not to answer." I set my glass on the counter to my left.

"Understood." He stands and pushes the stool back in before rounding the island. He's close but not touching me. I'm slightly shorter than him barefoot. He consumes the air around me. His broad, sculpted frame takes up space.

Damn my traitorous body and its memory! I may not want to react to him, but my heart and core don't seem to care. My body wants to find out if his kiss will make me melt into a gooey mess of hormones. I clench my thighs together, attempting to stave off the ache building. Then again, it's been quite some time since I've been with anyone.

"Why didn't you marry Patrick?"

Unconsciously, my nose wrinkles. My chest tightens, and my heart rate kicks up a few more notches. "He wasn't the guy for me." *Simple. Partially true.*

"Good. In my thirty-one years of life, I have one regret. I can blame it on youthful stupidity or altruism, but I won't though it's a facet of the truth. I was an idiot who failed to put us before my career aspirations. By the time I realized my mistake, you were dating Brandon and I chose not to intervene. As much as I wanted you, I refused to hurt you more and you seemed happy. Then, I planned to apologize for my grave error in judgment at Lor and Jack's wedding, but I was too late. You were engaged to Patrick. Yet, a few years later, here we are again in the same room except this time we're both single." He eliminates nearly all the space between our bodies although there wasn't much to take.

Tears threatened to fall.

"Tonight, for the second time in almost three years, I can breathe. The only thing those two evenings have in common is you."

I turn my head to the side and exhale slowly to will my tears away. "You hurt me. You crushed my heart."

He replaces his right hand beneath my chin and aligns our gazes. "I know, and there are not enough words to ease the pain I caused."

Despite my best efforts, a single tear streaks down my cheek. "I can't repair my heart again. It's why we can only be friends." *There... I said it out loud to him. Except, I don't believe my words.*

He dries my tear with his thumb, then scrubs his calloused hand down his still tan face. Colby pauses to lift my left hand between us before adding, "You still wearing my ring after nearly a decade says otherwise. Will you give me a second chance? Us... give us a second chance?"

CHAPTER FIVE

COLBY

Her silence speaks volumes but not in the way you would think. She needs time to parse and dissect her thoughts and emotions. "It was nice to catch up a little over dinner. Please consider my request. Good night, Annie." I press a kiss to the top of her hand and leave through the back door.

Walking away from her tonight was equally as hard as all those years ago. Yet pushing her to make an immediate decision won't go well for me. She's a thinker and a ponderer. Time is my friend and enemy. The last thing I want to do is lose more moments with her, but I'll wait as long as she needs to forgive me.

As expected, Lor and Jack are curled up on their couch when I reenter the house.

"How did that go?" Jack asks.

"Not sure yet. Well, she didn't turn me down flat. When did she start wearing my ring again?"

Our friends look back and forth between me and each other before Lor nods tightly.

Jack replies, "She slid it off her finger for Patrick to put the engagement ring on."

I drop my head and absorb the information. Despite the time, distance, and pulverizing her heart, she never stopped loving me. The same holds true for me.

Lor's phone vibrates on the ottoman, and "Jules" flashes on the screen. She unravels herself from Jack's embrace, slides her phone from the table, and walks into the office.

"Have a seat. That may take a while," Jack instructs.

I comply and lower myself into the deep chair diagonal from him.

"What's your plan?" he asks.

"My plan?"

"To get your girl back."

I grin at him. "Working on it. I need her to forgive me and trust me again before anything else. It will require time and effort, which I'm willing to do. I'm going to start by showing up for her, whatever that looks like these days."

"It was easier in high school. I agree."

"You and Lor are going to have to give me insight."

"True, and we will. You know her better than I do despite the intervening years." Jack points out. "Please accept my words at face value. Let's say for the sake of argument you're successful and woo your way back into her good graces and perhaps even her heart. Have you thought about what happens very late this season or next season when you can play?"

"Not yet. Like I said, working on it. Do they still have coffee on Saturday mornings on the deck?" As far back as sophomore year, Lor and Annie would meet for hot chocolate and donuts at a local café. Now they choose one of their decks.

"Yes, but not tomorrow. Jules is visiting her parents."

"Do they live in the same house?"

"No, they moved about an hour away," Jack informs me.

"Is The Wired Puppy open?"

"Yeah. It's where Jules fills out the crossword on Sundays until it's warm enough to be outside."

She does the puzzle in the park. A glimmer of hope appears in my mind. "Thanks, Jack."

"Happy to help. My wife and I are rooting for you… both of you. If any couple is meant to be, it's you and Jules."

"Appreciate the support." I push off the arms of the chair and shuffle toward the staircase.

About halfway up the stairs, Lorelei rejoins Jack in the living room. "Colby?"

I pause my ascent. "Yeah?"

"Whatever you said to her struck a nerve."

Inside I'm jumping for joy but playing it cool. At least I hope I am. I won't share my words with our friends. If Annie chooses to tell Lorelei, it's up to her. "I meant what I said."

"If you aren't completely in, don't pursue her. I don't think she can survive again," Lorelei warns me.

Having her reiterate the depth of the pain I caused all these years later makes my heart constrict. "I'm in, and I will never hurt her again." With assurances offered, I finish climbing to the guest room and flop onto the bed. I consider walking downstairs to get her phone number but decide against it. She should give it to me herself... willingly. Then again, I've pulled up her number from high school numerous times but never had the courage to press send.

I open a browser and start planning to get my girl back. For now, a stroll down memory lane will be a great place to start. Within fifteen minutes, I set up a delivery for tomorrow and order some supplies for Sunday morning. Content with the steps I've taken so far, I shuck my shoes and drift off to sleep.

The next morning, I borrow Jack's car to personally request my surprise for Annie's crossword solving. I walk into The Wired Puppy with a bag in hand and take in the décor. It's been updated, but it's cozy and comfortable. The walls are a pale yellow and adorned with photos of the surrounding area and town memorabilia, including a photo of the graduating seniors from Summit Creek High.

"Good morning. How can I help you?" A young girl with a mass of raven curls and a name tag with Kylie etched on it greets me when I step to the counter.

I place an order and ask to speak with the manager.

"Is everything okay, sir?" Kylie asks.

"Yes, of course."

"Good morning, how can I help you, sir?" The manager overhears without lifting her head. It takes me a moment, but I recognize her. She looks exactly the same as she did in high school with her long chestnut hair tied back in a severe ponytail.

"Stacie?"

She gazes up at me. "Hey, long time. I hear congrats are in order and a bit of I'm sorry as well."

I chuckle. "Thanks. Most people aren't sure what to say. Did you take over for your mom?"

A gloss of sadness passes over her face.

"Did I say something wrong?"

She shakes her head. "My mom passed away about four years ago."

"I'm sorry."

"No way for you to know. How can I help you?"

I explain what I want to do for Annie.

"Going all out, huh?"

Annie deserves the world, and I will give it to her. If she'll let me. "Starting at the beginning again."

"I'll personally make sure it's perfect. Good luck," she offers.

I hand over the bag. "Appreciate your assistance." I collect my order and step outside. Slowly, I walk along the sidewalk and take in how much and how little has changed in the intervening years.

Summit Creek is a small town in Delaware. The town is situated near a state forest with hiking trails and a lake with a dock and beach. Annie and I spent tons of time sitting on the dock talking about anything and everything including our future. One I crushed in epic fashion when I told her we should break up soon after graduation. I knew the distance would be a challenge for her and I didn't want her to be lonely, worry, or wonder about me. Although other factors played into it as well. My choice hurt her more than I ever thought possible.

As I wander down Main Street, I see the hardware store is unchanged. The Tipsy Tomato has had at least an exterior facelift since I visited last. That may not be true. I was here for the wedding a few years ago but didn't walk through town. I stood up for Jack and left the next morning to meet my team in New York for a doubleheader.

I cross the street and step into Rae's Books and More. Much to the surprise of Hatton and some of my other teammates, I'm an avid and voracious reader. I spend the next few hours meandering the aisles of the bookstore, filling the provided tote with new books to pass the time when Jack isn't bending me into a pretzel. Not exactly a correct metaphor, but it feels that way sometimes. Truthfully, as long as I can handle everyday activities without pain, I'll be fine. Someday I want to chase my kids in the backyard. Do I yearn to get behind the plate again? Absolutely. Is it guaranteed? Definitely not. Will I be okay if Hausman plowing into me ends my career? I'm not sure.

My phone vibrates in my pocket as I check out a few books by some of my favorite authors, including Harlan Coben. I thank the clerk and exit the store. I cross the street and settle in the driver's seat of Jack's car.

The sender catches me by surprise. Her number is still the same.

Bluebird: You remember?

I started calling her "Bluebird" our sophomore year. Not only does the endearment illustrate her gorgeous eyes but also my belief she would soar as an educator. I smile before I reply. *Me: I thought about you daily. Still do. Yes, every detail.*

Bluebird: Thank you. The peonies are gorgeous.

I ordered the fifty stems in varying hues of pink and red from a florist in the city. Not sure when, but she mentioned peonies were her favorite flower, but she couldn't afford them.

Me: You're welcome. How was your visit?

The infamous dots appear, disappear, and reappear a few times before stopping for good.

Me: I didn't mean to pry. I asked if you would be home today to deliver the flowers personally. Jack mentioned you were seeing your parents.

I hope she'll reply quickly but doesn't. *Damn.* I may have taken a few steps forward and one back in the span of three minutes. *Way to go, Colby.* Dismayed, I drive home and collapse onto the couch.

Jack enters the room and asks, "You good?"

"Not sure. Physically, I'm fine. Only a little tired."

"Looking for advice or do you want to wallow?" he asks.

"I want to ask your opinion, but I feel like I'm violating Annie's trust by doing so."

"What happened?"

I share about the flowers and asking about her visit and wait expectantly for him to comment, but he doesn't. "Well?"

"The flowers were a nice gesture. All I'll say is her lack of response has nothing to do with you. Her visit wasn't great. I have no more details."

I nod tightly. "Let me know if I can help with dinner."

"It's all set. We're eating around six."

"Okay." I climb the stairs, wiggle into the chaise lounge near the window, and crack open one of the books I purchased. I join Jack and Lor in the kitchen to offer help, despite him declining earlier. With the table set, we eat mostly in silence. Once we clean up, Jack invites me to a movie.

"We're going to the cineplex. Want to join us?"

"No, but I appreciate the invitation. Aside from physical therapy, it's my offseason."

Lorelei laughs. "What would you be doing in sunny Florida, alone during the offseason?"

"Same thing I'm going to do here minus the glorious, warm sunshine."

She raises an eyebrow, expecting more details.

I comply. "Grab a water and finish the book I bought this morning and possibly start a second one."

"Boring, old man," Lorelei quips.

"Yup, and proud of it. See you later or tomorrow." I climb the stairs with a bottled water in hand and settle into the chaise. Near eight, I see a flicker of light. At least I know she's safe at home, physically at least. From Jack's advice, I gather her visit didn't go well. I have no right, but I wish she would talk to me. *You need to earn it back,* I remind myself. I bury my nose in my book and make it to the turning point of the story. My phone chimes beside me, and I ignore it until I get to a chapter break.

Hatton: How are things up north?

Me: Living the PT dream. You?

Hatton: I'm in Texas with my family but wanted to check in.

Me: Thanks, man.

My phone rings in my hand. I'm surprised when I see her name on the screen. "Hi, Annie. Everything okay?"

"Yes. No. No." She exhales sharply. "I wanted to apologize for not answering you earlier."

"If anything, I owe you an apology. I overstepped."

I imagine her silky hair falling over her face as she disagrees with me. "You didn't. I opened the lines of communication myself when I thanked you for the stunning peonies. I'm not ready to share."

"With me or with anyone?"

"Anyone. I haven't shared with Lor yet. Only that my visit wasn't good."

I feel the urge to run across the grassy expanse between us, haul her against me, and comfort her. There are a few flaws in my plan. First, I'm not allowed to run. Second, she isn't ready for that. "I'm sorry, Bluebird. Do you want to talk or be alone?" The last thing I desire is to end the call, especially since she reached out to me.

"Will you sit with me, but I don't want to talk?"

"Sure."

Nearly a minute passes before she asks, "Are you coming?"

"On my way." I scurry faster than I should downstairs to make it seem like I moved immediately. Frankly, I thought she meant over the phone. When I step out into the backyard, her back door swings open. Once inside, I follow her to her living room and take a seat on the couch. Annie sits beside me, lifts my right arm, and wordlessly curls against me. For what seems like an eternity but more like fifteen minutes, silence surrounds us. I take the time to examine the parts of her I can see and feel. When we were together, she smelled like strawberries or vanilla. Now, her perfume is heavier, deeper, but still sweet smelling. Her blonde hair is shorter than it was years ago, but it remains silky soft. The V-neck she's wearing is oversized, and I have a direct view of her full breasts. I chastise myself for looking, but she's inexplicably more beautiful now than before.

"Colby?"

"Yeah."

She lifts her gaze to mine. "Thank you for coming."

"I always will." I consider adding whether we're a couple or not but don't. "I'm sorry I made you believe otherwise."

Her eyes widen, but she doesn't say anything further. Instead, she shifts into my lap and sets her head on my shoulder with her hands flat against my chest. I surround her with my arms and tighten my hold on her. In under a minute, her hands fist my shirt, and sobs wrack her frame. Annie crying and in pain guts me. The heaves lessen over the next thirty minutes to whimpers and short, sharp breaths.

"Come on, Annie. Let's get you into your bed."

She agrees wordlessly against my chest. This moment is heaven and hell at once. She was upset and called me. I'm grateful to be earning her trust again. However, she's upset, and that pisses me off. With a modicum of grace, Annie moves to her feet. With my hand on her lower back, I guide her upstairs to her bedroom and tuck her into her bed.

"Thank you, Two. It's nice to know you'll still catch me."

My breath hitches when she uses her old endearment for me. Two is the number of a catcher on a baseball position chart. I lightly kiss her forehead and whisper, "I meant what I said, Bluebird," before exiting her room. Did she hear me? Not sure. Either way, I plan to exceed her expectations of me. I check the locks at the front door and ensure the back door is secure as I close it behind me. Whatever the issue is, it's big. Tonight is the second time I've seen Annie crumble. The first time was my fault.

CHAPTER SIX

JULIANNE

Bright and early the next morning, I wake securely tucked into my bed. Wishing yesterday was an awful dream with a sweet and nerve-racking ending is what I want. However, I know for certain my father's illness is serious, and my time with him is starkly limited.

As much as I would like to ignore the facts, I asked Colby to sit with me last night. It felt... perfect. True to his nature and word, he didn't push me to share. Being in his arms while struggling with the diagnosis was torture of the best kind. It would be easy for me to throw open the door to my heart. Easy to divulge the fact, no man will measure up to the one man I judge all others by... him.

Aside from additional calls and visits, I can't do anything for my father. I would drive back today except they're busy. Instead, I dress, grab the paper from my stoop, and make my way to the café to work on the crossword.

"Good morning, Jules. How can I help you?" Kylie asks.

"Morning. My usual, please."

Stacie steps through the kitchen door. "Morning, Jules. I'll finish this one, Kylie." She frowns but steps back. "I'll bring your order to you. First, though, this is for you."

Now, it's my turn to frown. "Thanks, Stacie." The concern in my voice clearly evident.

She smiles. "Don't worry, I know the sender personally."

Intrigued, I take the gift bag to my booth in the corner. The little girl in me wants to tear into this package and find out who it's from. I realize it can only be one person… Colby. I pluck the tissue out of the bag and find a crossword dictionary, a package of erasable pens, and a card with the words *"Annie, in case you get stuck. Colby"* written in his familiar handwriting. How and when did he pull this off?

Stacie approaches with my coffee and breakfast order.

"When did Colby come in here?"

"Yesterday morning, ten or so. Don't hold me to the time though. I lose track while I'm working," she replies.

"Thank you."

"Enjoy," she says and walks away. For the next hour, I work on the puzzle and get stuck on a seven-letter word for calumniate. Before opening the book, I text him.

Me: Thank you.

Two: You're welcome. Are you stuck already?

Me: Perhaps. Are you?

Two: Maybe. Why don't you use your new book and look up six across.

Me: LOL. I can't figure that one out either.

Two: Tarnish isn't it.

Me: Neither is asperse.

Two: Is it time to call it?

Me: It is the last one I need. You?

Two: Same.

I flip the book open to and search calumniate. I literally laugh out loud when I see the answer. I snap a photo and send it to Colby before texting.

Me: I'm ashamed of us. We can come up with two other words but not the easiest. Slander.

Two: Sometimes the answer is right there, and we don't see it.

Or feels out of reach in say Florida. *Me: I appreciated your company last night.*

Two: I'm here for you. Anytime, anywhere, I will come for you whether you need to talk or sit in silence. I'm there. Just ask.

Me: Are you joining us at dinner tonight?

Two: Here or at your place?

Me: There.

Two: Yes.

Me: See you later then.

I sigh and finish my now-cold coffee. After clearing my space, I walk to my car. On the way home, I pull into the park and sit in the lot for a few minutes. I'll be able to get back out here and complete my puzzle each week, hopefully soon. I stop at the market for a few items. After parking in my garage, I step into my kitchen with my order in my arms.

I promised dessert for dinner tonight, and I still need to prepare it. Twisting my hair into a topknot, I craft the crust and filling and slide the dessert into the fridge in the nick of time. It takes a minimum of five hours to cure.

To pass the remaining hours, I shuffle to my office and review the single resumé I received for the athletic director position. I was hoping to have one person fill both roles, but I may not be so lucky. This candidate is for the staff position only. Charlotte Percy is a former Olympian and gold medalist in soccer. Currently, she serves as director of coaching for the local professional women's soccer team.

Could she do both? Probably. It's certainly worth an interview. I open my laptop and send an email to my assistant Reina to schedule it as soon as possible. I clear the rest of my inbox and consider changing for dinner. I don't, and about thirty minutes early, I cross our backyards with dessert in hand and let myself into their house.

I should be used to stumbling in on Jack and Lor making out in their kitchen. I was until Colby arrived. I've wanted the same with him since we were teens. My friends break apart, and Lor puts the pan into her fridge.

"Hey, guys."

Lor hugs me. "How are you doing?"

I shrug. "Still processing, I guess. It's a lot."

"We're here for you," Jack states.

"Much appreciated." I follow Lor into the dining room with silverware and serving utensils. When I turn the corner, Colby hits the bottom step of the staircase. *Holy hell!* Despite my state of mind last night, I could tell he's fit. *Of course he is, Julianne.* His chest beneath my hands was rock-solid, and his arms tight around me felt like home. Now, however, he's wearing gray sweatpants, a running hoodie, and a backward hat. The hat has always been my kryptonite, though I never mentioned it to him. I vaguely recall him having a few choice words with Coach during high school when he demanded he wear it properly. Colby declined, indicating he couldn't under his catcher's gear. Preventing myself from staring is much harder than I anticipate.

"Hi, Annie." His greeting breaks into my thoughts.

"Hi." I consider thanking him again for the book and flowers but think better of it.

Jack joins us with lasagna and garlic bread while Lor leaves to grab the pitcher of iced tea. I take a seat at the table, and Colby sits to my right. We eat together about once a month on Sundays. Dinner is one of the line items we were able to keep from our seventh-grade fearsome foursome life plan. Well, the three of us anyway.

The only sounds are of silverware hitting the plates or polite niceties. I know it's for my benefit. When I finish my first helping, I inhale sharply. "I'm grateful for the three of you."

Colby shifts slightly, setting his left leg against mine. The warmth radiating off him is comforting. If anyone recalls how I handle issues, it's him. Unconsciously, I lower my hand to grip the hem of my sweater. It's another one of my coping mechanisms. I shouldn't be surprised when I find Colby's, palm up, poised to hold mine. I glance at him discreetly and set my hand in his.

My eyes flutter closed as I take a deep breath. "My father…," I tighten my fingers in his hand before continuing, "has pancreatic cancer."

"Oh, Jules. I'm so sorry. What is his prognosis?" Lor asks.

I drop my head and will the tears away but fail. I swipe the wetness from my cheek with my free hand. Sharing with my friends lessens the burden a little. At the same time, Colby lifts our joined hands to his lips and kisses the back. "Abysmal and he's choosing not to get treatment."

"Anything you need, we're here," Jack offers.

Colby doesn't reiterate his words from last night, but I know without a doubt he'll walk beside me through this regardless of our relationship status. I acknowledge his offer and lean into Colby.

"Can I ask how long, or did they not share?" Lor asks.

"The doctors gave him three to nine months," I answer. When I let the information settle again, I slip my hand out of Colby's, push away from the table, and run to their guest bathroom. Thankfully, I make it before losing my dinner. I'm not in there long before there's a soft knock on the door.

"I'll be right out, Lor."

"Not Lorelei," Colby replies. His words were growly but not in an angry way. It's purely him. "Can I come in?"

No. "I would rather you not see me like this."

"It won't be the first time, Blue."

When we were in high school, three weeks before graduation, I got food poisoning at one of the year-end festivities. "It's open," I manage with limited reluctance.

The door opens, and Colby enters the tiny bathroom. The room instantly feels smaller and exponentially warmer. Wordlessly, he sits beside me with his left leg outstretched on the cold floor before smoothing my hair over my shoulders.

"Can I get you anything? Water, towel, a dry shirt to cry on, perhaps?"

A small smile curls up at the edge of my mouth. He could make me smile more easily than anyone else. "I need to sit here for a few minutes to be sure."

"Okay." He takes my hand in his and drags his thumb in mind-numbing circles to soothe me.

Five minutes later, someone knocks and says, "There's a water bottle out here for you."

"Thanks, Lor." I settle back on my heels, attempt to stand, but fail.

"Give me a second," Colby asks. He sets his hand on the wall, bends his right leg, and pushes to stand. He retrieves the water before extending his hand to me. I grab it and join him on my feet. We're as close as we were in my kitchen on Friday. His cologne or fabric softener or whatever envelopes me. Our gazes lock, and we both lean in.

"Umm, probably not the best idea right now." I cover my mouth with my hand.

His brow arches with intrigue. "Kissing is an option?"

"Perhaps, after a long, honest discussion about a few things."

"When you're ready, I'll be there."

I study his chiseled face. He's utterly serious. "If it takes until after he's gone?"

"I would prefer to stand beside you going forward and not to lose any more time with you. Either way, I'll be there."

Colby seems familiar yet unfamiliar. He's physically different. I'm sure his life experiences have molded him, but is the goofy guy who put french fries atop his lip at the diner still in there?

Only one way to find out, Julianne. Let him in… again. I wash my face and hands.

"Ready?"

With pursed lips, I nod. His hand settles on the small of my back as he ushers me to the dining room. Colby pulls out my chair and waits for me to sit. I appreciate his manners, always did, but this time I feel cold without his hand on me.

"Would you like to skip dessert?" Lor asks.

"You can serve it, but I'm not going to have any," I reply.

Jack pops up from his chair and walks into the kitchen. A few minutes later, he returns with three large portions of the Oreo cheesecake.

"Annie," Colby murmurs.

I turn my head, effectively blocking the others from reading his lips. "Yeah."

"You remember?"

I breathe deeply before answering, "Yes, every detail with painstaking precision—the good and the bad."

"Leaving you is the only regret I have in life. I would be ecstatic if you give me a second chance."

My eyes flutter closed. "We'll talk. Then figure things out. Okay?"

"Absolutely." He kisses high on my cheek, links our hands on my thigh, and digs into his slice.

Jack and Lorelei are silently eating their cheesecake while Colby and I make plans to at least discuss a relationship. The truth is, I would run headlong into a second chance with him except... my heart. All these years later, my heart isn't fully recovered from the first time he left. I can't handle another devastating breakup, especially once I lose my father.

CHAPTER SEVEN

COLBY

After dinner last night, I escorted Annie straight up to her bedroom and tucked her in. Leaving was difficult. I want to be there when she wakes up in the middle of the night to soothe her. The news about her father's health is devastating. The pain she shared is only the beginning. *Not the time yet.*

"Let's go," Jack grouses from the kitchen.

"Why are you grumpy this morning?"

Jack frowns at me. "I'm not grumpy. I'm tired. After your session, you can hang out. Then I'll bring you back at lunch."

"Okay." Jack drives to his office.

We greet his coworkers, who should be used to my presence at this point. I've been here each day in the morning. Shaking my head, I follow him to the therapy room and begin my exercises under Jack's watchful eye. For now, we're working on strengthening my quads and range of motion in my knee. Given my experience with rehabilitating my knee, I feel great. Despite the heightened severity of this injury, my progress is—in my opinion—stellar.

"Can I ask your opinion on something?"

"About Jules? I'll listen and then decide if I should weigh in?"

"Why wouldn't you?"

"Honestly, my wife and I are in a tough spot between the two of you. We both have information and confidences that we would like to keep."

"I understand. You can choose not to offer your insight after you hear my question. No hard feelings either way."

Jack motions with his hand for me to go ahead.

"My invitation to the ring ceremony and gala was forwarded to me yesterday."

"You want to invite Jules instead of requesting one of Madeleine's fix ups?"

I scowl at him. "Yeah, but I don't want her to feel like I'm taking time away from her father."

"It's a good idea. It'll allow her to see your baseball life, and you'll be able to introduce her to your teammates and friends in Florida."

"My what?"

"Yeah… the celebrity, the house, and the cars. Your life is different near the team. You aren't, but the forces around you are. Up here, you're gossip rag and reporter free, at least so far. Near the ball club… not so much."

I lift my leg and continue the extensions while we chat. "Arguably, you're right. With my injury though, no one wants to interview me. It's one plus at least."

"It can't hurt to ask her and talk about it," Jack offers.

"Thanks. When we're done, will you bring me to the dealership instead of the house?"

Jack frowns. "Sure, but why?"

"Easier to buy a practical car than ship mine up here for my recovery."

"No problem. Let me know if you need a ride at the end of the day."

I agree and continue letting him torture me with the slow pace of his exercise plan. Jack has my best interests at heart. However, despite grasping the reality of my injury, anything less than the entire season would be nice. Then again, it would mean leaving Annie. My gut tightens. Even at this early stage, leaving her again is not something I desire to do.

By the end of the day, I purchase an Audi Q7 in Navarra blue and drive myself home after informing Jack. I consider stopping at Annie's but instead park off to the side of the driveway and reach out to Madeleine's office while I ascend to my room.

"Good evening, Colby. How can I help you? How's the knee?" her assistant asks.

"Hi, Simon. We're making progress with my knee. Thank you for asking. I wanted to reach out and let Madeleine know I do not, I repeat do not, need her to set up a date for the gala." My date should be Annie or no one.

"No problem. I'll be sure to inform her."

"Thank you, Simon."

"My pleasure. Have a lovely evening."

"You as well."

I smile with that small hurdle handled and text Annie.

Me: How are you? How was school today?

When I don't get an immediate answer, I walk to the window as normally as I can with this brace on my knee. I note there aren't any lights on in her house. Despite the chilly temperatures, I grab a hoodie and take a seat outside and mull over my options regarding the gala and how to pull it off. I agree with and understand Jack's concerns, but the stark reality is… I want Annie. No. I need Annie back in my life. Since I arrived, I'm less grumpy, especially with my injured state. She brings life into my normally boring days and I'm grateful.

Research may help me with this plan. I google her school and then navigate to the calendar. Her spring break nicely coincides with family day and the gala. Opening day is a bit early, but my team is away for the six games. The team will be recognized on the field before the first home game of the season and the rings distributed at the gala later the same evening. Should I hedge my bet and invite her parents as well? I would prefer to be alone with Annie, but if getting her there means Edmund and Caroline are joining us, it's fine with me.

With a few steps forward, I return inside and prepare dinner. I wrack my brain, trying to recall if Jack or Lor mentioned they had plans this evening. As I warm some leftovers, my mind wanders to seeing my teammates again. I want to share my baseball life, as Jack calls it, with Annie and introduce her to my coworkers. However, going home means I will see my absence with the team in full living color. I'm not prepared. Having Annie beside me will absolutely lessen the blow.

I pour the food into a bowl and take a seat at the island. When I finish my dinner, I clean up and climb the stairs. With a new book in hand, I sit on the bed and crack the spine. I'm only a few pages in when my phone alerts me to a message.

Bluebird: I'm doing. School was fine.

Me: Want to talk or stew more?

Bluebird: I don't want to talk, but stewing isn't a good option either.

Me: Understood. If you want company in the silence, let me know.

Bluebird: Not tonight. Thanks for the offer.

Me: You're welcome.

Bluebird: Night, Colby.

I frown but stay put. The tarnished white knight in me wants to trudge across their backyards and demand she talk to me. However, I know her, and it'll backfire. She needs to decide she wants to and ask me. I can't push her. I also know her response, and lack of talking isn't personal to me. She's introspective about each problem she comes across.

Instead, I shop. I fill a basket for her, including a fluffy blanket, fuzzy socks, gourmet hot cocoa, and two mugs like the ones in her kitchen. After scouring the internet, I learned they are Rae Dunn, which is a popular brand. I customized one with 'Bluebird' and one with 'My Cocoa Mug'. I also found a necklace with a platinum bird with a sapphire heart hanging from its beak. All the items will be here when I get home on Friday. I also ordered another bouquet of flowers. The bouquet is mixed but includes peonies. I sent them to the school instead of home this time.

The rest of the week passes much the same way. I threw in another stop at the bookstore for more books midweek. At this rate, I may finish my 'to be read' list before opening day. My heart climbs into my throat at the thought. The reality is I'm not playing when the season starts. Truthfully, it hit me hard when I realized I should be reporting for spring training in a few days.

I wallow and sulk for the remainder of the afternoon. Lor and Jack are bickering about their vacation plans in the living room. I slip past them and climb the stairs. After therapy on Friday morning, I scoop up the packages and prepare Annie's basket. Near four in the afternoon, I walk across the grass and around her house to the front.

I set the basket on the ground and close the side gate behind me. As I do, a rail-thin guy strolls casually toward the front door.

"Can I help you?" I ask.

"I came to check on Julianne. We had a date last week and canceled it because of traffic. She hasn't responded to my messages to reschedule yet."

"She isn't home. I'll tell her you stopped by…."

"Jimmy Bolden." He studies me. "You look a lot like the catcher from Florida… Somerset." Jimmy doesn't remember me from elementary school… interesting.

Ever since the win and my face being plastered on the front page of sports magazines and internet sites, people recognize me more frequently.

The kicker is the headlines read *A Bittersweet Victory* or *Victory and Pain*. "I get that a lot. I'll let her know you stopped by."

"Thanks. Much appreciated. Julianne is a rare find."

I don't like the underlying tone of his words. "Meaning?"

"She's beautiful, in her thirties, has a good job, and has never been married before. Most importantly, she doesn't have kids."

"You don't want kids, Jimmy?"

Annie wants a houseful. Though that tidbit of information was from when we were much younger. I wonder if it's changed. I'm confident children are in her future plans, but the number may have changed given the passage of time. *My fault.*

"No, hell no."

"You mentioned she has a good job, but do you know what it is?"

"Yeah, she's a principal at some school for uber-rich, trust fund babies."

Settle. Calm. Partially true. Through gritted teeth, I reiterate, "I'll tell her you stopped by."

"Thank you." He turns on his heel and trots back to his souped-up truck. I would like to remind him we're in the Mid-Atlantic not the Deep South.

After waiting for him to pull away, I pick up the basket. Brushing off the bottom, I set it on the chair near Annie's front door. I consider waiting for her to come home, but I refuse to intrude on her space. Deep down, I want to be her shadow. There will be another breakdown or two before she's ready to share and talk. I need to be there to hold her, dry her tears, and comfort her. I need her to rely on me… again.

I turn to walk away and freeze when I hear my name.

"Colby?"

I glance around, but she isn't here. Then her laughter echoes around me.

"Doorbell camera. I'm notified when there's motion on my porch."

I turn and bend forward so my face takes up the entire view. "Smart."

"What are you doing on my porch?" she asks.

"Dropping off a gift for you."

"On top of the gorgeous flowers?"

"Yes."

"Thank you for the flowers. The delivery was the talk of the main office today."

I smile. "You're welcome. Please let me know when you get home."

"It'll be a while. The staff has happy hour tonight, and I need to show my face."

The worry in my chest lessens slightly. "Either way, I would appreciate a call when you're safely tucked into your home."

"I will."

I turn to leave. Her voice draws me back.

"Colby… thank you for asking Jimmy the right questions."

I frown. She heard our conversation. *Doorbell camera.* "You're welcome. Talk to you later." I descend the steps carefully and walk to the house, which is also still empty.

I down some leftovers in the fridge and wait for her call. As the hours pass, I mentally add the time it would take to get from a restaurant near her school to home at this hour. I recalculate at least every thirty minutes. The increased worry is new for me. Then again, I was eight hundred miles away and had no idea about her movements.

My phone rings near eight in the evening. Relief cascades over me when I see her name on the screen. "Hi, Annie. How was your happy hour?"

"Fine. Not my favorite thing to do, but it's important for my staff to know I'm not a stick-in-the-mud."

I laugh. "Can't have that. Still a homebody?"

"Very much so. You don't need to send me gifts."

"I want to. If I can't be there with you, I need you to be as comfortable as possible."

"I want to talk about an us, but with the news of Dad's illness and work… I don't have enough bandwidth."

"Completely understand. Just know, I will continue to take care of you from here unless and until you tell me to stop."

"I appreciate you and your concern for my well-being."

"Good. Want some silent company?" My stomach knots up as I wait for her to answer.

"Sure. No discussion about work, my dad, or us. Deal?"

"Deal. I'll be there in ten."

"The code to the back door is 040109."

My birthday, April first, and hers, September first, together. Interesting. Yes, sports fans, I was born on baseball's opening day.

"Okay."

I tug on a hoodie and slides before walking across the grass again. I input the code and enter. "Annie," I call out.

"Coming," I hear from upstairs. Within a minute, she steps into her kitchen. The pajamas from the last time I was here were cute. These border on sinful. Ninety percent of her lean, toned legs are exposed by the tiny shorts. She has a V-neck shirt with a fluffy sweater over it. I'm sure she thinks she looks terrible. It's the furthest notion from the truth. Annie is stunning no matter what she wears.

"Would you like a cup of cocoa?"

"Yes."

She busies herself pulling down the mugs. Despite my desire to see what her stretching reveals, I close my eyes. My imagination of the curve of her pert ass and the—

"Colby, you okay?"

"Uh-huh. What's with the coaching books and baseball information? You know more about baseball than most of the players in the league." I noticed the books on the island when I walked in.

She shakes her head. "Not talking about work."

I'm intrigued but raise my hands in surrender. "What activity are we partaking in tonight? Cards, Boggle, or a movie?"

"Movie. Concentration and high-level thinking, which are required to beat you in a word game or cards, are in short supply."

I follow her to the living room with my cocoa in hand. Interestingly my mug from the basket I dropped off earlier. Without hesitation, she hands me the remotes and draws her legs beneath her in the corner of her couch. I've got you, Annie. With an old favorite, *Letters to Juliette,* playing on the screen, I take a seat beside her. About fifteen minutes into the movie, she uncurls and drapes her legs across my lap.

A memory of a time in the past moves rapidly to the front of my mind. We were in my Civic at a drive-in movie. I don't recall the movie, though. She twisted in the passenger seat and set her legs over mine. I spent the rest of the evening dragging my hand up and down her silky, smooth skin, inching higher with each pass. Later the same night, I tasted her for the first time in my backseat. I manage to control my breathing to avoid tipping Annie off to the memories in my head. Either way, a repeat performance is not an option tonight as much as I would like it to be. My self-control is through the roof. I haven't kissed Annie in over a decade. Yet my fingers are tingling to find out if her skin is as soft as it was all those years ago. Hiding my erection in these joggers is impossible.

Her head lolling to the side catches my eye thirty minutes later. She's sound asleep. Despite the turmoil roiling in her body, she looks at peace. I'm sure it isn't the case. Carefully, I extricate myself from beneath her and guide her to a reclining position on her couch. When I turn to grab a blanket from the chair, I hear my name.

"Colby." Her voice is soft and sleep addled.

I drape the blanket over her, and answer, "Yes."

"Thank you for being true to your word. It's a lot...."

"If time is what you need, then I'll give it to you."

"Can I ask one question before you go?" She shifts against the back of the couch, allowing me room to sit beside her.

"Anything."

"Why did you leave me?"

A crushing weight lands on my shoulders while a hundred daggers pierce my chest. No reason not to spill the complete and unvarnished truth. "I couldn't bear you giving up your aspirations for mine. By the time I realized you were my dream, I was too late and hurt you deeply. I didn't think I deserved a second chance. Now, is our opportunity, and I don't want to let you go."

Stunning Annie silent isn't a frequent event. She attempts to speak a few times and fails. Finally, she manages, "Good night, Two."

I lean closer and kiss her forehead. "Sweet dreams, Bluebird." Before leaving, I rinse our mugs and set them to dry in the rack. I lock the back door, closing it behind me, and exhale slowly. Baby steps are progress, right? Only one way to find out... if Annie lets me in.

CHAPTER EIGHT

JULIANNE

In the wee hours of the morning, I traipse upstairs and fall into my bed. I would like to say I've been sleeping since Colby left, but I haven't. The only thing holding me back is me. Taking the risk he'll hurt me is a huge leap. Then again, it can't be worse than dating at thirty. Could it? *No.* Dating now is horrid, especially since I hate the apps. I believe him. I trust him despite our past. He has been true to his word since he arrived for therapy.

Instead of trying to sleep, I change and walk five miles on my treadmill before dressing to visit my dad. It isn't until I open the cabinet for my travel mug that I notice Colby washed our dishes from last night before he left. It's unfair for me to compare the version of him in my mind... the one who crushed my teenage heart into a million pieces and the grown-up version. Grown-up Colby is beyond words. He's still an exceptional listener, and he's not pushing me faster than I need to go. I'm grateful. I refuse to squander this chance for us.

His response to my question was more than I expected. Brutal honesty was always something we gave each other until the moment he left. Now, knowing the true reason makes my heart ache more. A swath of blame should be added on my side of the ledger for not reaching out at any time in the last few years.

I push away my thoughts and pull out of my driveway. A new Brett Young song plays through my speakers as I drive to my parents. About halfway there, I exit off the interstate for more coffee and gas. Before I leave the station, I call my mother.

"Morning, Jules."

"Morning. I wanted to see if you need anything. I can pick it up before I arrive."

"Oh, sweetie. We're in New York visiting Tom and Pam for the weekend." Pam is my aunt, and Tom is her second husband. Like my parents, they couldn't have children. However, my aunt and uncle chose not to adopt.

"Oh. Why didn't you tell me?"

"You already visited at your normal time this month. We will see you next weekend as usual."

"Have fun," I mutter.

A rush of emotions course through me at once. I've been keeping Colby at arm's length because of my father's illness, among other things. Yet, my father seems content to maintain the status quo as if there isn't an expiration date on his life with Mom and me. *Understood.* With that notion in mind, I make a bold decision. I'm going to let him in slowly. How though? Honestly, I have been spending time with him but not truly letting him in again. I take the next exit and turn back toward Summit Creek.

When I reach home again, I check my work email and find three potential candidates. Unfortunately, Charlotte, the first candidate, took a promotion at her current employer and declined to interview. The new candidate is Kyle Nager. While he applied for both positions, he doesn't meet the minimum qualifications for the director job. While I stew on the possibility of hiring two people, I open the next resume in my inbox.

The final option is Katherine Williamson, who is looking to relocate to be closer to her siblings. Currently, she's the athletic director at a private school outside Seattle. Her credentials are impeccable. I schedule an email to my assistant, requesting a video conference interview for as soon as possible.

With that handled, I dig into the coaching books and information I bought and culled from my research. A few hours later, my phone chimes.

Lorelei: Hey, you home already?

Me: Yup. Long story.

Lorelei: Want to talk about it?

Me: Nope.

Lorelei: Care to join us at the soirée tonight?

Me: No. Thanks for the invite though.

Lorelei: Welcome.

Before I think better of it, I call Colby.

"Hey, Annie. How are you today?"

"Not sure. Mixed, I guess. Are you free in an hour for the evening?"

"Yes." His answer is unequivocal and unwavering.

"How much walking can you handle?"

"Walking is no problem. I can't jog, run, or hike yet. Well, I can jog and run, but Jack would have my head. Why?"

I laugh softly at his self-deprecation. "I'm planning on the fly."

"Very unlike you, beautiful."

I smile at the compliment and skim my fingers over the pendant he gave me, which includes a bird and my birthstone. A detail I'm certain was purposeful. "I know." When we were dating in high school, every date was meticulously scheduled by me well in advance and executed to perfection. "Want to go to the forest with me and walk the lake loop?" On the outskirts of town is a state park. There are numerous hiking trails as well as a flat, gravel path around a large lake. The irony is we had our first kiss on one of the benches surrounding the lake isn't lost on me. It was exactly how you would expect a first kiss to be... inexperienced, fumbling, and unfulfilling. Kissing and other exploration with Colby only got better the longer we were together.

"Yes. I'll raid Jack's closet for a jacket and gloves. When do you want me to pick you up?"

"Whenever you're ready. I only need to add more layers."

Forty minutes later, Colby knocks on the front door. He escorts me to the passenger side and waits for me to settle in. As he backs down my driveway, I ask, "Did you transport your car up here?"

He looks at me briefly and grins. "No, I bought it a few days ago. Less hassle than transporting one of mine."

I chuckle. "How many do you have?"

"Cars? Five, including this one."

"Not bad. I expected more."

"Can I ask you a question?"

I shift in the buttery soft leather seat. "Sure."

He lowers his hand to cover mine. "Please don't take this the wrong way, since I'm grateful and moderately hopeful to talk about us, but... why the abrupt change of heart?"

My eyes flutter closed. I catalog how amazing my hand feels beneath his. The warmth radiating from him has never been matched by any other man. There weren't many, but every other one was an actual frog. Not the fairytale frog who turns into a prince. I share how the beginning of my day went and the call with my mother.

"I'm sorry."

"For?"

He parks in the bumpy lot and looks over at me. "Your parents didn't share their plan to handle your father's illness as nonexistent with you."

"Me too. I'm taking their decision, which is theirs to make, as a sign. A directive to live rather than put my life on hold. They certainly aren't interested in cobbling together extra time for me to spend with my father. I get my two visits a month and no more."

"Why did you pick here to talk?" he asks softly.

"Most of our relationship was spent here, and we weren't always making out."

He chuckles. I reach for the handle.

He tightens his grip on my hand. "I'll get your door, Annie." He releases my hand and rounds the car. The cold, hard ground crunches beneath my feet. The sliver of air between us is charged with unrequited potential and desire. Heavy, blissful lust that weighs more than our past sits in my heart. He offers me his arm, and I loop mine through his.

We turn right and walk side by side in silence nearly halfway around the lake. Initially, I was checking his gait to be sure he's fine.

"How is your therapy going?" I ask.

His step stutters briefly with his gaze pinned to mine. "Is that what you truly want to know?"

My shoulders drop. "No, but I'm easing into this conversation."

"Okay. One easy question, then a hard one."

"I can work with those rules."

"Jack is exceptional. I feel great. Am I in shape to catch Hatton's fastball or be behind the plate for nine innings? No, not yet."

"I'm sure it tears you apart to admit you're human."

"It does. Physically anyway. Though I've been feeling older in the last few years. Emotionally, I began owning my humanity when I realized leaving you would permanently change my life."

"It happens to the best of us. Hatton's fastball is something to tout, that's for sure."

"You watch my games?"

"Yes, as many as I can. Despite my broken heart, I've followed your career under the guise of my love for baseball rather than admitting my need to know you were alive and well... even if you weren't mine anymore."

Abruptly, he stops walking. "Annie, to this day, I regret leaving you. I take full responsibility for it. Could I blame youthful stupidity? Sure. Who meets the one they're meant to spend the rest of their life with during Little League? It's rare, and I own hurting you. I also bear the blame for not speaking up when you were with Brandon. When I saw Patrick's ring on your finger at Jack and Lor's wedding, my bruised and battered heart ached and shattered again. I was confident our chance was gone."

I can't help myself. I need to know. "Is that when you started dating every young starlet you could find?"

He shakes his head. "No. Each woman was set up by my agent for their benefit not mine. I never dated any of them."

Containing my eye roll is impossible. "Sure."

"Why would I lie about that? We're here to talk about us, a potential us. The reality is I spiraled after finding another man's ring on your finger."

"You don't drink excessively or do drugs," I state emphatically.

"I don't. I mean emotionally. I locked myself in my house, became a hermit, and only went to work and events I was contractually obligated to attend. After the first few solo events, Madeleine asked me to escort a new up-and-coming actress named Elsie Snow. I agreed. We literally posed for photos and stood next to each other all night. She took a separate car home at the end of the evening. Same goes for Estelle Gomes, and Angelica Swisher."

"Have you dated anyone else for more than a few months?" I force the words from my lips.

"No. Why didn't you marry Patrick?"

"I already told you why."

He eliminates more space between us and cups my face with his free hand. The electricity in his touch far exceeds my memory of the same. I set mine on his chest, and by the slimmest of margins, I refrain from kissing him, despite a yearning in my heart I only ever felt for him.

"Maybe you could share the real answer now?" he asks while his hand glides down and stops on my shoulder.

"You want the whole truth?"

"It's why we're here isn't it? To decide if we can be together again. To figure if we can mend the cracks in the foundation we started building over a decade ago. If you will allow me to heal the hurt I caused by choosing my professional dream over us."

The tears I'd been fighting finally break free. A few roll down my cheek. Colby leans closer and kisses them away.

"When I took your arm walking out of the church at Lor and Jack's wedding…." I attempt to take a step backward.

His grip tightens on my shoulders, preventing me from moving. The heat pinging between us is…

"Keep going, Bluebird. We need to share everything."

I breathe deeply and continue, "A shot of heat and familiarity raced through me." *The same kind of heat rushing through me right now despite the nearly chaste hold he has on me.*

"Same for me. Until I looked down and saw a ring on your finger that wasn't mine. To top it off, I knew without question you wouldn't pick his engagement ring."

Colby is absolutely correct. Patrick bought a gaudy yellow diamond with a gold band.

"True. More importantly, I tried to imagine leaving that church, our church, on my wedding day. I didn't see my fiancé beside me. I saw you."

"Why didn't you tell me?"

I purse my lips and wrinkle my nose. "Lor and Jack never broke down the walls we implored them to erect until recently. I didn't know you—"

"Neither did I."

We stand, unmoving, in silence for a few minutes before I speak again. "What do we do now?"

"We try again but slowly."

I tilt my chin upward to kiss him, but he turns his head, and I end up planting my lips on his cheek. "What the...?"

He laughs heartily. "I want to kiss your lips to see if they're pillow soft like in the past. I will, just not tonight."

"Why not?"

"We're doing this right, Bluebird. What do you say to visiting one of our old late night date spots?"

"If you mean Tipsy Tomato, I'm completely in."

Colby presses a lingering kiss to my forehead, and we walk back toward his SUV. "Are you free tomorrow morning?"

I raise an eyebrow. "Depends on how early you're thinking?"

"Can we work on the puzzle together at the café?"

Attempting to contain my smile is futile. "Yes. I normally get there at nine."

"I'll pick you up in plenty of time."

"It's a date."

He frowns briefly.

"What else?"

"It kind of goes against the whole slow mantra, but... will you attend the gala and ring ceremony with me?"

A twinge of pride and a slice of anger tangle in the pit of my stomach. True, it's his first championship win, but...

"Stop wondering about the things we missed. It's a long list and not fun to dwell on. Trust me, I've done it plenty over the years."

"When is it?"

"April 5th."

It's during break. I was planning to rent a cottage somewhere and unplug for a solid week. Spending time in Florida with Colby is much more appealing.

"Annie, please share what you're thinking," he states as he opens my door.

I sit and wait for him to settle into the driver's seat. We were good together regardless of our young age. Reading me seems to be a skill he still possesses exactly like he knew I wasn't fully truthful about Patrick. "Yes, but…."

"No but. Whatever you need to travel to Florida with me, I'll make it happen. Better yet, I'll plan everything. Would you be willing to spend the entire week at my place? I can show you around, and you can meet some of the guys. They are also hosting a family day at the stadium the day before the ceremony."

"Okay. Yes. Yes." It's new to have Colby in charge of things. I kind of love it.

He leans over the center console and kisses my cheek. "Crispy pepperoni still your favorite?"

"Yes. Has yours changed?"

With a sexy grin on his face, he says, "No, but I'll share with you."

Instead of pushing away the butterflies and hope swirling in my belly, I savor them. I trust Colby's words.

CHAPTER NINE

COLBY

Last night, we closed down the Tipsy Tomato. Like we did in high school, we crossed the street and had milkshakes at the diner until curfew. We don't have curfews anymore, but I walked Annie to her door after midnight. The self-control it took not to invite myself into her house was monumental. The girl I knew bloomed into a stunning woman, and I refuse to mess up this time. I may be one of the most well-known names in baseball, but my private life is exactly that… private. I have dated a few women since Annie, but none were her.

At eight the next morning, I climb downstairs and find Lorelei sipping coffee in the kitchen.

"Late night?"

"I'm sure you already talked to Annie. Whatever she chose to share is what you're getting."

Lorelei wiggles her finger at me and says, "Nope. Not how this is going to work. As I mentioned we are rooting for you… hard."

"We appreciate your support. Annie and I are stepping into a relationship slowly."

"Uh-huh. How is inviting her to spend spring break with you at your home in sunny Florida and attending the ring gala not precisely the opposite of that?"

I frown. Worry cascades through me. Did I push her too fast? Then I recall her displeasure at me rebuffing her kiss. "We're adults now, Lor. Are those your words or hers?"

"Mine."

Relief washes over me. "I want her to meet my teammates and be with me for the ceremony. As you know, I have four guest rooms she can choose from."

Lor waves me off when Jack enters the room. *Interesting.* It appears they aren't in agreement about my date to the gala.

"Morning, Colby."

"Jack."

"I'll be back later."

"Have fun." Jack's words follow me over the threshold.

Before I pick her up, I send a message to Simon, my agent's assistant, requesting some information for the gala. If we're attending this party, we're doing it right. *It may be the only one I get.* I'm not wallowing about my injury exactly. Therapy is progressing well. Walks are good for me, especially ones with Annie regardless of the hard conversation. However, with my teammates reporting for work, a sheen of sadness settles in my heart.

A little early, I knock on Annie's front door. A few minutes later, she hurries down the stairs, disarms her alarm system, and throws it open.

"Morning. I… umm… come in. I'll be ready fast." She turns to hurry back upstairs. As she does, I notice her clothing. Her pajama pants are threadbare with all the major league baseball teams on them. As I look closer, I realize they're mine from high school. She kept them this entire time. What other items does she have stashed in her closet? The door between us opens a sliver more.

I reach out, encircle her forearm with my hand, and she stills. Closing the door with my foot, I haul her into my arms. "Breathe, Blue. We don't have an appointment."

She inhales deeply, and her hands flatten on my back. "I'm never late," she mumbles against my shoulder.

"You're not late. I'm early. What's really going on, Annie?" It takes me a few beats of silence to determine the thoughts in her gorgeous head. "You were afraid I wouldn't show?"

"Maybe."

"Julianne, please look at me."

She shakes her head but concedes. Her piercing eyes shift to meet mine.

"I would never squander my chance to love you again." *I never stopped loving Annie, but now isn't the time.* No other woman ever came close to the perfection of her. It's possible she hasn't either, given her penchant for wearing my ring and my clothes. I eliminate the space between us and kiss her lightly.

"Now we can kiss?"

"Call it a moment of weakness. What other clothes of mine do you have in your closet?"

A fierce blush blooms on her cheeks. "I have your championship hoodie, your letterman's jacket, and a few T-shirts. Before you ask, you can only have your coat back. The rest won't fit this version of you."

"Are you saying you find me attractive?"

"You were good-looking in high school, Colby. The grown-up version of you is sexy as…."

"Interesting. My thoughts about you are similar. Get dressed, gorgeous. The puzzle isn't going to solve itself."

"I'm going."

We arrive at the coffee shop, place our order, and immediately start the puzzle.

"Are we doing this old school?" I ask.

"Yes," Annie replies. At her response, I shift my chair beside her, and we tackle the puzzle together. Two hours and some lively debate later over a nine-letter word for ability ensues. You would think this would be an easy clue to answer. I came up with "expertise" and "handiness" while Annie proposed "dexterity." We were both wrong. She pulls out her dictionary, and we determine the answer should be "adeptness."

With the ease we had during the first part of our relationship, we talk about current events, music, and books.

"Is the topic of work an option?"

She wrinkles her nose when I finish asking.

"We don't have to talk about your job if you don't want to."

"You're curious about the coaching books?"

I slide my fingers between hers on the table. "Yes."

She shares the vacancy at school and the lack of viable replacements. Certainly, not one candidate for both positions.

"You're going to be the baseball coach?"

"I'm preparing as if it'll be necessary. We have a few seniors who were scouted last year. They deserve a proper coach. If it's going to be me, I need to be ready."

"Annie, you know more about baseball than some of my teammates."

"History and stats, sure, but coaching, not so much."

"I happen to know someone intimately familiar with the game of baseball."

"Do you? Will assisting me in any way violate your contract?"

Damn! I didn't even think of that. "That's why you didn't want to talk about it?"

"Partially."

"Plus, you're worried the team will get attached to me if I help out and I'm able to return to playing."

She drops her head as if her thoughts would offend me somehow.

"Annie, I'm not angry. You were protecting them and, more importantly, yourself. Would you be okay with me asking Madeleine if I'm able to help out?"

"Yes. Thank you."

"What time do you get home on normal weekdays? Are you free on the weekends for the foreseeable future?"

"Around five if I leave as soon as school ends. Whatever I have planned, I would be happy to bring you with me."

"Sounds perfect to me. Ready to—"

I hear the words before I'm able to locate the speaker. "Yes, it absolutely is Colby Somerset. Didn't your parents teach you anything? He's the greatest baseball player to play at Summit High… like ever. Hell, his picture is in the locker room and the trophy case."

Annie heard them as well. "Go. I'll clear this and then we can leave."

After a kiss atop her hand, I hand her my keys. Then, I greet the two young men a few tables over.

"We didn't mean to interrupt your coffee," the taller, lanky one admits.

"No problem. What's your name? What position do you play?"

"Milo and I'm a pitcher. This dude"—he points to his tablemate—"is Billy and plays catcher."

"Nice to meet you both."

"You made an amazing tag in the final game. Sorry about your knee though." Billy joins the conversation.

"Thank you. Eventually, my knee will be good as new. When does your season start?" I asked, but the question stings a bit.

"We"—Milo motions between himself and Billy—"never stopped training. To answer your question, team practice starts in a few weeks. Then we have one week of games, spring break, and then the rest of the season."

"Great! Best of luck to you both."

"Thank you," they reply in unison.

I exit the coffee shop and join Annie at the car. We spend the next few hours chatting while we prepare dinner for the four of us at her place. Jack and Lorelei leave soon after we eat. I hang out for a while longer, talking about my teammates, the gala, and our second first date.

"Are you free on Thursday night?" I ask.

"Yes, actually. It's my last day of school for the long holiday weekend."

"To clarify, you're free Thursday evening to Monday evening except for Saturday when your parents are set to visit, correct?"

"Yes. What are you up to?"

Giddiness courses through me. I intend to soak up every minute I can with her. "Please don't fill up your free time. I'll plan everything for our second first date and second second date. You get the idea."

A look of trepidation crosses her face.

"The concern on your face is priceless. Unlike before, I can handle setting up a date among other things."

"Okay. Please let me know the attire for our first date when you are set," she states.

"I will." Taking her hand in mine, I tug gently and eliminate the space between us. Julianne flush against me is a heady experience. How she feels now has nothing on during high school. Lust zips through me. The ache to kiss her until we can't breathe is palpable. However, I promised to go slow, and I will, even if it kills me.

"You should go before I lure you into breaking your dating conditions." Her whispered words near my ear send shivers down my spine.

"You're temptation personified, Bluebird." I hold her close for another moment, press a kiss to her cheek, and leave. Before entering the house, I take a seat on the patio despite the cool temperature to will my erection away. Also, I'm not in the mood to talk about Annie and me with our friends tonight. Dating Annie again is amazing and I want to continue being with her for the rest of my life. If she'll have me that is.

Thankfully, they already turned in when I get home. I scribble a list of calls and arrangements to make tomorrow and get some sleep myself.

CHAPTER TEN

JULIANNE

The parking lot at school is nearly full when I arrive the next morning. All night, I tossed and turned, thinking about Colby, which gave me a late start. Balancing the warm and fuzzy feelings with the memory of the pain he caused is difficult. I want to surrender and believe we could have it all. I promised myself and, more importantly, him I would. Cautious optimism is my inner monologue when it comes to Colby.

"Morning, Principal Silva," my assistant states when I walk into the main office.

"Morning."

"Here is your schedule for the day."

"Much appreciated, Reina." I glance at the sheet. "Please show Mr. Nager into the conference room when he arrives."

The phone rings, and she acknowledges me before she answers the call. Stepping into my office, the first thing I see is the gorgeous flowers Colby sent last week. I smile, own how good I feel, and get to work.

"Coach, pleasure to meet you." I greet him a few hours later in the conference room.

"You as well. I'm grateful for the opportunity to discuss the athletic director and coaching positions with you."

"There seems to be some misunderstanding. Could you give me a moment?"

"Of course."

I wake my tablet and check the confirmation Reina sent to him. "This interview is for the head baseball coach position only. The email from my assistant indicated the same as you don't meet the qualifications for the staff position."

"Oh, I see." His face falls, showing his marked disappointment.

My first impression of him isn't great. Not only did he not read his email, but he isn't grateful for the opportunity to be the coach. "Would you like to continue this interview?"

"No. Thank you for your time."

I extend my hand to him and escort him from the building. As we walk, I struggle to contain my frustration. I realize this isn't a professional sports team, but I expect my potential staff hires to be thorough nonetheless. Furious, I stomp back to the main office. Arguably, you can't hear my shoes on the Berber carpet.

"Julianne, the interview with Miss Williamson is confirmed for two this afternoon," Reina shares when I walk into the main office. When I don't answer or indicate I heard her, she asks, "Everything okay?"

"Yes, of course." I flop into my high-back leather chair with a huff.

Less than a minute later, Reina buzzes me. "Mr. Somerset is on line three for you."

I frown. "Thank you." Why is he calling the main office? Before I answer the call, I pull out my cell phone. There are a few text messages and a voicemail from him. "Hi, Colby."

"Hi, beautiful. Busy day?"

"Frustrating. You?"

"Jack went hard on me this morning, but I will endure the therapy to heal. I have some good news, and it sounds like you need some."

"Good news is always welcome."

"Want to share what went wrong first?"

I take a settling breath and share my meeting with Mr. Nager but don't divulge his name.

"Not the best way to show up for an interview."

"No, it isn't. Two, please brighten my day with your news." I imagine his gorgeous smile while he replies.

"I spoke with Madeleine on my way back from therapy. As long as I don't break Jack's rules, I can assist in an unofficial capacity."

"Makes sense."

"Are you willing to let me help you, Annie?"

Without hesitation, I answer, "Yes." Giddiness courses through me. Not only will the team get a professional catcher, but we will also spend more time together.

"Great. How about I make dinner for you tonight and we can talk about it? Before you ask, it isn't our second first date. That will be Thursday."

I laugh softly. "Okay."

"Do you mind if I let myself into your house to get started before you arrive?"

"No. The alarm code is the same as the backdoor keypad."

"I hope your afternoon interview is better than this one," Colby offers.

"Me too. See you later."

Colby deserves the credit for the smile on my face as I handle some administrative issues before my interview with Kate Williamson. She's well-spoken and has great ideas how to handle the hypothetical issue I posed during our talk. She'll be visiting our campus in person during her spring break, which luckily is the week before ours.

As soon as the last bus pulls away, I stride to my car and head home. With music blaring, the drive passes quickly. When I step into my kitchen, Colby doesn't hear me. I notice his earbuds and watch him unabashedly for a few minutes. The muscles of his back and arms twitch and tense as he chops something at the island. I set my bag on the counter and wrap my arms around him from behind like I did when we were younger. *Sweet mercy!* The contours of his chest and abs are insane! My palms are met with ripples and ridges, and he's fully clothed. Tingles zip from my head to my toes.

He sets down the knife, plucks out his earbuds, and turns until we're facing one another. Our gazes lock. The ribbon of sexual tension between us is stretched taut to the point of shredding.

"Annie." His gaze drops to my mouth.

"Colby." I lick my lips.

His voice strained, he says, "Bluebird," then drags his thumb over my lower lip, cupping my face.

"Two." I flatten my hands on his back, draw him closer, and kiss him. My brazen action is met with momentary surprise and then complete surrender. We open to each other in slow, intense increments. I wet his lips with my tongue before darting forward into his mouth. The intensity of our kisses increases exponentially. His large free hand curves around my waist, his fingers bruising my skin. Ignoring his hard length is impossible. I clench my thighs together to quell the building ache as my brain imagines how he will feel... Kissing Colby wasn't like this in high school. Then, it was sloppy and uncoordinated. Now, pure, overwhelming pleasure skates up my spine and swirls in my chest. The fact we're both completely clothed boggles my mind. Rather than wonder about his experience, I tug his lower lip between my teeth. The growl vibrating between us is new as I add enough space to look into his cerulean eyes again.

Silence surrounds us for a minute before I muster the ability to ask, "It wasn't like that before... was it?"

"No, it wasn't. Not even close. It's never been—"

I set my head on his chest and whisper, "For me either." The weight of our admissions has us putting the brakes on for the time being.

He kisses the top of my head and releases me. "How was the second interview?"

"Excellent. Much better than the first. She's going to visit in person in a few weeks."

"Nice. Do you still get comfy when you get home for the evening?"

Of course he remembers. He was stuck waiting for me with my parents in the family room. "Yes. I'll be right back." I grip his shirt and tug his lips close again and kiss him softly. As I climb to my bedroom, I struggle to refrain from sharing my inner thoughts. Feelings and emotions that include: I want to kiss him repeatedly and at least daily to I'm a fool for not reaching out to him sooner.

"I can hear your thoughts down here, Annie." His baritone voice follows me.

I giggle and change into leggings, a tank, and an oversized sweater.

Colby is carrying two plates of food to the table when I return. "Sit. What would you like to drink?"

"Iced tea, please." It's weird not needing to cook, but I could get used to it. Both the meal and the company.

He sits beside me, and we enjoy our dinner.

"This is tasty."

"You sound surprised."

"I am, maybe a little. I assume you have a chef or prepackaged meals for you at home."

Colby grins. "I do, sort of. As you know, my mother was a terrible cook and my father even worse."

"I recall. She burned toast, and your birthday cake was undercooked and gross."

"Yes, it was. Marta is my housekeeper. When I first hired her, she would also prepare meals for me. However, there was a catch. She made it a condition I would let her teach me to fend for myself. In the off-season for almost three years, she spent a few days a week with me teaching me to cook."

"Awww, that's sweet."

"She's like a surrogate mom. Marta is still my housekeeper, but she only cooks when I request something specific. Otherwise, I do it myself or eat at the facility."

"You continue to surprise me each time you share about your fancy life in Florida."

He sets down his fork and threads his fingers into mine. "My life isn't fancy at all." He lifts his shoulders and tilts his head a bit. "Well, some would say my cars are fancy, but otherwise I live frugally. You'll see when you visit."

"Shocked the number is only five. I guess I will."

"How many did you expect?"

"You had huge car dreams. I remember you had your heart set on the Shelby GT500 from *Gone in 60 Seconds*."

"I did."

We finish our meals and talk about baseball and coaching.

"Do you have a roster and the stats from last season for me to look at?" he asks.

"Yeah. Those are in the green folder. What are the others?"

"The red is for the junior varsity players. The team lost three starters who need to be replaced."

"Key positions?"

"All are key positions, aren't they?"

"Point taken."

I smile. "The third baseman, right fielder, and the third pitcher in the rotation graduated last year."

"You are…."

"What?"

"Amazing."

My nose wrinkles, but I hold his gaze. "At my job, sure. Everything else is a work in progress."

"I realize some of your self-doubt is my fault. You're not only amazing at your job but anything you set your mind to and always have been. I'll show you every day if you'll allow me the opportunity."

I want to give him a true second chance, but I'm terrified to make a mistake. "You hurt me deeply. I can't go through the pain again."

He rises to his feet and offers me his hand. I take it and stand as well.

He kisses our joined hands and replies. "I will keep showing up every single day until you're confident I mean 'as long as you'll have me.'"

Lifting my chin slightly with his free hand, he lowers his mouth to mine. A sweet kiss and he pulls away.

"I believe you. Trusting your words is harder than I anticipated."

"I understand. I will prove it until you're confident in me… in us."

"Thank you," I mumble against his chest.

"No, thank you."

He holds me in my dining area. He hasn't wavered from his words. It's up to me to let the past go. I suppose our second first date is as good a time as any. The problem is if kissing Colby exceeds every man before him—including him—what will being with him do to me?

We clean our dishes, and Colby kisses me goodnight and leaves. My feet are rooted to the floor, and I'm longing for more kisses.

CHAPTER ELEVEN

COLBY

The closer the end of the day gets, the more my anxiety increases. I'm off-the-charts nervous about spending time with Annie. This is my chance to prove I'm the man for her. I haven't been this anxious since our first date all those years ago. Without a doubt, she was out of my league then and still is now. We've taken baby steps forward. We share dinner after work and talk about the team. The tryouts are set to start next week.

There are some benefits to being me and coming from a small town. I recreated our first date, down to the minute, as best I could. Well, except for the part where we're both adults now.

At precisely 5:37 p.m., I ring the doorbell at Annie's. Yes, I was late all those years ago.

"You're late... again," she accuses.

"I know. Tonight, will closely mirror the original as best I can."

"Including a tardy arrival?" Annie winks at me.

"Technically, I have been on the front porch watching the clock for the last ten minutes. Being late on purpose isn't the same thing as actually being late, is it?"

She gifts me with a genuine smile. "No, it isn't. I appreciate your attention to detail. To be clear, which first date are we going on?"

I frown at her. "I didn't compliment you the last time, and it was a misstep. You look gorgeous, Annie." I shared our date would be casual. She paired fitted dark jeans with a royal blue V-neck sweater and booties.

"Thank you. Go ahead, ask what I mean?"

I reach out, take her hand, and grin at her. "What do you mean?"

"When did we first go out?"

"September of senior… ah. I see."

"Our first date with only you and I was senior year."

"True. I forgot about our chaperones. They were hugely overprotective." Until the end of junior year, Annie's parents required us to hang out at her house, or they accompanied us on our dates. That summer, we were allowed to go out in groups only. It seemed over the top then, and I hated it. I would do anything to spend time with her outside of school. I complied with their request. Now, if it were our daughter, I might consider it briefly and then trust in our potential offspring.

I open her door and wait for her to settle into the passenger seat.

Before I pull out of her driveway, she adds, "Your car was not this fancy in high school."

Containing my laughter is impossible. "Funny you should mention my old Civic."

"Because?"

"It's in my garage in Florida."

Delight shines in her eyes. "You kept it? How? It's been almost fifteen years!"

"Absolutely! The memories in that car are too important to let rot in a junkyard."

Again, Annie is speechless. I'm not sure if it's a good thing or not yet. I park in front of the cinema, and we walk inside with our fingers threaded together. We held hands the first time but not linked like this.

"Good evening, Mr. Somerset. Miss Silva," the usher greets us. If I recall correctly, his father, Johnny Butler, was one of our high school classmates. This date may tip off the community to my presence, but honestly, I don't care.

Annie whispers, "What have you done?"

"Good evening," I reply and escort Annie to the concession stand. "As I mentioned, I tried to recreate our first date alone as closely as possible." To do so, I needed to find a copy of the movie as well as order some of her favorite candy because it isn't easy to find now. I have to give the staff credit. They made it appear as if Annie's favorite candies, Necco wafers—chocolate only—and Nerds are always in the display case.

"How did you?"

I tug her closer and whisper near her ear, "I remember everything, Annie. Reliving the good times is one way to start over. Only now, we're going to skip the part where I was an idiot of epic proportions." I kiss her cheek and order the rest of our snacks.

Since we were young, this theater has changed hands and been renovated. To be honest, the luxury seats, which include date sofas, are an upgrade from the stiff seats of our teenage years. I select the sofa three-quarters of the way from the screen in the center.

"What are we watching?" she asks.

"Are you testing me, Blue?"

With a wink, she tucks her legs under and leans into me. "Just curious if your recollection is correct."

I never knew what it was when we were young, but Annie's need for physical touch is unchanged. Truthfully, having my hands on her is unparalleled. Sidling closer to her, I reply, "My memory is perfect." Goose bumps skitter across her skin as the opening credits begin.

"*Trouble with the Curve*," she states.

"Yeah. I recall we came to see *Twilight,* but it was sold out, and we chose this movie out of the remaining options."

She presses a light kiss to my lips and burrows deeper into my arms. Throughout the movie, I keep glancing at her. I've seen this movie repeatedly and can quote nearly fifty percent of the dialogue. Then again, I've watched almost every baseball movie at least once. Like the last time we watched it together, Annie is enraptured until the end credits roll.

"Ready to continue our date?"

"Yes, I'm starving."

"Who said anything about food?" My grin is a mile wide.

She shoves me lightly. "You said we were recreating our first date."

"So?"

"That means we pick up a pepperoni pizza, eat it under the bleachers at the high school, and barely make it home by curfew."

"Your memory is excellent. Let's go." I offer her my arm. She loops hers through it, and we make a stop at Tipsy Tomato before driving to our high school.

We won't be able to eat under the bleachers because they were replaced with enclosed ones about six years ago. Instead, I grab a few blankets I pilfered from Lorelei's linen closet and hand them to Annie. I follow her to the Stallions logo in the center of the field with our pizza and a bag filled with other necessities. I spread the blanket out and set up two electric camping lanterns to offer some light and a second thick blanket to cover us. The last time we did this was in the late summer. Annie was wearing cutoffs that showcased her ass and a tee with my number on the back.

"It's chilly for our re-creation, but it's been perfect," Annie offers.

I smile and steal a kiss.

"Food first, then kissing. Isn't that how it went the last time?"

A wide grin curves at my mouth. "Yeah."

"Are you up for sharing more about your last few years, or do you want to leave it alone?"

She pauses with the slice of pizza near her lips. "Nothing more really to tell. I'm a simple, boring girl."

She's nothing of the sort. She's everything. As much as I didn't like Jimmy, some of his words ring true. Annie is a rare find. My unicorn. "I don't believe you." I scoff.

Annie raises an eyebrow in my direction. "Truly. Aside from a date here or there, I'm a homebody. I go to work, and I take a yoga class every so often. The second weekend of the month I go visit my parents and on the fourth they come visit me. I have coffee with Lor on Saturdays in the yard and do the puzzle at the coffee shop on Sundays."

"Sounds like my life."

"Ha. Now who is leaving out fun details." Her eye roll is impressive.

"While it's true, I play a game for my career. If I'm not at work or a required event for the team, I'm home." I consider adding alone but don't. "As you already know, I also complete the crossword weekly. Our travel coordinator makes sure I have a copy of the newspaper if we're traveling."

"That's nice of her." The twinge of jealousy in her voice is adorable.

"Him. It's probably one of the most mundane requests he gets."

"Fair." She polishes off her slice and snuggles closer to me.

"Cold?"

"No."

Without hesitation, I clear my plate and turn dim the lanterns. We maneuver onto our backs, side by side, with our hands linked. In silence, we stare at the stars. For these minutes, the hurt from the past melts away, and we're us again.

"Can we pull this off?" Her question is barely audible.

I glance her way and note her gaze is skyward, as if looking at me when she whispered her question would change the answer. "Yes."

"When you're able to catch again?"

"Yes."

"Florida is far away, Two."

I can hear the unasked questions. What about my career? What will I do when you're traveling for work? "It is. I want to share my life with you, Annie. I always have, even as a skinny, teenage boy who didn't know he would reach the major leagues. When I saw the picture of my future, you were beside me. Every. Single. Time. It took longer than it should have for me to see us clearly." Before I question my motivation, I shift and hover over her beneath the blanket. "Can we answer the 'what-ifs' together?"

Rather than nod, she cranes her neck and kisses me hard. Slowly, I lower myself on top of her, leaning toward my right. The intensity ratchets up quickly. She slips her ice-cold hands beneath all layers of my clothes. The caress of her skin on mine has never been surpassed. Her mouth consumes me. Each nip, bite, and tug on my lower lip has me reminding myself we're at the beginning despite my insane—though purposefully chosen—drought. I travel along her jaw and down her neck with my mouth as low as her jacket will allow. Before I ask, she snakes one of her hands between us and unzips her jacket.

"Please continue," she urges.

With a grin, I pass over her collarbone and back toward the middle.

A deep, gruff voice from my left calls out, "Who's there?" The beam of a flashlight pans over us.

We freeze. I take stock in our clothing and note we're disheveled but both fully clothed.

"Evening, sir." I carefully push to my feet and offer Annie a hand to hers.

The officer approaches and flashes the light in our faces for a moment. "Somerset and Silva. Why am I not surprised? When did you get into town? Are you two still a thing? Last I heard you we're off playing in the majors."

Annie greets Pat, our classmate from high school, and attempts to keep our relationship private. "Nice to see you again."

"I should take you both in for trespassing on school property," he states with a hint of levity in his voice.

"That won't be necessary. I have been here a few weeks, and we wanted to visit one of our old haunts together," I explain.

"Honestly, I saw the SUV first and noted it was too pricey for the janitorial staff. Then I saw the two of you making out like teenagers."

"We appreciate you checking on us. We'll be on our way," Annie assures him.

"Good to see you together. You give the rest of us hope," he admits. "Go home. I really don't want to be the one to bring in the town major leaguer and his high school sweetheart for trespassing and public indecency."

"Night, Pat. Much appreciated." Annie offers.

When he is out of earshot, I bury my head in the crook of Annie's neck and laugh heartily. After a minute, Annie notices Pat is waiting for us to leave the field. We hastily gather the blankets and our garbage. I wave politely as I guide Annie into her seat. As I pull away, Annie starts cracking up.

"Did he really threaten to arrest us?" She's laughing hard enough for tears to stream down her face.

"Yeah, he did. We can chalk it up to a great story we can tell our kids one day."

At the mention of children, Annie sobers quickly and swallows hard.

I reach over and take her hand in mine. "Please share."

"It isn't important."

"How you feel is of the utmost importance."

She glances out the window, at me, and back.

"Is your number still the same?" My question is near a whisper. The only other sound is her measured breathing.

She shrugs.

"I never had a number per se. The only part of fatherhood of any consequence was having you as my children's mother."

Her head whips in my direction as I pull into her driveway. "What? How?"

I park and twist in my seat to face her as best I can. "It seems farfetched, I understand. My intention was always to come back for you. You know the rest."

"No, I don't. Aside from discussing I wanted more than two kids, we didn't dig much deeper. I suppose that level of depth falls into teenage love relationships."

I take her hands in mine and kiss them. "Perhaps, but now… this isn't teenage love. You and I both realize that. Although we're not ready to say it out loud, this is meant to be. We are meant to be. I knew when I gave you the ring on your finger. It will be true every single minute until I ask you to be mine for the rest of my life."

"Colby." My name sounds like a plea and a prayer at once. A plea not to mess with her heart… again. A prayer my words are honest and true. "I'm terrified to be wrong again."

"I know, and it's completely my fault. Whatever it takes for you to trust in me—in us—I'll do it. I chose wrong, and we lost too many dates like tonight." Releasing her hand, I swipe the single tear rolling down her face with my thumb. Her tears have gutted me since the first time she soaked my shirt with them all those years ago. The notion I caused this one and more I didn't see is heart-wrenching. Eliminating the space between us, I kiss her cheek and then her hands.

I pause on her front porch after escorting her home. "Good night, Annie." With a sweet kiss on her lips, I wait for her to lock her front door and reengage her alarm before walking back to my SUV. A small surge of pride swells in me. Our second first date was perfect. It can only mean one thing; Annie and I are meant to be. I can't screw us up.

CHAPTER TWELVE

JULIANNE

First thing in the morning, I tug on my shoes and a jacket and take a walk in the brisk air. Exercise will help clear my head. I hope. I tossed and turned last night. Hell, the last time I looked at the clock was a few hours ago. This walk will help me grasp everything going on in my life from my dad, to finding a coach and an AD, as well as the swirling and gut-twisting feelings Colby unearthed with one date.

I exhale and start with my dad. Nothing I can do except see him when he's available. His choice to live rather than fight for more time… is his. In his position, I'm not sure I would choose the same. Grappling with Dad's decision is one of the many reasons I decided to try again with Colby. The operative word being try, at least until last night. I need to do more than try. As hurt as I was all those years ago… I believe him when he says he's grown. I agree his choice to leave me and pursue baseball alone was partially altruistic. As much as I don't want to admit it—to myself, much less Colby—I would've forgone school and followed him around from game to game and team to team. I mean he was in the minors for three years. Where would we be as a couple? Where would I be professionally? Likely not the principal of a prestigious private academy. *Sigh.*

Filling the positions at work is progressing. I hope Kate is enamored with the school when she arrives in two weeks. Rounding the block, I turn left and continue walking. Aside from sharing a backyard with Lor and Jack, the neighborhood is beautiful and secluded with underground utilities, wide sidewalks, and genuinely nice people. To be fair, my encounter with Mrs. Henderson a few doors down is comical.

"I see that baseball player stopping by. Don't let him hurt you again, missy." As you can tell, she's a Summit Creek lifer and a nosy biddy. Her gravelly words made me attempt to slow down my rapid descent into Colby's world. Attempt. Ha.

"I appreciate your concern, Mrs. Henderson. Have a lovely day." I wave and continue walking. My mind spins with memories of the past both good and bad, flashes of our recreated first date and run-in with the law, and the possibilities of a future with Colby. A future I wanted desperately at the young age of seventeen and if I'm being honest with myself, still want now. As I consider what our future might look like, I turn up my sidewalk. Approaching my house, I find Colby sitting on the front porch.

"Morning, Bluebird."

"Hi. Shouldn't you be at physical therapy?"

He rises to his feet, brackets my waist with his large hand, and kisses my cheek. "Yes, but I pushed it back when you didn't answer my text, call, or the front door. You shouldn't walk without your phone."

I shake my head, pluck my phone from my pocket, and wave it at him.

"Still need your silent time, huh?"

A knot of emotion coils in my chest. *He remembers.* When we were younger, at least once a week, he would sit with me in the quiet. Sometimes he would hold me and others we would simply sit with me until I was done sorting, mulling, or deciding. "Yes. Thank you for checking on me."

"You're welcome. Can you be ready to go out for the rest of the day around one?"

"What are you up to?"

"Taking care of the planning for our trip. Some of it requires lead time," he responds immediately.

Trust him. Believe him. Our second chance could turn out to be everything you ever dreamed of. "Yes. I can."

"Perfect. I'll pick you up then. The first part of our day is casual. The second part requires a dress and heels."

"Will we be coming home tonight?" I swallow hard at the idea of finding out if being with Colby again after all these years is better than before, much like kissing him is. It must be. *Right?* Not only is he absurdly hot, but the two of us had to gain experience between then and now. Inwardly, I shake my head. My sexual encounters after him were dismal and frankly, unfulfilling. I've learned the fine art of orgasming solo.

"Yes. We need to be here when your parents arrive tomorrow."

"I'll be ready. Don't keep Jack waiting."

"Yes, dear," he replies, kisses me lightly on the lips, and walks to his SUV where he waits until I'm safely ensconced inside my house. After downing a bottle of water, I shower and stand in my closet, trying to figure out what to wear for my dates today. There's a pile of casual clothes on my bed, dressing bench, and on the chair. "Yes," "no," and "maybe" piles, to be more specific. The dresses are in a pile on the floor of the closet. The mess keeps growing. I pick up my phone and call Lorelei.

"Hey, Jules. Everything okay?" she asks when she picks up.

"Yes. No. Mayyyybe. Yes."

Lorelei laughs. "What did Colby do?"

Now, it's my turn to laugh. "Nothing bad." In fact, he seems to be doing everything right.

"You're feeling some sort of way because you want to go out with him and continue to do so. Your clothes are strewn around your room because none of your clothes are good enough."

"Scary accuracy, Lor."

"As you know, we want you to be with Colby. Jack and I know it has been hard on both of you. My husband and I have compared notes but didn't share with you or Colby. Per your individual requests, I might add. You could wear his MLB pajama pants with his championship hoodie, and he would still be proud to have you beside him. Wear your low back, little black dress with the high slit. Walk forward with caution, and let the man love you again."

"Is it truly that simple, Lor?"

"For you and Colby? Absolutely. I wholly believe you were meant to be in high school. The only change to today is age, wisdom, and some experiences both of you would have rather skipped."

"You're the best friend a girl could ask for. Love you."

Lorelei replies, "Same goes, gorgeous. Love you."

With my newfound confidence in pursuing an adult relationship with Colby, I tug on jeans, a V-neck with a matching thin cardigan, and court shoes. To be fair, I knew everything Lor told me, but hearing it from her was helpful. Then, I pack my dress, slingback shoes, and makeup into a travel bag with barely twenty minutes to spare.

Precisely on time, Colby knocks on my front door. "Hi, sweetheart."

I greet him with a kiss and ask, "How was your appointment?"

"I think Jack took it easy on me today. Ready to go?"

"Sure."

"Want to share where we're going?"

He takes my bag from me and opens my door. "We're meeting Kelly Cavallaro Barnett in Philly for my tux and your dress for the gala."

"The famous couture designer?"

He raises an eyebrow.

"First, how do you know Kelly?" I ask.

"She's designed my suits and tuxedos for the last three years. When did you meet Kelly?"

"I shared about my siblings." He nods. I continue, "My sister, Jillian Blackthorne Cruz, has a brother named Jake. Jake—also adopted—is married to Norah Cavallaro."

"Kelly Barnett is your quasi sister-in-law?" His voice drips with surprise.

"Yeah."

"Have you met her?"

"Not yet."

"Anyone else in your new extended family I should be aware of?"

I laugh softly. "Worried your celebrity status will be eclipsed?"

He shakes his head. "Jordan is a class act. I would put him and I about even. Kelly and Nicholas Barnett are A-listers as well. Seriously, though?"

I lift my shoulder as I consider his question. "I guess Connor's wife is a celebrity. Well, she used to be."

"Who is Connor?"

"I will make you a chart before you meet them all. Connor is Jake's partner in Blackthorne Security. Not actually related except they're best friends since basically birth, and Connor's sister was Jake's first wife. Anyway, Connor's wife is the singer, Carys."

"She's hot!"

I shoot a look at him. Although his opinion is on point.

"What? It's true."

"She's stunning in everyday life as well. She uses her given name Callie." The rest of the ride passes quickly given the time of day we're traveling. We arrive in the city earlier than necessary.

Colby pulls into the Rittenhouse and hands the valet his keys. "Please bring the bags to our suite."

"Of course…."

"My apologies. Our reservation is under Somerset."

"Very well, sir."

I wrinkle my nose but say nothing.

"Want to take a walk? We have an hour until we need to meet Kelly."

"Sure." With our hands linked, we stroll across the street. When I was young, my family didn't travel for vacations or day trips like other families. Rittenhouse Square is a large park in the city with lush greenery and wide walkways. Given the season, the greenery is filling in. There is a statue of Billy the goat as well as a lion crushing a serpent.

"We need a room to change for dinner and if we choose to, after dinner," he states, allaying my fears, especially considering I asked if we were staying the night.

"Okay." We circle the park in silence, and it's refreshing.

"I don't want to spoil anything, but what do you typically do when your parents visit?"

I giggle. "It's all very old school and boring. Honestly, I get more out of phone calls than seeing them in person. It's as if when they left, they forgot how awesome Summit Creek is. When they arrive around ten, we have coffee and a small snack to tide them over until lunch at the café or the deli. Then they leave."

"When and why did they move?"

I inhale sharply and gather my thoughts. Colby guides me over to a bench. After the intervening years, he's like thinking, rightfully so, this story isn't a good one.

"You don't have to share."

"I do. It was a difficult time for me. When I graduated from college and I was looking for a job, they encouraged me to look everywhere."

"You were set on staying in Summit Creek?"

"Yes. Limiting my horizon—their words, not mine—wasn't going to bring you back to me."

Colby covers my hands with his, listens intently, but offers nothing.

"I took a position in Philly, and they ran with the information. Sold their home in Summit Creek and bought a townhouse near the water about twenty miles from here. The school offered three months to decide if the position was a good fit or not. I didn't love the position, the school, or the faculty."

"You chose to leave the job after the probationary period and move back home?" he attempts to fill in the rest.

"Sort of. A few days after I signed the contract, my house went on the market. I put in a full price cash offer immediately, sight unseen."

"You knew before your first day, you weren't going to stay?" His tone is incredulous.

"Yes."

"Why?"

My eyes flutter closed. *Admit it to him. Tell him.* "I still had hope for us then. I wanted to share a home with you and a backyard with Jack and Lorelei."

"None of us were together at that point. Right?"

I drop my head in agreement. "No. Like I said, I was hopeful." My eyes still cast toward the ground.

Colby sets his fingers beneath my chin and lifts until our gazes meet. "You weren't the only one filled with hope. It paid off."

"It is looking like my gamble was completely worth it."

"Despite the strain on your relationship with your parents?"

I shrug. "I told them before they purchased their townhouse. It was a conscious choice for them."

"That must have hurt."

Sharing with him makes me feel a bit lighter. Until now, only Lorelei knew all those details. "Yeah, but I needed to have my own life. The one I hoped for anyway."

Colby leans closer, adding, "Bluebird, we're going to get there together."

"Promise?"

"Promise." His soft kiss is soothing but doesn't leave room for escalation to behind closed-door levels. We don't have time. We hurry to the hotel and go directly to Kelly's suite. He knocks on the door.

As the door swings open, I'm shocked to see Cruz answering.

"Cruz?"

"Jules. How are you?" He ushers us into the room. "I'm well. Working."

"Where are my manners? Colby Somerset, please meet my brother-in-law, Javier Cruz."

Cruz takes Colby's extended hand. "Pleasure. Congrats on the championship win."

"Thank you."

"Kelly will be out in a minute. She took a call from a producer. They are working out a timeline for her next movie," Cruz shares.

"No problem," I reply. We chat until Kelly breezes into the room. She is a replica of Norah minus a few inches in height. Chestnut hair and wide brown eyes complement a flawless complexion and curves most women would covet.

"Hi, Colby. Nice to see you again. You must be Julianne," Kelly greets us.

"Nice to see you again, Kelly," Colby replies.

"It's a pleasure to meet you." I share my relationship to Cruz with her, although she may already know. "Norah speaks highly of you."

Kelly's smile widens. "She's my favorite sister too." There are only two sisters. "Julianne, there are a few racks of dresses in the bedroom. Sift through them and see if there is a style or fabric you like. I can take Colby's measurements and fabric choices while you browse."

"Great. Thank you." I cast a quick look in his direction. A gorgeous smile appears on his chiseled face. His smile was one of the first things I noticed about him. In high school, it was devilish and made him seem like a bad boy. Now, I know he has a heart of gold and wants to give it to me… again. I step into the large bedroom, and I feel like a princess. Gorgeous couture dresses surround me. I scan them and note there are numerous styles and colors to match most skin tones and body types. It's probably a good thing there aren't prices on these gowns. I groan softly.

I promised to let him handle the planning for our trip. This is part of it. Extravagant? To me, yes, but not to him. I know precisely how much Colby is worth, which doesn't matter to me in the slightest. His last contract was widely publicized and broke records. In fact, his contract terminates at the end of next season.

Ignoring the potential cost, I pull three dresses after scanning the racks. The first one is a floor-length, mermaid-style dress in burgundy with embroidered details. I zip it and check it out in the mirror. It's nice. Immediately I chastise myself. It's stunning and looks fine on me, but it isn't the one. My second option is a strapless gown with a fitted bodice in sage green with delicate embroidered flowers. As I struggle with the zipper, there's a knock on the door.

"Annie, do you need help?" His deep, sexy voice washes over me.

"Yes, actually."

Colby steps inside and latches the door behind him. "Wow, you look…."

I'm facing a huge mirror, holding the dress against my body. "I'm not sure about this one," I offer. "Can you zip it?"

He stalks over to me, and the desire in his eyes is unmistakable. He bends and moves closer. The warmth of his breath on my skin sends shivers through me. Colby sets a column of kisses along my spine as he tugs the zipper upward. "I stand by what I started to say. You look gorgeous."

I purse my lips and frown. "This one isn't it."

He unzips the dress, turns me in his arms, smiles, and kisses me lightly. "Which dress is next?"

"I'm not changing with you in here." My voice isn't even convincing me.

"I've seen all of you before, Bluebird."

"I'm not sixteen and perky anymore." The second half of my response trails off.

"You're more beautiful now than you were then. I'll turn around if it will make you more comfortable."

I can feel my cheeks heat with his words. "Okay."

He turns his back to me. I slip out of the sage dress and step into the third gown. I choose not to see if he's peeking. Handling his gaze on my body right now is a lot to process. Truthfully, it was my favorite of the three I chose. The dress is lavender silk with gray undertones. There's slight ruching at the waist and a mid-thigh slit. I'm able to zip myself because it's on the side, not in the back. The straps are a tad loose, but otherwise, it fits as if she tailored it specifically for me.

"You can turn around." I adjust the skirt and thwart my inclination to fidget.

Colby is speechless. His stare is penetrating. The desire from before has morphed into one more deadly for my heart and soul. I've seen this expression twice in my life. The first time was when Jordan introduced me to Alex and the second when Jill introduced Cruz. The look of awe and "I can't believe she picked me" etched on their faces. The air in the room is exponentially hotter than it was before he joined me. Somehow it has increased more with this dress.

I eliminate the space between us and set my hand on his chest, his hard, sculpted chest. Am I imagining things because it's been too long since a man has touched me? No, he's ridiculously fit.

"Two, please say something."

A light knock on the door nearly drowns out his response.

"You're stunning," he manages.

"Thank you. Come in," I reply.

Kelly joins us. "I see you've narrowed it down."

"Yes."

"Is anything pulling or tight?" she asks.

"No, but the straps are loose around my shoulders."

Colby hasn't said anything else, and he remains stock-still in his spot.

Kelly looks between us again. A sly smile curves up at the corner of her lips. "I'll grab my pins and be right back."

The desire zinging between us doesn't lessen in the time it takes for Kelly to return.

"Colby, can you give us a minute?"

Wordlessly, he nods, kisses my cheek, and exits the room.

"I met you today for the first time. Colby and I are acquaintances at best. However, I happen to know when a man is head over heels in love. When I first met Nicholas, I refused to give in to the swirling emotions in my heart to see if the sparks were real. Circumstances beyond our control forced us to be in close quarters. The look on my husband's face was a replica of Colby's the moment before he kissed me the first time." She pins the left strap and moves around me to the right. "Please take some unsolicited advice from an old married lady. Whatever is holding you back, let it go. You won't have any evidence if it's real until you tangle up your sheets and have your first disagreement."

I stifle a laugh. "We were a couple in high school."

"Oh. He wants a second chance, and you're scared."

"You're precisely on point."

"My advice holds. Don't let past hurts cloud what could be an amazing life together now."

"Is offering stellar advice a Cavallaro thing?"

She smiles. "Norah is exceptional at seeing all the angles."

I whisper, "You are too."

"You can change. We'll work out delivery details once you've put on your casual clothes again."

"Thank you, Kelly."

"You're welcome. We're family. It's what we do." Once the door clicks closed behind her, I step out of my dress. My dress. Tamping down the happy dance in my heart is not as easy as you might think. With my casual clothes on, I join them in the sitting room.

"Ready for our date?" Colby asks.

"Of course." I know something is up. Concern and worry zing through me. His voice is flat, and he's politely rushing me out of here. I hug Cruz. "Please give my best to Jill and a kiss to Hallie."

"I will," he replies.

Without allowing me a proper goodbye with Kelly, Colby ushers me out the door.

"What's wrong?"

"Your phone rang a few times. The caller was Jefferson Hospital."

"Oh." My heart plummets to my feet, and fear expands in my chest.

CHAPTER THIRTEEN

COLBY

My stomach bottoms out when I see the name of a local hospital flash on Annie's phone. *Damn!* She isn't ready. Then again, I'm not sure anyone is prepared to lose a parent. Despite their strained relationship, I know it's going to hurt.

Unsure what to do, I escort her to the elevator and press the button for our floor. With our hands linked, I lead her into our room as her call connects. As I requested, there are numerous bouquets of flowers in our room including peonies and roses.

"What's going on?" Annie listens for a minute. "We are nearby." She waits for a response. "Okay." She ends her call and pinches the bridge of her nose. It's endearing and a mannerism she has had as long as I can remember.

Drawing her against me, I hold her and smooth her hair away from her face. "When you're ready, we can go see your father."

She shakes her head against my chest. "Not my dad." Her words are muffled in my shirt.

"Your mom?"

Her head moves slightly before she adds, "She fell."

"It's going to be okay, Annie."

"Is it? He told me not to bother coming to the hospital because I can't do anything for her. What am I missing? Why wouldn't I?"

Adding some space between us, I tilt her chin upward. "Do you want to go to the hospital?"

"Yes."

"Then, that's what we'll do."

"You don't have to join me. I'm sorry about our date."

"Of course, I'm coming. I'm here, Annie. There's absolutely no chance you're handling this alone." My gaze bores into hers, leaving no room for her to mistake my intentions. "I'm with you every minute of every day whether it's a good one or a horrible one. I'll be beside you. If you need me to hold your hand or your heart… I'm in. I'll wait until you're fully ready to accept my words as true."

She swipes her tears. "He might turn us away, and we'll miss our dinner reservation."

"All I care about is you. What do you want?"

Annie inhales sharply. She's steeling herself to protect her heart from the pain this may cause. This moment isn't the first time I resolved to never hurt her again, but it is the most recent. She deserves the world, and I'm going to give it to her. "I need to go to the hospital regardless of my father's opinion."

"Why don't you freshen up and we'll leave?" I suggest.

Before she walks away, her hand cups my jaw, and she draws me in. Much like the last time we kissed, emotions spill over and the tension between us increases a thousandfold. Lust, desire, pleasure, and a host of other carnal feelings course through me. I've wanted to kiss Annie with reckless abandon since the day I gave the right away. Reluctantly, I pull back. Before releasing her, I say, "Please know, I want to kiss you until you can't breathe and still want more. Now isn't the time." I press my lips to her forehead, and she steps away.

The ride to the hospital is short and silent. We enter through the emergency department.

"Good evening. Could you direct me to Caroline Silva?" Annie asks.

The young, ginger-haired nurse is staring at me instead of addressing Annie's question.

A few moments longer than necessary pass before I state, "My wife asked you a question." My words and tone are curt. My intention is unmistakable—back off and do your job.

Annie squeezes my hand.

The nurse startles out of her stupor and directs us to Mrs. Silva. We're a few steps away from the desk, and a frail version of her father steps into the hallway.

"Julianne, I told you not to come," he admonishes her.

She's struck speechless and not in a good way. How could she not come? Family is everything to Annie. Doesn't he realize this?

"Sir, Annie can make her own decisions. If you didn't believe she would come here after you shared Caroline's condition, you're sorely mistaken."

Mr. Silva retreats into the room he exited, and we follow before he replies, "I wasn't speaking to you." He sets his sights on Annie. "What is he doing here? It's bad enough you came, but you brought him." Mr. Silva points his arthritis-riddled finger in my direction. "Didn't you learn anything the first time he crushed your heart and spat out the tiny shards? He will destroy you again."

A stab of guilt and pain slice through me.

A shudder cascades through her. "Dad." Annie's voice is shaky and laced with anger.

I don't give her a chance to respond. "You don't know me, and clearly you don't know your daughter well either. Right now, the only man hurting her is you."

Mr. Silva freezes at my strong reaction to his treatment of my woman. Yes, mine, for the rest of my life.

"You will not speak to me like that, young man."

"Sir, I kindly ask you not to disrespect Annie in the manner you are either. She deserves respect and the ability to visit her mother in the hospital if she chooses."

Annie tightens her grip on my hand again. "Where is Mom?"

"They took her for X-rays," Mr. Silva answers.

"What happened?"

Mr. Silva shakes his head and replies, "She fell down the stairs and landed on her hip."

Annie nods. "Okay. How are you feeling?"

Her father ignores her question and takes a seat near the window.

"Are you going to answer me?" she presses.

"No. I've made my choice, and you won't convince me otherwise." His words are terse and unbending.

"I asked how you're feeling. I have no intention of attempting to change your mind again. It was hard enough the first time. You can decide how to live your life and so will I."

Her father points directly at me. "With him?"

"Yes."

"That is a mistake of epic proportions much like meeting your siblings." Mr. Silva restates his position.

I understand his disdain for me. He's protecting his daughter and her heart from potential repeat heartbreak. I can't comprehend his mistrust of her siblings though. The tension in Annie's body increases with each sentence he utters. I sidle closer and glide my hand around her lower back.

"Dad, you have made your opinions abundantly clear before and reiterated them today. You don't agree with my decision to embrace my biological family or Colby. Fine. I get to make those choices and bear the consequences, if any, good or bad. The same way you can decide to forgo treatment for your cancer."

There's my feisty woman! I dig my fingers into her hip a bit deeper.

"I see. Well, if you wish to see your mother, you can wait until she returns. I'll be in the private family room down the hall." Mr. Silva rises and exits the room without looking back.

I turn her into my body and collapse my arms around her. "I'm proud of you, Bluebird. I'm sure standing up for yourself was difficult."

"Thank you. Surprisingly, it wasn't. Choosing me and what I want was easy. Owning my decisions and the potential repercussions is something else."

"Fair."

"Your wife?" she asks.

"I have never appreciated the stares and tunnel vision part of being a sports figure. I'm not even sure she knows who I am. Aside from the fact the title should be accurate in this moment but for my idiocy, and I hope it will be true eventually. Either way, my words and the title shifted her attention to you where it should've been the entire time."

Before Annie can respond, Caroline is wheeled back into the room. "Julianne, you're here." Her words are both questioning and thankful.

"Mrs. Silva, let's get you back into bed," the nurse requests. Once she's settled, the nurse adds, "The doctor will be in to discuss a plan for you soon."

"Thank you," she replies.

"How are you?" Annie asks.

Caroline waves off her daughter's concern. "I'm fine. I fell, and your father overreacted."

"Well, I'm glad we were close and could make it here tonight. You'll be able to follow doctor's orders without guilt."

"What were you doing in Philly?"

"We came to meet with his tailor for the ring gala and have dinner."

"How lovely." Then Mrs. Silva stares me down. "You're back?"

Without hesitation, reservation, or equivocation, I answer, "Yes."

Annie wrinkles her nose with a vengeance. "Mom, I can't fight more tonight."

"More?" Caroline inquires.

I set my hand on Annie's forearm, and she looks up at me. "If I may." She arches an eyebrow and tilts her head in acquiescence. "Mr. Silva and Annie had words when she chose to come here against his expressed wishes. In addition to his disagreement with my presence, his displeasure with her choice to meet her siblings was shared as well."

She glances at Annie. "I see. Well, my husband doesn't speak for me. As for her siblings, I think it was a great idea. Edmund does not." She turns her attention to me. "If you hurt my daughter again, you will answer to me."

"Yes, ma'am." At least I have acceptance from one of Annie's parents.

"Good. How's the knee?"

Apparently, my word is enough. For that, I'm grateful. "Making progress each day."

"Any chance you'll get back to Florida this season?"

"If I do, it won't be until near season's end. I guess it depends whether or not the team makes the playoffs. Quite frankly, I wouldn't want to upset the chemistry by attempting to step in at that time though."

"You have always been a class act on the field, Colby."

The dig about mistreating Annie doesn't go unheard. "Much appreciated, Mrs. Silva."

Annie acknowledges my statement.

"I'll go get your husband and give you a few minutes to chat." I kiss Annie high on her cheek and leave the room. It doesn't take long for me to locate the waiting room. A frail version of the man I knew long ago is sitting in a chair staring blankly at the wall. He turns his head in the direction of the door when I enter.

"I thought you would be gone by now." His statement is biting and angry.

"Why? Because you were rude and disrespectful to Annie and me?"

He looks away from me like a petulant child.

"Your wife is in her room." I turn on my heel to leave but stop in my tracks and add, "Hurting Annie is my only regret in life. She's willing to give me a second chance. I won't screw it up." I leave the waiting room and walk back toward Caroline and Annie.

"Excuse me?" A boy with his casted arm in a sling stops me a few doors away. "Are you Colby Somerset?"

I crouch to his level. No shot of pain or discomfort in my knee. *Thanks, Jack.* "I am. What happened?"

Astonishment and glee appear on his face. Meeting one of your sports heroes is a big deal to a kid. I remember as if it were yesterday. I met Buster Posey and Brian McCann, both of my modern-day favorites, at one game about ten years ago during batting practice. It was one of the best days of my life.

"In my game, the runner crashed into me," he shares.

A frazzled brunette stops behind him. It appears my young friend slipped his mom. Relief passes over her features when she catches up to him.

"Where do you play?"

"Right here in Philly."

"Cool. What position?"

"Catcher." He looks left and right, then left again. "Same as you, Mr. Somerset."

"Did you get the out?"

"Yes. Just like you did in the World Series."

I raise my hand for a high five, and he complies. "Well done. What's your name?"

"Tucker Canello."

I pull my hat off. "Pleasure to meet you. How old are you?"

"I'm ten."

I rise to my full height and ask for a Sharpie at the nurse's station. I autograph the hat and hand it to him.

"Thank you!" Joy ripples through him so profoundly he's nearly bouncing up and down.

"You're welcome." I shake his mom's hand before they leave. When I gaze up, I see Annie leaning against the doorway of her mom's room. The look on her face is divided. I can only guess her thoughts. I'm fairly confident, she's smiling because Tucker is happy. Also, she's sad because we should have a child by now about the same age. At least in a perfect world, we would. I approach her and kiss her lightly without a care for who may see, specifically her father. The irony is I would appreciate his blessing to marry Annie.

"That was hot as hell."

I wink at her. "Which part?"

"All of it."

I grin at her. "How are you?"

She waves me off. "I'm fine. The doctor indicated there were no breaks. Mom has a large contusion on her leg. They are discharging her as we speak."

"Good. Stay here or go home?"

Annie tugs her lower lip between her teeth.

That's hot as hell! "Whatever you want to do is fine with me."

"Okay. We can talk more when we're alone."

I lean in and whisper, "Oh, I like this even more." I eliminate most of the space between us and attempt to slide my arm around her waist.

Annie swats my arm and offers her goodbyes to her parents. "I'll see you in a few weeks. Please follow the doctor's orders." Annie pointedly looks at her mom.

"I will. Colby, don't forget what I said," Mrs. Silva states.

"I won't."

Caroline nods tightly. As we leave, the nurse from earlier returns with her discharge instructions. Hand in hand, we exit the hospital.

"What do you want to do?" I ask, settling into the driver's seat.

"Can we go home in the morning?"

I kiss the back of her hand. "Of course. Dinner? Are you hungry?"

"Does the hotel have late room service?"

I hand her my phone. "Not sure. The reservation link is in my email. Can you check? If they don't, we can grab takeout before we get back there."

"What's the code to unlock it?"

"0901," I answer but keep my eyes on the road.

"My birthday?"

"Yeah." Silence surrounds us for a few minutes. Her surprise, well, surprises me. She has my birthday for her backdoor.

"The hotel has twenty-four-hour room service. Is that okay with you? I know you planned a dinner out."

"Our date was never about dinner. It's about us spending time together to reacquaint ourselves with each other."

"Okay. We can order when we get there." She puts my phone in the cup holder and links our hands. The remainder of the drive is quiet. Contemplative Annie is back for the moment. Earlier today, I saw glimmers of our future. Now with her dad's terse statements, I feel like we took a step back, at least a small one.

CHAPTER FOURTEEN

JULIANNE

My nerves are on edge despite staying being my decision. Colby was willing to drive home tonight. Why am I nervous? Inwardly, I remind myself. *You purposely chose to stay with him overnight.*

"Ready to talk yet?" he asks.

"I'm thinking about us, not my parents."

He turns his gaze to mine briefly. "Question still stands."

"I don't know where to start."

He pulls in front of the hotel and hands the valet his keys. Stillness in words surrounds us in the elevator but not in actions. Colby's hold on me is tight and supportive but not oppressive. Once our room door clicks closed, Colby kicks off his shoes and draws me into his arms. His lips are on mine before I can take a breath. I decide to see how far he will let me go before stopping me this time. Our tongues tangle, and we dance toward the bed. Dipping my hands beneath the hem of his shirt, I smooth my palms up his abdomen. My hands are met with hard ridges and divots beyond my comprehension.

"Holy crap, Two. Do you work out more than once a day?"

A devilish grin curls up at the corner of his mouth against the curve of my neck. "No. My training regime has been consistent since the minors." He lifts my shirt over my head. "You should talk, Annie."

Containing my laughter is impossible. "I don't exercise at all. I walk and nothing more. Occasionally, and I stress occasionally, I go to a yoga class with Lorelei. Frequent exercise, no thank you."

Colby chuckles. "I'll work out enough for both of us."

"Deal." Dragging my hands down, I gather his shirt and push up. Each inch of skin is rewarded with a kiss. As I climb, he grips his shirt at the back of his neck and hauls it over his head. When I reach his chest, I notice a tattoo. Intricate script letters form the word "Moonshot" inked into the skin at his ribcage. When I realize what it means, I'm overwhelmed with emotions. Ones I tried to lock away. The same feelings which caused me to end my engagement to Patrick.

"When did you get this?" I manage to ask.

He exhales sharply and kisses my forehead. An intimate gesture I've never experienced before Colby. "On my eighteenth birthday."

"We weren't together then."

"I know. I couldn't have you wearing my ring with the same engraving without having a matching one myself."

"How did you know I never took it off?"

"I didn't. I had to believe you still loved me even if we weren't together."

"Colby." His name is a whisper from my lips.

"It's always been you, Annie. My heart and soul will always be yours."

With his words, the final bricks in the wall protecting my heart fall to the ground. Our lips collide, and we make quick work of the rest of our clothes except for our underwear. I push my concern of being nearly naked with Colby from my head. I try to anyway.

"As I said, you're more beautiful now than before." He lowers the strap of my black lace bra down my arm and follows with his tongue. The wetness he leaves behind raises goose bumps on my skin. Each touch increases the intensity of us. I should be scared out of my mind. He's barely touched me, and I'm ready to combust. Let's not forget the fact, no man has ever made me feel as much as him. Warmth cascades through me when he's within arm's length, my heart races, and snippets of the best memories move forward in my mind.

Perhaps I didn't recognize it our first time together, but I know for certain the two relationships between then and now don't come close. He unclasps my bra, pulls it between us, and drops it to the floor. If I thought his mouth on me was amazing, I didn't account for how phenomenal being held in his strong arms nearly naked is.

"Your skin is impossibly soft, Annie. You feel incredible against me." His large hands move in opposite directions with light touches along my back. Tingles skitter outward and down to my toes.

All I can manage is to drop my head in acknowledgement. My words escape me, and I'm not sure I'll ever get them back. He wraps one of his arms around my waist and climbs onto the bed. We wiggle to the middle before he lowers to his forearms, hovering over me and leaning mostly onto his right side.

"Do we need to switch positions?" I whisper.

"Maybe, but we need to talk about something first."

"Okay." My reply is laced with concern.

"It isn't bad, not exactly. It took a more than a year, but when I decided to date someone…" He shakes his head. "Before I dated anyone, well, to be honest, this only applies to three women, I was clear and upfront. Intercourse wasn't an option. They believed it was because I didn't want to have a child before I was ready. It was only partly true."

"What is the truth?"

"I refused to be with any woman other than you."

"For all these years?"

He drops his head, and his eyes close briefly. "Yes." His hand moves from my waist and cups my face. "Initially, it was easy. I was still in love with you. I didn't want to be with anyone else. When I couldn't take the edge off myself, I set up my rules."

He has been pining for me for nearly a decade. *Wow!* "Are your rules the reason you slowed me down when I took control?"

"Partially."

"Why else?"

"Habit. Fear. Jealousy."

"Of who? Patrick?"

"Yeah."

I push up onto my elbows beneath him, and our chests meld together again. *Holy hell!* "No reason for you to be jealous. None, at all." Adding it has been a few years for me won't help this conversation either.

He arches an eyebrow but doesn't press me for more details. It makes sense. I wouldn't want them if the situation were reversed.

"We figured it out the first time with moderate success. With our gained knowledge of likes and dislikes, we will do it better now."

"Slowly," he adds.

"How slow are we talkin'? The ache from your hands alone is a lot to process."

"We will absolutely take the edge off tonight." Without another word, Colby burrows his arm between me and the bed, then flips our positions.

"Your knee?"

"Doesn't hurt. Being cautious is all." His eyes glaze over briefly. "You're—"

I interrupt what I assume will be a compliment with a kiss. His hands bracket my hips. The thin layer of lace and cotton between my heated center and his hard-as-stone length is useless. Rocking back and forth, I increase the friction between us. Ripples of pleasure roll forward faster than I would like. Colby uses his abs of steel to sit up and sucks my taut nipple into his mouth.

A murmur of need vibrates through me. Colby sucks harder and cups my other breast with his hand. An undercurrent of bliss spirals in my belly.

He releases me with a pop to demand, "Take what you need."

His words pierce the tenuous hold I had on my emotions and body. Moments later, white-hot pleasure explodes, I shatter, and then collapse on top of him. We're not completely naked, and the… Sweet mercy! I'm screwed. Being with Colby again is going to ruin me, considering this blew my mind.

"Sorry, I'm crushing you."

Colby's fingers dig deeper into my hips. "No, you feel better than I remember, and it was amazing before."

I lift my head from his chest and kiss him deeply.

He pulls back and says, "As much as I would like to stay in bed with you, we should order food. I vaguely recall you not being very pleasant when hangry."

I chuckle, kiss him again, and climb off the bed. He rummages through his bag for shorts while I tug on a shirt and nothing else. Ten minutes later, we place a large room service order and wait for it to arrive. We chat about my parents and more specifically my father's reaction to Colby being back in my life.

"Does it bother you?" he asks.

"No. I make my own choices. I'm choosing to give us a second chance at forever."

Unfortunately, our heart-to-heart is cut off by our food delivery. We settle at the rolling table and eat mostly in silence. Comfortable, effortless silence like early in our relationship. We cuddle on the bed and watch a movie until I fall asleep nestled in the crook of his arm.

When I wake the next morning, I'm draped over Colby. It feels like home. I'm scared and optimistic at the same time.

"Morning, Annie."

I crane my neck. "Morning. How long have you been awake?"

"A little while. I didn't want to disturb you."

"I sleep well in your arms, always have."

"It didn't happen often before."

"No, but the short naps on the couch were perfection."

"They were. Breakfast in bed or on the way home?" he asks.

"In bed, definitely."

After a kiss, he's standing and ordering. A smorgasbord of food arrives within the hour. It's as if Colby doesn't know my food likes and dislikes. Untrue. Perhaps he's starving like me. We talk about the upcoming season—both of them—while we eat.

"Why are you staring at me like that?"

He answers, "Staring is an awful word. I'm memorizing each curve and freckle across the table."

"Perhaps you should study more thoroughly in the huge shower." I point to the bathroom.

With a mischievous but sexy grin, he gulps the rest of his coffee. Taking my hand in his, we step into the bathroom. Colby doesn't waste any time and discards the shirt I slept in. I follow and push his shorts and boxer briefs to the tiled floor.

Holy hell! I felt him last night, but I don't recall Colby being this large. Then again, we were so young. As I unabashedly ogle, he reaches around me, turns on the water, and tests the temperature. Colby smooths his hand down the center of my back, over the curve of my ass before gripping tightly. His mouth meets the slope of my neck. Together we step into the glass enclosure.

Water cascades over us, heightening each nip, caress, and kiss he bestows on my body. I stabilize myself against the cool wall and thread my fingers into his thick, soft hair.

"Colby." His name sounds like a call for relief. Maybe it is.

He ignores me. Travelling lower, he kisses my hip down to the tops of my feet. Worry floods my brain about his knee, but the overwhelming sensations from his mouth and hands have me casting my concerns aside rapidly.

Rising to his full height, Colby widens my stance with his good leg and pins one hand above my head. He teases my aroused core with his fingers. I surround his hard shaft, stroking in time with his finger gliding forward and back. A soft whimper escapes my lips when he pushes two fingers inside me. My head falls forward, meeting his.

"How long, Annie?" he whispers.

"A man...?" My thoughts are cut off by the building bliss from his fingers. "Since I broke off my engagement. My vibrator... a few days."

"You haven't had sex... either?"

"No. Please make me scream."

Without another word, his pace increases rapidly, and the friction ratchets up the pleasure spiraling in my belly. I match his rhythm and speed, stroking faster.

"Annie."

I bow away from the tile as the pressure builds, and my inner walls pulse around his fingers. "Don't stop."

"You either."

Stars explode in my eyes and my core when he presses his thumb on my clit. "Colby." I grind against him, allowing the shudders to consume me as he orgasms in my hand.

We take a seat on the bench until our panting decreases to normal breathing.

"When we're together again, can we make sure we have no plans for a decent amount of time thereafter," I murmur against his shoulder.

"Yes. We're going to need it to make up for missed opportunities to scream together."

I laugh. "Is that even possible?"

He shrugs. "Don't know, but we're going to try like hell."

Near noon, we start the trek home. I'm not sure it qualifies as a trek. Summit Creek is about ninety minutes away from the city. Either way, we spend the rest of the day together and meet the next morning to solve the crossword at my place instead of the café.

CHAPTER FIFTEEN

COLBY

Our date morphed into heavy and honest conversation. Not only did we talk about us, but I shared my history with her. This morning, I wake up and text Annie.

Me: Good morning, gorgeous.

Her response is usually immediate because she's getting ready for work. Ten minutes later, I walk across the yard to her house. I enter the code and find her alarm still on. I silence it and climb the stairs to her bedroom.

She's a vision even sound asleep. Unfortunately, the peaceful expression on her face will disappear when I share she's running late. It's one of her pet peeves. I sit on the edge of her bed and slide the pad of my thumb along her cheek.

Her eyes flutter open, and she groans and buries her face in her pillow. "Morning." Her greeting is muffled.

"Morning. You need to get moving, gorgeous, or you'll be late for school."

"Ut-uh. My alarm didn't go off yet."

I lean forward and press a kiss to her temple. "It's after six."

With a serious frown on her face, she lifts her head and checks the clock. "Damn!"

"Time to get out of your cozy looking bed. I'll make you coffee and breakfast."

"Thank you."

"Of course." With expedience I didn't know she possessed, Annie is showered, dressed, and ready to go within twenty minutes. "You have seriously decreased your time to get ready."

She smiles and laughs softly. "The principal can't be late."

I set a travel mug of coffee, a bagel with avocado and tomato, and a bagged lunch in front of her. Rounding the island, I draw her close and kiss her deeply as if I can't get enough. It's the truth. "Go, Bluebird. I'll see you for practice after school."

She grabs her tote and keys and slips into the garage. I finish cleaning the kitchen, put some chicken in the fridge to defrost, and show myself out the back door. When I re-enter Jack and Lorelei's house, I find them in the kitchen waiting for an explanation.

"What?" I ask.

"Did you sleep at Annie's last night?" Jack asks.

"No. I went over there this morning when she didn't answer my text."

"Uh-huh." Lorelei answers.

"What's with the questions? Aren't you two team CJS?"

Lorelei laughs, and Jack frowns because he doesn't get it. "We are. We think you're going a little slow, that's all."

"Will one of you share what CJS means?" Jack asks.

"Colby and Julianne Somerset," his wife answers.

"I thought we wanted them to get together but not instantly?" Jack asks.

Lorelei shakes her head. "We're past that stage, babe. Aren't you paying attention?"

Jack shakes his head and looks at me. "Don't be late. I assume you're leaving from the office for practice this afternoon?"

"I am."

"Please promise me you won't do anything stupid."

"I promise. The last thing I want is to jeopardize my stellar progress. I mean, it was pain free when I crouched down to—"

"No! Stop. I don't want to hear!" Lorelei demands.

Glad to know Annie doesn't share intimate details with our friends. I laugh heartily. "I don't kiss and tell. If you would let me finish my sentence, when I crouched down to greet a fan at the hospital, I was completely pain free."

Jack states, "That's the goal. We're past the two-month mark in your rehabilitation. I'm ecstatic about your progress."

"Have you shared your opinion with the team?"

Jack tilts his head. "Yes, but not in the way you think. I provide the weekly report they requested without any hint of my personal feelings out of it. I don't want the front office or you, for that matter, to focus on the progress. Are you ahead of where I thought you would be? Yes, a little. I stress… a little. I've kept the information to myself."

"Much appreciated. I'll see you at my appointment. I need to pack for practice." Happy with Jack's report, I climb the stairs and locate the items I need for the rest of the day. After grabbing a protein shake on the way out the door, I park at Jack's office in the nick of time for my appointment. Today's plan calls for the stationary bike and then some massage.

The ride to Point Academy is traffic free, and I arrive earlier than necessary. I park alongside Annie's car and head into the office.

"Good afternoon. How can I help you?" A young woman greets me.

"Hello. I have a meeting with Principal Silva," I answer her.

"Your name, sir?"

"Colby Somerset."

Her eyes widen when she recognizes me. "My apologies. It's a pleasure to put a face to the voice on the phone. Right this way."

"Thank you...."

"Reina." She knocks on Annie's door.

"Come in." Annie's voice calls. She looks up when Reina steps into her office.

"Good afternoon, Mr. Somerset." Annie rises from her tufted leather chair with her hand outstretched. "Thank you, Reina."

"Principal Silva." I skillfully stifle a laugh as the door clicks closed behind me. "You look exactly as I thought you would in your professional world—in control and admired."

"Got a kick out of that one, huh?"

"Calling you Principal Silva? Maybe a little." I tug gently on our clasped hands.

Annie crashes into me with a sweet sigh. I greet her with a light kiss.

"Do we need to go over the ground rules?"

I frown at her. "No. No kissing near the players."

"It will be difficult, but it's the right call. Want a tour?"

"Definitely," I reply.

Annie leads me down a stately corridor and turns right. Each brush of her hand makes me want to find a darkened corner to break the rules and make out with her until we're panting for breath. I won't, but I want to. The buried rebel in me desires to muss her up at work.

"Two, don't do it."

I feign dismay. "Who me?"

She arches an eyebrow in my direction.

"Fine. I was thinking it, but I'll be professional on school grounds. It might kill me, but I will."

"Thank you. I never said it would be easy for me to do the same."

When our hands brush again, I grab hers for a brief moment and release it. To say I'm shocked by the athletic facilities is inaccurate. The clubhouse rivals a few major league stadiums, and the field is exceptional. "Annie, this is spectacular."

"Yeah, it is."

The clubhouse has a state-of-the-art gym as well as a training room and huge locker room for not only the baseball team but, from the signage, every varsity sport the school offers.

"How old is the turf?"

"It was replaced three years ago." When we step onto the stellar field, I see a young man sitting in the dugout. "Mr. Simonson, shouldn't you be in class?" Annie approaches the young man.

"I have study hall now. Mr. Jones gave me a pass."

"Want to share what's going on?" Annie asks him.

"My grandfather died last night, and this is the only place I feel normal right now."

I grip her hand to get her attention. "Let me talk to him. What's his first name?"

Annie nods curtly and replies, "Tyler" and backs away.

"Hey, Tyler. Mind if I sit with you?"

He looks up at me and frowns as if he's seeing things. As if I can't truly be standing here at this moment. I suppose his response makes sense. Why would I be here? I wouldn't be but for Annie.

"Principal Silva, are you punking me?"

"No, Mr. Simonson. Why do you ask?"

Tyler looks me straight in the eye. "Are you Colby Somerset?"

"Yes."

"How could you know he's my favorite active baseball player?"

His favorite player? A sense of calm settles over me. I wonder if my idols felt this way when I met them.

Annie smiles. One that lights me up from the inside but reassures Tyler.

"I didn't. Mr. Somerset is here to assist your team this season."

"No way," Tyler replies.

I drop my head and acknowledge Annie's statement. "Can I join you?" I ask again.

"Yes," he replies.

Annie takes a few steps away to offer the appearance of privacy. Can she hear our conversation? Perhaps, but she won't betray Tyler in any way.

"What year are you, and what position do you play?" I ask.

"I'm a senior and was second in the starting pitching rotation last year, but with a new coach, I'm not sure."

"Well, I think your coach will make her decisions based on performance during preseason."

"Her?"

"Yeah, Principal Silva is your coach."

He glances at Annie and then at me. "Real talk, does she know anything about baseball?"

I laugh heartily. "Principal Silva," Annie takes a few steps closer to the dugout. "Which team leads the league in runs this pre-season?"

"As of last night… Texas."

Tyler tilts his head. "Who has the lowest ERA?"

Annie smiles and replies, "Shane McClanahan of Tampa Bay."

"How many years has it been since a back-to-back World Series win?" I ask her.

"It's been twenty-three years since a team has won back-to-back World Series titles. The Yankees won three in a row."

"Let's try a coaching question. How does a pitcher like Tyler improve his control, merely as an example, of course?"

"That isn't a short answer. Step one would be to figure out what speed your location is failing. Then you need to slow down and pay attention to your mechanics to successfully locate your pitches and document your misses. Determine the speed at which you fail to locate as well as you'd like. Following that you would gradually—"

"Wow!" is all Tyler manages in reply.

"I get why you need to be here. It's the only place you feel safe and calm, right?" I offer.

Tyler nods.

"Yeah, me too. Always has been." Arguably it's the only place I felt safe and calm since I hurt Annie all those years ago. When we were together it was her. I'm hopeful we can surpass where we were before. "Want to sit in the quiet or tell me about your grandfather?"

"Quiet, please." True to his word, Tyler remains silent until the bell summons him to his next class. "Thank you."

"You're welcome. I'll see you after class for practice."

Tyler nods tightly and rushes away. I exit the concrete dugout and fall in stride with Annie.

"I need to finish up a few things and change. Want to wait in my office?"

"Sure."

Over the next forty minutes, Annie downs the rest of her lunch, answers three emails, and dresses for practice. Once the last bus leaves, we head into the coaching office to grab the necessary gear. She's running around like the Energizer Bunny. I have no doubt her nerves are off the charts. To calm her and to be honest, to soothe the aching need in my chest, I pin her against the wall and kiss her breathless. She responds without a second thought. Annie sets her hand on my chest and adds space between us when she recalls where we are.

"I know. No kissing in front of the players. There aren't any in here, and I needed to help you relax."

Annie rolls her eyes.

"Don't disagree. I know you're nervous, and kissing helped. Admit it."

Her eyes flutter closed briefly, then she mumbles, "Yes. It did."

I press my lips to her forehead and let her slip out of my arms. The players filter onto the field over the next fifteen minutes.

Precisely at the beginning of practice, Annie steps onto the field. "Good afternoon. In addition to being your principal, I will be your coach this season."

A host of groans rumble through the players.

Tyler silences them. "Guys, hear her out. She has skills."

Annie acknowledges Tyler's words and continues, "My goal was to find you the best coach available. None of the candidates were up to the level necessary to handle the job and bolster this team to the top of the league. All I ask is you give me and my assistant coach, Colby Somerset, a chance."

Unintelligible chatter rolls through the players.

Colby states, "Thank you, Coach Silva. Gentlemen, let's get warmed up and show Coach why you deserve a spot on the roster."

Tyler and a teammate lead the players through standard stretches and proceed to short throws while Annie and I watch.

"The catcher?" I ask, indicating the player beside Tyler. Despite memorizing the roster, I can't tell who they are yet.

"Yeah. Mikhail Telford." Once the team finishes warmup, Annie directs, "Let's work on some fielding. Pitchers and catchers, please go with Coach Somerset to the bullpen area."

"This is awesome! Colby Somerset is our coach."

I fall in step with him and Tyler. "Telford, right?"

"Yeah."

"I'm here to assist Coach Silva. She's your coach."

"Dude, I asked her some pointed questions earlier. She's smart. Give her a chance," Tyler urges his teammate.

"Okay. What could she possibly know about baseball?"

I expected some hesitance from the players. It makes sense. "Listen, I understand your skepticism. Coach Silva played baseball starting when she was six until high school. She tried out for the baseball, but they wouldn't let her play because there was a softball team."

"That's messed up!" Tyler states.

"I agree. She would have been an amazing teammate."

Telford was listening carefully. "She was on you teammate when you were younger?"

"Yeah, she was." After reassuring the guys a bit, we have a moderate pitching practice, and I study their mechanics and how to place them in the starting rotation in between glances at Annie with the field players. She was scared to take on this role, but she's a natural. Once the guys trust her, it will be great. It's the first practice, but it's clear some of the players were working in the offseason while others were lying on the couch, including the ace pitcher from last season, Beckett Fisher.

Annie blows her whistle, and we hustle to meet her near home plate. "Gentlemen, good start for the first practice. We'll see you again tomorrow. I intend to have a roster set by the end of next week. Mr. Simonson, please stay back for a moment."

A chorus of "Thanks, Coach," echoes around us as the guys take off.

"What's up, Coach?"

"Great first day out. Do you know the schedule for your grandfather's services yet?"

"No. My mom and her siblings were planning today."

"Please let me know the details when you do. Don't worry about missing school or practice."

"Thanks. I will." He takes off and catches up with his teammates, who are nearing the clubhouse.

I reach for her but let my hand drop. "Feeling better about being thrust into coaching?"

A sneaky, sly smile curls up at the corner of her mouth. It's sexy, and I want to kiss it off her face. "Yeah, this was so much fun! I didn't realize how much I missed the game. I mean, it's one thing to watch you and study the box scores. It's something else to get dirt under my fingernails again. How about you? Was this hard?"

"My knee is fine. No pain at all. Is it hard to be on the field? No. It's pretty awesome. Would I prefer to be behind the plate in Florida right now? Is that what you're truly asking?"

She inhales sharply.

The truth is I would give up playing for Annie. She would hate me for it, but I would do it. I don't need more money or fame. Quite the opposite, in fact. I would be fine here with her. "I won't lie to you. I miss the game and some of the guys. I don't miss the drama and the front office politics. Right now, I'm focused on rehabbing my injury and rebuilding our relationship, not what happens if I can catch later this season. The season isn't even underway yet."

She exhales slowly.

My words strike a chord. I'm spot-on, and she's shaken by my candid words. "All I can do is promise to share my progress and anything that goes on with the team when it happens. Does that work for you?"

Her eyes flutter closed briefly before she mutters, "Yes."

"What do you say we go home, cook dinner, and discuss our team?" I suggest.

"Sounds perfect!"

We stop by her office and then to our cars. "I'll follow you."

Today has been amazing. About halfway into the drive, a call comes through the Bluetooth in my SUV.

"Hey, Hatton. How's it going?"

He groans. "I hate my new catcher. Any chance you're miraculously healed?"

I shake my head. "I'm sorry, man. Making progress, but I'm not in catching shape yet. How bad is it?"

"For starters, Easton Bolton is a rookie. Well, technically, he's in his third year but first in the majors. He doesn't set up well when I don't take his pitch suggestions. Ugh! I never thought I would wish for an old-timer."

I laugh heartily. "Much appreciated, Hatton. Maybe I can talk to him when I'm there for the ceremony and gala."

"Really, you would do that? You're coming?"

"Yes, I'll be there to accept my ring with the rest of the team. Of course I'll offer some of my wisdom. I want the team to succeed even if I'm not catching for you."

"Cool. I'll see you soon. Thanks for the talk, old man."

I grin though he can't see me. "Anytime, kid." Ending the call, I consider if I can't get back there this season and dispel the notion immediately. I've accepted Jack's prognosis and treatment schedule. I will stick to it and be sure my knee is fully healed before I play another game.

I park in front of Annie's garage and step inside before she closes the door. Over dinner we discuss the first practice and our impressions of a few players.

"Fisher is out of shape. Simonson spent the offseason working on his speed and placement. Even though we've only had one practice, Simonson should be your ace, then Stricker, Fisher, and Roberts. Your team isn't deep enough for a five-man rotation. Telford is probably the better catcher, but Carson has a better attitude," I share.

"Dropping Fisher to third?"

"Yes. He hasn't been working in the off season. Simonson and Stricker have."

"Okay. I'm not surprised about Fisher. His father gives him what he wants, hand over fist, because he's absent. I mean, no one in high school needs a brand-new sports car to drive, which was promptly replaced after he got into an accident."

"Noted. What about the position players?"

"Meyers will certainly retain the shortstop position, and Jones will nicely fill in the third base spot. The outfield is a disaster."

I chuckle at her choice of words, and we discuss her team more in depth. Then we curl up on her couch and watch opening day baseball. Mine is away to start the season. It's a weird feeling being here instead of playing, but I'm okay. To be honest, I would prefer the team I'm working on with Annie. Perhaps Haussman plowing into me was the best thing to ever happen to me.

"Is it hard to watch?" She asks quietly, as if the volume of her words impacts their meaning.

"No. I wouldn't give you up to be behind the plate right now."

Her gaze bores into mine. I'm completely serious. There's no waver or inflection in my voice, and she recognizes the same. Unsure how to handle my admission, Annie snuggles against me and promptly falls asleep. I trust Jack to rehab my knee to the best of his ability. Will I be able to play again? I hope so, but if the cost is losing Annie again, I'll move on. Whether that means retiring or asking for a trade, I'll do it.

CHAPTER SIXTEEN

JULIANNE

It has been nearly two weeks since the start of practice. Daily after therapy, Colby drives to school, we have lunch, and then run practice together. Normally, we would jump right into games, but the schedule this season is wonky due to spring break. I need to get through one more day of school. Ideally, before I leave, Kate will accept the athletic director position and practice will run smoothly. Then the true test will begin. Nine days with Colby... alone... in Florida. My emotions zip back and forth from elation to terror. First, let's get through the workday.

When my feet hit the bottom step, I hear my alarm chime. Rounding the corner, I find Colby stepping inside with breakfast in hand.

"Morning, Bluebird."

I kiss him more deeply than he expects, but he indulges me. "Morning, Two. You were up early today. Why?" I indicate the bags from The Wired Puppy.

"I went to sleep instead of packing last night."

I smirk at him. "Oh. My bad."

He shakes his head and draws me closer. "Nothing to feel bad about. I appreciate you sticking to going slow. It wasn't an easy yes."

He's correct. It hasn't been. My vibrator has used extra batteries since our second first date in Philly. "Have you looked in the mirror lately?"

The blush on his cheeks is seriously cute. "You have to know without a doubt you're better looking and more fit than the majority of guys your age."

"So I'm old but hot?"

I bury my head into his sculpted chest and reply, "Not old but absolutely hot."

"Noted. Eat your breakfast, sweetheart. I'll make our lunch. Before I forget, take these." He hands me the keys to his SUV.

I frown. "Why?"

"I'll have a car bring me to practice, and we can leave together for the airport. Would you prefer your car instead?"

"No, forgot is all." I didn't forget. Overall, he doesn't flaunt his wealth, but his car is worth three times as much as mine.

"Annie, please share what you're nervous about."

He saw right through my flimsy excuse. My eyes flutter closed, and I take a deep breath. "All of it." Exhaling sharply, I add, "We can't discuss it now."

"Why didn't you share before?"

I shrug. Truth is… I never stopped loving Colby. He was my first everything, and the prospect of sharing those feelings again makes my stomach knot and roil. The reality is I'm not sure if it's fear or anger or both.

Drawing me into his embrace again, he whispers near the shell of my ear, "We'll talk about each and every concern you have about us."

"Most of it is me." His cologne is strikingly similar to when we were younger. It still soothes me. With one last whiff, I add some space, kiss him, and rush out the door with my breakfast and coffee.

About halfway to school, I realize how luxurious it is to drive Colby's SUV. More so when he calls me, and I answer through Bluetooth. I didn't connect my phone but yet somehow… Colby.

"Hey, sweetheart. You didn't grab lunch."

"Hey. Yeah. I can get something in the cafeteria for us."

"I'll bring it. Truly, are you okay?"

"Yes. I'm nervous about this trip."

I imagine him gripping the back of his neck with his hand. "Because of me?"

"Not exactly. I would prefer to have this conversation face-to-face if you don't mind."

"Okay. We'll talk tonight."

For the rest of the ride, I open the moonroof and enjoy the sunshine beaming down on me. It's still early but shaping up to be a gorgeous day, at least weatherwise.

I park in my spot at the same time as Alton Brown steps out of his car. He's a tenured science teacher and an exceptional mentor to our underprivileged students.

"Morning. Nice new ride," he states.

"Not mine. Borrowing it."

He nods, and we walk into the building side by side. "Have a great day," he mutters and continues down the hall without an answer.

"Morning, Reina."

"Morning. I'll be right in with your messages."

"Thank you." I drop my purse into my bottom desk drawer and lock it. Settling in my chair, I push away the lingering thoughts about Colby for now. I need to focus on Kate's on-site interview.

"Knock, knock."

"Come in, Reina."

She hands me a stack of messages and the mail requiring my attention. "I figured you would want to get this done before break. Miss Williamson is scheduled to arrive at ten this morning. Her flight landed safely, and her arrival is still on time."

"Perfect. Please make sure anything pressing is ready for me to review after lunch. I'm taking advantage of the break starting on a Thursday and leaving directly from here."

"I will. Good for you."

I flip through the stack of papers she left, and the next thing I know, Reina informs me Kate has arrived. I smooth my skirt and exit my office.

"Miss Williamson, welcome to Point Academy."

"Pleasure to meet you in person, Principal Silva."

"You as well. I thought we would start with a tour." Like with Colby, I walk Kate to the athletic facilities and explain along the way. "As I mentioned in our video conference, we offer soccer, basketball, and track to both our males and female students. Additionally, we offer baseball and softball, but only men's hockey."

"What is the status of the coaching staff for each sport?"

"At this point, the only vacant positions are the athletic director, assistant athletic director, and head baseball coach."

Kate asks, "Who is filling in?"

"I am for all three positions at the moment."

She nods in both acknowledgment and understanding. I take it to mean she would do the same thing to grant the students the ability to play. As we walk through the fields and I share the basics of the facilities, Kate is quiet and observant. She appears confident and capable.

It isn't until we reach her would-be office that she asks her next question. "Who would be in charge of hiring and firing coaches and support staff in my department?"

"You. If you accept the position, you'll select your second-in-command personally. I can block a hire, as can the board, but haven't had the need to exercise it since I joined Point Academy."

"Your school and amenities are top-notch. If we can negotiate an acceptable salary and benefits package, I will accept the position."

A huge sense of relief pours through me. Outwardly, I smile and suggest, "Why don't we head into my office and discuss the specifics?"

"Perfect."

After Reina delivers a tray of fruit and water for us, Kate and I come to terms for her new position. Her current salary is significantly less than it should be, and she's pleasantly surprised with my offer.

"Here is a letter of intent for your signature. I will have the contract drafted and to you by the middle of next week."

"I'm looking forward to working with you." She extends her hand, I shake it, and then she leaves.

Before I can retake my seat, Colby breezes into my office, hauls me into his arms, and kisses me hard. I lose myself in him despite where we are and my protestations against it. Our tongues tangle, and I resist the urge to slip my hands beneath his shirt by the slimmest of margins. We are interrupted when Reina knocks but doesn't wait for me to answer.

"Oh, I'm sorry. I'll come back."

I step back, gather my wits somewhat and ask, "What do you need, Reina?"

"Two teachers are breaking up a fight in the corridor near the cafeteria."

I rush past Colby, out of my office toward the cafeteria. By the time I arrive, Mr. Edson and Mr. Winkle have successfully separated the students.

"Please take him—" I indicate Stephon Kyle. "—to the conference room and him to the nurse's office," I point to Beau Daly. They escort them past me. When I turn, I find Colby leaning against the wall, watching me.

"Does that happen often?" he asks as I approach.

"No. This is the second fight during my tenure here. Those two have history."

"Meaning?"

"Respectively, their parents are divorced. The catalyst for the divorces was an affair between Stephon's mother and Beau's father."

"I see. Can I have the key to the baseball office? I'll hang out there until you're done."

We turn down the hallway toward the main office. "Sure. It's in my purse. Also, you may have to run practice, depending on how long this takes."

When we arrive, I ask Reina to pull their files.

"Already on your desk," she replies and retreats to her desk.

I immensely appreciate her anticipating my needs, and then we step into my office, and I retrieve the key for him. He takes it from my hand. "Two."

"Yes." His gorgeous eyes flicker with something I can't place. A notion I don't have time to deal with now either.

"Promise me you won't do anything crazy if you're on your own."

He laces our fingers and draws me against him with our hands bent between us. "I won't take any unnecessary risks running practice."

"Thank you."

"Try to eat if you can," he instructs. "I left lunch on your desk." With a chaste kiss to my cheek, he turns toward the door with his bag slung over his shoulder. Before he disappears, he looks back and winks at me.

I sit in my chair and pull up the video footage on my computer. I watch the footage twice, then grab the files and stalk to the nurse's office.

"He started it, Miss Silva." Beau lifts the ice pack from his cheek.

"I saw that on the footage. I also noticed you let him hit you. Why?"

"I don't plan on losing my epic spring break trip because of him," he answers with a wince. Beau has a split lip and a shiner blossoming before my eyes. "My dad is taking me and my sister to our cabin in Maine. Stephon and his mother weren't invited. It's my time. Stephon isn't happy he and his mother weren't invited, and he threatened to crash it. I told him to give it a shot, and then he sucker punched me."

"I'm going to speak with Stephon and his mother. Please stay here until Nurse Stanton says you can leave."

"I will. Thank you for watching before coming in here."

I leave the office and walk directly to the conference room.

I knock and enter the conference room. "Mrs. Kyle, always a pleasure to see you." Hopefully, the sarcasm in my tone is evident. "I'll keep this as succinct as possible. Your son incited a fight with Mr. Daly. After reviewing the footage and his history of failing to follow school rules, Stephon shall serve three days in-house suspension upon returning from break."

"What about Beau?" Stephon asks.

"You thought this would get him in trouble so he couldn't go on the trip?" I pose the question to Stephon.

His eyes widen in surprise.

"Yeah, I know about that. Any discipline I chose to mete out for Mr. Daly is between him and I. Do you have any questions?"

"No," Stephon answers emphatically.

"Good. Please grab your things from your locker and leave school premises," I instruct him.

I exit the room without waiting for a response. If I hurry, I might be able to clear my inbox and eat before practice ends. By the time I finish the new email and voicemails, only twenty minutes of practice remains. Rather than waste more time, I walk to the field and watch from a distance.

The boys are working on signs and situational decisions. Colby has a runner at third and a batter in the box. He calls for a suicide bunt. While they didn't pull it off, they followed instructions well. After a few other scenarios, he calls them in to a huddle.

I can't hear him, but they seem happy when they break.

"How long have you been standing here?"

"Ten minutes or so," I answer. "You look pretty hot as the coach."

Colby leans in and whispers, "Not as hot as you."

Desire zings through me, and heat pools between my thighs.

"Ready to go? We have a waterfront oasis to get to."

"So ready." I hope my bravado is strong enough. I want to leave here. Am I ready to be alone with Colby for the next week plus… I'm not so sure.

CHAPTER SEVENTEEN

COLBY

Parking in the long-term lot, I hop out of my SUV and open Annie's door. We pull our luggage from the hatch and enter the terminal.

"Good evening. How may I assist you?" a young, fit, blond man in a perfectly tailored uniform inquires. His name tag indicates his name is Austin.

"Colby Somerset and Julianne Silva checking in for a Pemberton flight to Tampa," I reply.

"Very well." He taps on the keyboard in front of him. "Your plane has arrived. I'll escort you to the private terminal for boarding."

"Thank you." I thread my fingers into Annie's after he takes our bags. Her hand is shaking. "What's wrong?"

"Not used to all this," she mumbles.

"Is that part of the issue from this morning?"

"Yes."

"What else—"

"Your flight attendant will be with you shortly," Austin informs us and promptly leaves.

Annie glances around the room to determine if we're truly alone. "It's one thing to know your car costs three times as much as mine and you have four spares in your garage. It's something else that everyone I'm going to meet is in the same income bracket as you are."

I smile at her and kiss her softly. "For the most part, most of the people I surround myself with are humble."

The gangway door opens, and we're ushered onto the plane.

"Mr. Somerset, welcome aboard. Miss Silva, it's a pleasure to welcome you to my extended family in person." Cash Morgan, our pilot, offers.

I'm sufficiently intrigued but offer nothing more than a simple thank you.

"Thank you. You as well," Annie replies.

We take our seats and the drinks from our flight steward. Once we're airborne, I ask, "How do you know Cash?"

Annie laughs. "I don't exactly. How do you?"

"I don't. Madeleine recommended Pemberton Airlines. My question still stands."

"The Morgan family is a client of Jake's."

"Cool."

"Can you ease my nervousness a bit and fill me in on the schedule for our vacation?" she asks.

Now, it's my turn to chuckle. Frankly, I'm surprised it took her this long to inquire. Giving up control over her schedule is not something Annie is adept at. "Sure. Tomorrow, we're getting manicures and pedicures on my deck. Then, we're having a quiet evening at home complete with dinner cooked by me." I wink at her. "Saturday is family day at the stadium. Followed by the first home game and gala. We're going to the game, and then we have a few hours to dress before the gala."

"Just throwing me in the deep end?"

"Didn't mean to. I'm grateful you agreed to attend with me."

"Even though we weren't together, I'm proud of you achieving one of your dreams."

"I would've preferred you beside me when it was happening," I offer quietly.

Her shoulders drop slightly. "Can't change that. All we can do is focus on how we look going forward."

"In your mind, what do we look like?" I ask, realizing the answer isn't simple.

She takes a deep breath. "I don't know what we look like. The only sure thing is I want to be with you."

"It's a start. What are you concerned about?"

"What happens when you can play again?" Her voice drops off as she asks.

I take her hands in mine. "To be honest, I don't know how much longer I'm going to play. I was considering retirement at the end of my current contract."

"Which is after next season, right?"

I wrinkle my brow. "Yes. Will it be difficult? Yes. Will it be worth it? Absolutely."

"What do you plan to do when you retire?"

"The only plans I have are to actually rest for a year before deciding what to do next."

"Fair. Which degree did you pursue in college?"

"Computer science and accounting."

She turns more fully in my direction. "Stuck to something boring like your parents suggested, huh?"

"Yes and no. I've always loved computers as you already know. However, I'm quite adept at accounting."

"If you were so inclined, I'm sure Madeleine would be willing to refer you to her clients who need wealth management assistance," Annie suggests.

"That's a good idea. Let's shift back to our vacation. Is there anything you want to do while we're away?"

"Not really."

"What were you doing for your vacation before?"

"Didn't I already share with you?"

"Nope."

Annie replies, "I planned to rent a cottage on a beach and unplug from the world."

"Is sand required?"

"Not necessarily."

"Perfect. I can work with that. I happen to have a pool and dock in my backyard."

"You have a dock but no boat?"

I had no doubt Annie would recall I dislike boats. When I was about twelve, we went on a man's fishing trip. My father, his brother, my cousin, and me because I didn't have a brother. Violet refused to go. The first few hours were fine, but once my cousin was bored, he started acting up. His father attempted to soothe him but was unsuccessful. He removed his life vest and jumped into the lake. Despite his father's pleas, my cousin decided to swim to the island in the middle of the lake. We followed him and attempted to get him back into the boat. We failed and he went under. It took three days for his remains to surface. Annie spent those three days glued to my side.

"Yup, still don't like boats." We chat for the rest of the flight about potential activities for after the gala. Admittedly, Annie is still the same as she was in high school. Willing to go out but equally as comfortable staying at home.

When we deplane, our driver meets us at the gate. "Johnny, nice to see you."

"Mr. Somerset, welcome home."

"Thank you. I would like to introduce Julianne."

He extends his hand to her, and she takes it. "Pleasure to meet you."

"You as well."

We settle into the town car for the ride to my house. Annie is quiet with words during the ride but actively watching the scenery pass by as I draw circles with my thumb on her hand.

"Please let me know when you need to return to the airport, Mr. Somerset," Johnny requests after setting our luggage on the sidewalk.

"I will. Have a great evening."

My heart constricts as I escort Annie inside my home. It's similar to hers except for the waterfront location and pool. Otherwise, it's cozy and comfortable. The true test will be when she sees her library. At some point in high school, we talked about our dream home. A private library was Annie's only wish. I built her one in my home. Crazy and presumptuous, perhaps. More accurately, determined we would find our way back to each other.

She hasn't uttered a word since she stepped inside. I'm not sure if it's a good quiet or a concerned quiet.

"You okay?"

"I'm speechless. Your home is… you."

I smile. "I guess. Let's get you settled in." I grab our bags and roll them down the hall. Noting she hadn't followed me, I stop and turn back. "You coming?"

"Uh-huh."

I leave the bags in the hallway, return to Annie, and draw her into my arms. I kiss her lips and add some space between us. "It's me, Bluebird. What's going on in your gorgeous mind?"

"Taking all of this in and trying not to go down the path of blame as well."

"Don't. Placing blame keeps us in the past." Truthfully, I've done it enough for both of us, deservedly so. "We're focusing on now and our future." Taking her hand in mine, I lead her to the luggage, and we each grab one. Should I offer her the guest suite? Yes. Do I plan to? No.

While large, the master suite isn't anything out of the ordinary. There's a sitting area with two comfortable chairs and a console table. Past that is the master closet which is almost as large as my childhood bedroom complete with "his" and "hers" sides with a huge dressing bench in the middle. The king-size bed has ultrasoft linens and a navy duvet.

"You can unpack in the left side of the closet and the tall bureau on the opposite wall is empty," I point out.

"Thank you." Annie wheels her luggage straight into the closet and gets to work. Her response leads me to believe she's still stewing.

Rather than giving her space, I follow her into the closet with my bag and begin emptying it. Each time we're looking at one another, I make a funny face or kiss her. Three kisses later, we're kneeling on the bench and making out like we're back in high school. *No!* Now is one-thousand times better. I tug her shirt overhead, revealing a sexy-as-hell red lace bra, and she wiggles out of her jeans. Her reflection in the floor mirror reveals her pert ass in a barely there thong.

"Damn, Annie!"

She frowns. "What?"

"Your lingerie was not like this before!"

She giggles softly. "It wasn't. I couldn't afford it. Lingerie is my splurge."

"I approve." I rise to my feet beside the bench and push my athletic pants to the floor. Bracketing her hips with my hands, I guide her onto the bench and sit on the floor between her thighs.

"What are you doing?" Realization flashes in her eyes.

"Any concerns about my knee?"

She arches an eyebrow at me. "No. None."

"Good. This is going to take some time. I wanted to be sure your focus was on the sensations I'm about to cause with my tongue."

Her eyes widen. She leans forward and kisses me deeply. "You seem confident in your skill set."

"Perhaps I am." Before her gorgeous brain goes crazy, I add, "The answer to the question in your head is three, including you." I draw my finger down her midline, out over her thigh, and down to the top of her foot. I repeat the same motion on her other leg and follow with my tongue. She's silent until the flat of my tongue caresses the crease between her core and her thigh.

"Two."

I switch sides and follow the same path up her left leg without touching her.

"Two." This time my name sounds more like a demand. The tilt of her hips toward me indicates the same as well.

Rather than answering, I dip my tongue between her folds, swiping upward before nipping her nub lightly. Each stroke varies and ratchets up the pleasure. She shifts closer to the edge of the bench, and her hands grip my hair. Hard.

I pull away, and she frowns. Lying on my back on the Berber carpet, I guide her to straddle my face.

She hesitates. "I'll crush you."

"You won't." I coax her lower, closer to me, and resume tasting her. I push a finger into her and pull her clit between my teeth.

Annie rocks her hips, spurring me on. "Sweet mercy."

I withdraw my finger and plunge forward rapidly. Her arousal coats my face as she grinds. I catch her gaze as she twists her nipples. Her core tenses as she shatters. Her body is shaking, and her legs pulse against my head.

Before the waves subside, Annie shifts back onto the bench. She's looking anywhere but at me.

"Bluebird, talk to me."

"That has never happened before."

I frown, knowing she doesn't mean oral sex. "Happy to have another first." I push up to sit again. "Not the right answer?"

She shakes her head. "Are you a ninja or something?"

"Why?"

"It didn't feel like that when it was you before."

I feel my cheeks heat. "I may have done some research while I was in the minors to maintain my street cred with the guys."

"You studied sex so you would sound more experienced?"

"Exactly."

"It paid off. That was intense."

"Like I said, happy to oblige. Let's get cleaned up," I suggest.

"But I want…" She starts to protest, but it falls away.

The reason for her deciding not to fight me, I'm not sure. Truthfully, I want her to feel as if she's the center of attention always, especially in here. Well, the bedroom anyway.

After a long, refreshing shower, we order Chinese takeout and fall asleep to *Bull Durham* in my bed. Tomorrow, we prepare for my first time with my teammates since my injury,

CHAPTER EIGHTEEN

JULIANNE

Near six the next morning, I slip out of his luxurious bed and pad to the kitchen. After my cup brews, I set one up for Colby. I disarm his alarm system and curl up on one of the loungers by his pool. Taking my time, I savor each sip and take in my surroundings. The inground pool is beautiful and off to the right of the dock leading into the bay. There isn't much traffic there right now aside from a few early morning kayakers. Flashes of last night filter into my mind. No one has ever made me feel so much. Truthfully, not even Colby himself. We were young and inexperienced, but the pleasure he drew from me, and we didn't....

Colby steps through the French doors wearing low-slung shorts and carrying a cup of coffee. "How did you slip out of bed without waking me?" he asks after kissing me.

"You sleep hard in your bed. Deeper than in Philly. I get it. I haven't slept that well... ever."

"Is it the bed or something else?"

My cheeks heat. I know it's our tempting and almost perfect sheet time last night. Technically, closet, but no judgment. "I plead the fifth."

He winks at me and takes a seat near my feet. I lift them and drape them over his thighs.

"Are you taking the week off from physical therapy?"

He sips his coffee. I never fancied myself an arm porn girl, but his flexed forearms are delicious.

"I'm going to attend via Facetime at nine. Then Isla and Steffi will be here for our spa treatments."

I smile and shake my head. "There isn't a salon for you to go to privately?"

"The last time I went for a pedicure, I was mobbed. True, it was between World Series games, but still."

"How did that happen?"

"Someone pranked me. I think it was Hatton."

"The ace on your team?"

I see the anguish the second the word "team" leaves my lips. "I'm sorry."

He shakes his head. "Don't be. It's hard being here and not having to report. Honestly, more difficult than I thought it would be. It doesn't help Hatton and Bolton aren't on the same page."

"I'm sure that sucks."

The look on his face is priceless.

"I know more about you and baseball and the combination of the two than anyone else, except maybe Madeleine."

"You are more attuned with me about everything, including baseball, than anyone else despite the intervening years."

I wrinkle my nose.

"Nothing to be uncomfortable about, gorgeous. Is there?"

"I may not have shut off my bots, which link stories about you to my inbox each morning… yet."

He chuckles heartily. "You were stalking me all these years?"

"Kind of."

"I'll allow it."

I roll my eyes at him.

"I'm going to work out with Jack in the gym. Feel like walking at the same time?"

"Sure." I rinse my mug after following him into the kitchen. Changing quickly, I descend to his lower level and find a massive personal gym he could easily charge a membership fee to use. "You didn't leave your house much, did you?"

"No, I didn't." His phone chimes, and he answers Jack's call. "Morning."

After I hear Jack reply, I tune them out. I stretch a bit and start walking at a moderate pace. Despite being at the lowest level of his house, the upper windows allow a sliver of the outside to watch as I walk. It takes restraint not to ogle Colby as he exercises with Jack. I chastise myself watching his muscles constrict during his session. *He's doing physical therapy, not a fitness competition.* Rather than distract him, I push in my earbuds and listen to my favorite podcast. I'm a little behind lately.

When I finish one episode, I've added another mile to my tally and decrease my pace. Colby stares at me from across the room while he stretches.

"What?"

"Nothing."

"Colby." His name sounds like a plea. I suppose it is.

He rises, stalks toward me, and hauls me into his arms. "I love having you here with me."

"Want to know a secret?"

"I love it—"

He cuts me off with a hard kiss, weakening my knees. Before he leaves me panting and wanting more, I pull back. "We don't have time to continue this now and shower before our appointment, do we?"

Colby frowns. "No, we don't. Come on, let's get you cleaned up before your appointment."

"My?"

"Our," he clarifies.

After a long, hot shower—alone—in the Carrara-tiled shower, Colby ushers Isla and Steffi inside to set up. Within fifteen minutes, our feet are soaking, and we're being pampered. When we're nearly finished being buffed and polished, his phone chimes with an alert.

"What's that?"

"The alarm notifying me someone is at the gate." He pulls open the app and smiles. "It's Marta, and it appears she has packages for you."

I raise an eyebrow in his direction. "My dress or something else?"

He shrugs and smiles. A smile which tells me it's more than my dress.

"What did you do?"

Isla and Steffi look between us and then one another.

"I said I would take care of everything, and I did."

"What else is there?"

"You'll have to wait until we're done and see," he replies instantly.

I don't miss the smiles on Steffi and Isla's faces. To be honest, I would be jealous of me too. When they finish with our spa treatments, my feet are smooth, and my fingers and toes are polished a soft pink.

Colby ushers them out and introduces me to Marta. "Morning."

"*!Hola! Señor Somerset,*" she replies and then bursts into laughter when Colby gives her a cross look. "Morning, *hijo.*"

Colby smiles and hugs her. "Marta, please meet Julianne."

I attempt to extend a hand to her, but she throws her arms around me. I was nervous to meet the people in Colby's life. The warm, friendly welcome from Marta is exactly what I need to get over my fears about not fitting in here. Also, the fact my parents are distancing themselves from me has me yearning for new connections. "Pleasure to meet you." She doesn't release me but turns her attention to Colby. "*Ella es la única. Si?*"

Colby nods tightly.

"*Ya era hora,*" Marta quips, causing a severe blush to appear on Colby's face.

My Spanish is a bit rusty, but I believe her words translate to "she's the one" and "about time." I believed him, but he shared about me with Marta, and I'm kicking myself for my stubbornness.

"Your deliveries are in the master bedroom. Let me know if you need your suit or her dress steamed."

"Thank you," Colby replies. He threads my fingers in his and leads me to the bedroom. "Why don't you pull your dress out and hang it? Then we will make sure you have everything you need for Sunday."

"I don't need anything else."

He closes the gap between us. "Annie, let me take care of you."

I settle my uneasiness with his generosity and steal his breath with a kiss. Moving to the garment bag with the KB Couture logo, I unzip it and gawk at my gown. I'm crazy excited about this event. Not true. I'm a twisted knot of emotions both good and fantastic.

Colby's arms slide around my waist from behind. "Ready for the rest?"

"Yes."

"Promise you won't freak out."

I twist in his arms and clasp my hands around his neck. "I won't freak out."

The skepticism in his eyes is warranted. He kisses me deeply and retreats to the packages Marta brought into the room. The sheer fact I've never seen any of these brands before should give me pause. The only difference between these and the things I brought with me to wear is the cost. Colby hands me two nude boxes with a brand name in script on the lid.

"I didn't know if you wanted to stay low-key or stand out."

"So you bought a pair for each?" A faint reminder of his wealth creeps into my mind. He's the second highest paid player in baseball. Being with him will require me to accept fancy shoes, right? Right.

"Yes."

I open the first box and find black pumps with a moderate heel and a red sole. I slip my foot inside, and it fits as if my foot were measured.

"How did you get the size right?"

"Lorelei did some recon for me," he admits.

"Makes sense to use the information available to you." I slip off the black shoes and open the next box. This pair is... wow! The same style shoe covered with crystals. "Colby, these—"

"Shoes. Either pair will look sexy as sin on your feet."

Not going to lie, these are insane. "You might turn me into a shoe person."

"Fine with me. What else do you need for the gala?"

"Nothing. I have a gorgeous gown and now fabulous shoes."

"You're missing accessories. I know how practical you are, and I kept it in mind for the jewelry." Colby reaches into a small navy-blue bag and produces a velvet box.

Slowly, I open it and find a stunning pair of drop diamond earrings. To be honest, these are perfect for the dress. "What do you mean?"

He extends his hand to me, and I set the box in it. He pulls one earring out and takes it apart. "These are convertible. A set of studs, which I noticed you didn't have despite wanting a pair as long as I can remember and a jacket for special occasions like the gala."

"They're perfect. You said jewelry?"

He smiles widely and hands me a long narrow box. Inside is a diamond bracelet, but it's dainty. It's a platinum chain and six bezel-set diamonds, evenly spaced. In short, exactly what I would pick for myself.

"I don't know what to say."

He closes the box, sets it aside, and draws me into his chest. "You speechless has been happening a lot lately, and I don't mean contemplative."

"I know. Thank you."

"No thanks are necessary. Now I think we're ready for this event. What do you say to one more surprise?"

"I don't need anything else, Two."

"Maybe not, but you deserve it, and it's about time you know it's here."

I frown and let him lead me through a pocket door in the master closet into a…. I kiss him hard and deep before taking the entire room in. While his home is cozy, it's clear a single man lives here. However, this library—my library—is distinctly feminine. The walls are a soft grey with floor to ceiling shelving with copies of books from my favorite authors including modern ones, a notion that makes me pause, arranged in rainbow order. There's a massive window seat overlooking the bay as well as a plush couch with a fluffy blanket and accent pillows in my favorite color—purple.

"You built me a library in your home when we weren't together?"

"Yes. It has everything you dreamed of when we were teenagers."

"I gather Lor and Jack assisted with this?"

He drops his head. "Yes. How can you tell?"

"There's no way for you to know my favorite authors from the last five years without one of them assisting you."

"As crazy as she thought I was, Lorelei was a huge help with the design elements."

"While I love the stuff for the gala, I truly do, this is the best tangible thing you've ever given me."

He furrows his brow as if considering my words more carefully. "I plan to regain the ultimate intangible one again."

You already have. Sharing my feelings out loud is more terrifying than I anticipated. To be fair, I never stopped loving Colby. Getting past the pain he caused is another matter.

"I do too."

"You never lost my heart, Annie. I shouldn't have, but I took it back for a while. It always has been and always will be yours." His arms collapse around me, and we kiss until Marta knocks on the door.

"I'm sorry to interrupt, but Miss Snow stopped by," Marta shares.

"Thank you. I'll be right out," Colby replies.

"Did you forget to tell Madeleine you didn't need a date?" Annie asks.

I laugh heartily. "No. I reached out to Simon personally. She lives across the bay."

"Cool. Her last movie was fantastic."

"Fangirling a little?"

"No, just stating a fact."

Colby greets Elsie with a hug. When she sees me, she adds, "I didn't mean to disturb you. I saw you on the dock yesterday and figured you were back for the ceremony."

"No problem. Elsie, please meet Julianne."

"Pleasure to meet you. Would you like a drink?"

Elsie is equally as beautiful in person as she is on screen, although her hair is a darker shade of blonde than her last film. "That would be lovely."

I walk into the kitchen and realize I don't know where anything is. Colby assists without making my lack of information obvious. I also note a timer on the oven. Marta must have cooked something for us.

Elsie takes a seat at the island. "Congrats on the win."

"Thank you."

"I see you aren't limping. Physical therapy going well?"

He answers, "Yes. Selecting Jack for my rehab was a smart decision. Plus, being away from the team has allowed me to focus more on myself and my rehab."

"I get it. No politics at home."

"Exactly. What about you? Where is your next exotic filming location?"

Despite my initial disdain for her since they went on a set up date, she seems lovely.

She laughs. "It isn't exotic at all. We're filming at a horse farm in Oklahoma in the fall. I have a decent break right now. I'm working on finding my next few projects and relaxing."

"Good for you."

Elsie swivels her attention to me. "What about you, Julianne? What do you do?"

It's nice of her to include me in their conversation. Perhaps she's like Colby and down to earth despite her profession. "I'm a high school principal."

"More power to you. I was tutored on set, but my brothers were terrors in school."

"I certainly have those moments with students here and there. Otherwise, it's fulfilling."

Her phone vibrates on the counter. "Shoot, my brothers are early. It was great catching up."

"You too," Colby replies, escorting her to the door.

"She seems nice, but she was surprised to find me here."

"Yeah, I gathered that too. Last I knew she was dating one of Madeleine's athlete clients."

"Hmm." I lift a shoulder.

As it drops, Marta rejoins us in the kitchen. "The dessert for tomorrow will be done in ten minutes."

"Thank you. I can take it out. I appreciate you coming over to make it for me."

"*De nada.* Have a wonderful time tomorrow and at the gala. You deserve it." Her words are for Colby, but she is looking directly at me. "I hope to see you more, Julianne. He's less grumpy than usual."

I stifle a laugh. "I hope so too. Have a great evening." Marta hugs us both and leaves. "I thought you were cooking?"

Colby steals my breath with one of his heart-stopping smiles. "It's for Hatton." As he shares, the timer expires. He pulls a decadent-looking dessert from the oven.

"What is that?"

"It's *Torta Negra Colombiana.* I brought one to spring training, and Hatton stole some. It's a rich chocolate cake filled with chocolate chunks and dried papaya."

"Sounds amazing."

"It is. Why don't you finish examining your library while I start dinner?"

"I want to do that, but I would rather help. If you won't let me, can I at least keep you company?" I plead.

He kisses me and guides me onto one of the stools at the island with his hands on my hips. "You can stay, but only watching."

"Deal." Watching him work in his kitchen is more than I bargained for. We never had the opportunity to live together. While arguably, we don't now, as adults I can see how we would work if we did. I'm shocked by his comfort level creating dinner from scratch.

"You make your own pasta?"

He winks at me. "Surprised?"

"A little."

Nearly an hour later, he sets our plates on the island and fills glasses with wine. Dinner is beyond delicious, and the conversation flows nicely. I've only been here for a little while, and I could see myself getting used to it and sharing my space with him.

CHAPTER NINETEEN

COLBY

The entire drive to the stadium, I've been swimming in my thoughts. Annie is taking in the scenery along the drive. I don't blame her. She's in a new place and always did soak up everything.

"Want to talk about how you're feeling right now?" she asks.

I lift our linked hands and kiss the back of hers. "I'm all over the map. I'm anxious and excited at the same time. It doesn't make sense."

"It does."

"How, gorgeous?" It isn't an endearment I use freely. I've always thought Annie was stunning. Today wearing cutoffs, a team shirt, and fashion sneakers is no exception.

"You're anxious because today and tomorrow are not how you envisioned them to be. You planned to be behind the plate and then rush to the gala to pick up your ring. Winning the game for your team made that impossible."

She's right.

Annie continues, "You're excited because you will be able to share a huge part of your life with me. It makes you happy and angry at the same time."

"At me," I admit.

"I know." She shifts in my direction as best she can in my McClaren. "Don't let any of that ruin the next few days. You should enjoy the events. You earned it."

"Thanks, sweetheart." I pull into the secure lot near the player's entrance. I round the car and open Annie's door. Then I hear my name.

"Somerset! Old man, you made it!"

We bro hug. "Hatton, be nice. I may have brought you a gift from Marta." I reach into the trunk and pull out the torte.

"Sweet." He extends his hand to accept the bag.

I shake my head and hand over the bag with the torte in it.

"Marta is the best. Are you going to share her contact information with me?"

"Never. Hatton, please meet Julianne."

"Pleasure. Are you keeping him on task with his rehab?"

Annie raises an eyebrow. "He's doing fine, why?"

"Good. I need my old-timer catcher back."

His words aren't a stab in the heart for both of us. For me, because I abandoned him. I'm sure it feels that way to Hatton. For Annie, because she is reminded I have a life here as well. Interestingly, she takes it in stride.

"He's doing the work. When he'll be back is not for me to decide."

Hatton won't hear it, but I did. I hear the underlying concern about our relationship being put to the test when I can play again. "I'm working hard, Cal. It's all I can do. Let's go inside and have some fun."

The team set up games and skill drills for the families. They have a ball toss, pitching from the mound, and a drill to attempt to throw out a stealing baserunner. There are bounce houses for the kids and other outdoor games. Later there will be a mascot race too.

"Ready to meet a whole bunch of stuffy people?" I whisper near the shell of Annie's ear.

"Behave."

"Yes, dear."

Annie laughs, I take her hand, and we enter the walkway.

"Want a tour first or second?"

"Whatever works. You do what you need to do. I'm in no rush."

Without a doubt, Annie is absorbing the sights, sounds, and people around us. Over the next few hours, I introduce Annie to a host of people. After grabbing bottled waters, we greet some of my teammates and the owner.

"Somerset, glad you could make it," Mr. Wilson states.

"Wouldn't miss it."

"How is the physical therapy going? The reports are shallow and unremarkable."

Fury builds in my chest. I've read Jack's reports. They are on point and perhaps a tad conservative. Before I answer, Annie squeezes my hand. "I'm making progress in line with my therapist's plan."

Thankfully, Madeleine emerges from the dugout with her husband and Simon beside her.

"You aren't grilling my client, are you, Mr. Wilson? This is a family event." Her voice is as sweet as pie but laced with enough sting for him to back off. Also, Christoph's presence makes most people pause despite Madeleine's reputation and prowess as an agent.

"Of course not, Ms. Wi... Mrs. Anderson."

"I thought so. Have a great afternoon. Colby, would you follow me?" Madeleine states.

"Absolutely." I gently lead Annie behind Madeleine down the right field line.

"Sorry about that," she states when we join her. Her gaze locks on Annie. "You must be Julianne. It's a pleasure to put a face to the name. Not only does Colby talk about you, but Jordan and Reese do as well."

Annie takes Madeleine's extended hand. "Pleasure to meet you."

Madeleine introduces her husband, Christoph, and her assistant, Simon.

"Mr. Somerset, you failed to mention she's stunning," Simon gushes, holding Annie's free hand.

A fierce blush creeps onto her face. "Stop."

Simon shakes his head. "I call them like I see them. You're beautiful."

Annie drops her head and thanks him.

"How is your rehab going?" Madeleine asks.

I frown and ask, "I thought Jack was copying you on the reports."

She tilts her head in question. "You mean the bland, boring statements merely illustrating you have been showing up for the last eleven weeks or so. Words exemplifying you are precisely on point with his projected plan of nine months."

I glance around us and step closer to her. "I'm progressing faster than the reports indicate. However, Jack didn't want to share with the team in case I have a setback."

"Understood. It's a solid plan. I'm going to be honest with you. The team is high on Easton Bolton."

"The front office and management may be, but the players aren't."

She raises an eyebrow. "Please share."

"Want to take this one, Annie?"

"Sure. Bolton is no match for Colby in fielding percentage and batting average at the same point in his career. Hell, not at this point in his career either. Bolton's passed balls are most in the league, allowing for runners to advance into scoring position. While I understand it's only been two series, the numbers don't lie. If you extrapolate the figures over an entire season, he's mediocre at best."

Madeleine is floored. "Where did you find her?"

"She was the only girl who could play baseball in Summit Creek. We were attached at the hip starting when we were six," I reply and press a kiss to Annie's temple.

"Her assessment is likely true, but it won't stop them from pushing you to the bench until it's clear they were wrong," Madeleine indicates.

"Right now, my only focus—careerwise—is healing from this injury and getting back behind the plate."

Annie deflates as the words leave my mouth. Inwardly, I shake my head. I shared my plan to finish this contract with her. She knows I won't handle being the bullpen catcher well at all. "Ready to test out your arm, Annie?"

"So ready!" she replies.

With a flourish, I lead Annie to the line for the throwing competition.

As we approach the plate, she stretches. "You good?" she whispers.

"Yeah."

"Want to try again?"

"I'll be fine. This is hard."

"We can go whenever you want," she offers.

"Maybe after I throw out this runner."

She steps to the front of the line and dons the catcher's gear.

"Hot, Annie. So... fu... freaking hot!"

"You sure about this, darlin'?" The third base coach asks her.

"Absolutely."

I understand where he's coming from. Annie certainly doesn't appear as if she has an arm. She looks like she stepped off the pages of a fashion magazine although she doesn't believe it to be true. She's about to prove Coach Jensen wrong.

Coach prepares the players. "Runner, ready?" The runner at first drops his head. "Pitcher?" He offers a curt nod. "Okay, darlin'. Let's see what you can do."

With a proud smile, I step back. Annie crouches in my spot behind the plate. The pitcher throws a fastball as the runner takes off. Without hesitation, Annie heaves the ball to the fielder.

"Out!" Coach Jensen shouts. "Have to say, I'm surprised."

Annie pumps her fist into the air before throwing her arms around me.

"That's my girl! Well done, Bluebird."

She lifts her shoulder. "Thanks. Let's go home."

"Sure you don't want a tour?"

"I'm game if you are, but I get the feeling you're ready to leave," she murmurs while I unclip the chest protector.

She sees me. Always has. "I am."

"Then let's leave." Nearly an hour later, we pulled out of the stadium lot toward the house. "Do you have a spot here?"

"You mean that isn't my house?"

"Yeah."

"No. I have a spot I share with an amazing girl. It's the only one I need."

"Colby."

"It's the truth, Annie. In fact, we should go there when we get back to Summit Creek. Did I miss something?"

"No. I haven't been there since you left."

I pull into my garage and kill the engine. "We will go back together."

"Okay." Normally, I would go for a run to get rid of my anger and anxiety. Can't do that yet. "I'm going to swim to tire myself out. Want to watch?"

Annie grins at me. "Sure."

Fifteen minutes later, I dive into my pool and swim laps. With each stroke, I attempt to push away some of the feelings roiling in my gut. Bolton is not better than me. Even if you compare us at the end of last season. He's a baby. Annie's analysis was correct. Perhaps I should skip the game tomorrow and only attend the gala.

Nope, can't do that. I accepted the invitation to the pre-game announcement. Donning my uniform and not being able to catch is going to be torture of the worst kind. I've lost count of how many laps I've completed. When I reach the far end of the pool, I see Annie's legs dangling in the water.

"What's wrong?"

She shakes her head. "Nothing exactly. My mom called. Dad is declining faster than he would like. He cancelled their visit on the weekend as well as any going forward." Anger, fear, and possibly preemptive grief flicker on her gorgeous face.

I consider what she's wearing before making my next move and decide I don't care, and she won't either. With my weight evenly distributed, I grip her hips and guide her into the water with me. After a sweet kiss, I grab the float and climb onto it, and she follows, curling up against me.

"We can fly to Philly instead of home. Better yet, we can leave as soon as Cash can get here."

Tucked against me, she feels as if she belongs there. She always has. Inhaling sharply, she replies, "I appreciate the offer, but no, you deserve to accept your ring with your team. Besides he said he was done with visits. My father doesn't want me to see him decline any further. I'll be lucky to get a phone call."

"I'm so sorry, Annie."

Muffled against my side, she replies, "Me too."

While this is an inopportune time, I catalog how she feels in my arms. I've done it before, but now—our second chance—I'm absorbing each little detail about grown-up Annie. For a woman who doesn't like working out, her legs are lean and toned, and she has a tiny waist and breasts, which are slightly large for her frame. Honestly, she's my walking wet dream.

"Are you feeling a little better?" Her words are quiet.

"About today and tomorrow… I guess. I knew it would be difficult to be here. I wasn't expecting it to feel like tomorrow is the last time I'll be with my team."

"Would you prefer to be rehabbing here instead?"

I hear the hurt in her voice and dispel the notion immediately. "No, absolutely not! I trust Jack. I was expecting to feel more welcome."

"I understand. Mr. Wilson wasn't very nice. It was amazing when Madeleine put him in his place."

"Yeah, it was. Want to rinse off and relax in your library?"

"Sounds perfect with one small addition."

I raise an eyebrow at her. "What are the chances you have the ingredients to bake cookies?"

"One hundred percent."

"Marta is amazing!"

I laugh heartily. "I requested them. Does that count for anything?"

"Absolutely. I pay in kisses. Does that work for you?"

"Hell yes!" Annie shifts over me and plants a hard kiss on my lips. Being with Annie may blow my mind. No, not may. It will blow my mind.

CHAPTER TWENTY

JULIANNE

Walking on eggshells is something I'm not used to doing. Not with Colby or anyone else. I tell it like I see it… always. For a guy who is about to receive the prize for winning the championship for his profession, he's surprisingly reserved.

"Want to talk?" I murmur against his bare chest after the alarm goes off for the second time.

"Nope, I'm good."

I kiss his flank and push up to look at his chiseled face. "Please elaborate."

A sly smile grows. "I have a fresher perspective this morning."

"Do tell."

"Would I have preferred a better welcome from Mr. Wilson? Yes. However, I won't allow it to impact the importance of today. I earned the right to be here, and I'm going to celebrate with my amazing woman beside me."

"Yours, huh?"

"I refuse to let you go again. Work for you?"

"Yes." My voice said "yes," but my heart tripped. Going down the "what if" trail isn't a good plan. We will figure out the future together. Whatever it looks like. I take a deep breath. "Where are we sitting today?"

"For the ceremony, I'll be on the field. You will be in the dugout with the wives, although there aren't many."

"Okay and for the actual game?"

"I reserved seats in the bleachers, but we were invited into the owner's box as well."

"Intriguing."

"Why?"

"Mr. Wilson was a jerk to you yesterday. Why would he invite you into his box?"

"To make it appear like everything is fine behind the scenes," he replies instantly. The edge in his voice is unmistakable. He's faking this bravado for today. Unfortunately, I have to let him do it.

"Any chance you have another gift for me?"

"Perhaps. You don't already have one?"

I purse my lips. "Not for this team." Without another word, he cages me beneath him and steals my breath with his mouth. I pull away and ask, "How long do we have until we need to leave?"

He twists his head to read the alarm clock again. "Slightly more than an hour, why?"

Not enough time for me to make him come with my mouth. Without considering any further, I slide my hands between us and slip them into his boxer briefs.

"Annie." My name sounds like a growl.

I ignore him and stroke his length a few times before he shimmies his clothes off. "Change your mind?"

"Making it easier. Why now?"

I take his length into my hand and stroke him again. "Considering how long it's been since we've... you know... we need to catch up to make you last longer when we are together again. Ideally, sooner rather than later."

"Smart. No pressure though." He turns so we're side by side.

"There's more than enough of that right now." I wink at him and increase my speed.

He drags his tongue down my chest, burying his face between my breasts. With a skill I've never experienced before, he tugs the strap of my tank down my arm with his teeth and pulls my puckered nipple into his mouth. His free hand coasts over my belly and into my sleep shorts. "You're soaked, Annie."

"Like I said... pressure."

"What were you thinking about?"

"Accepting we can't change the past and deciding what I want for my future."

"Which is?"

"You."

Without hesitation, he slides his fingers along my core, building the intensity more before plunging two fingers inside me. Each time he reaches deeper, I stroke downward. Soon the swirling pleasure erupts, and we orgasm at once.

Our gazes meet, and we burst into laughter. "Didn't think that one through, did we?"

He shakes his head. "Nope, but it was worth it. Use the sheet to clean up a bit, and we'll change the bed later."

Given our delayed departure, we scurry around and barely make it to the stadium on time for the ceremony. Colby is wearing shorts for now and me a pristine jersey with his name and number 8 emblazoned on the back.

He hurriedly changes in the locker room. He emerges as the staff whisks the wives and family members toward the dugout. "Annie."

I pause and wait for him to weave his way through the people.

"Thank you for being here with me despite everything."

I cup his face with my hand and kiss him softly. "No place I would rather be. I'm proud of you, Colby."

"Thank you. Me either." He leans closer to say something but stops himself. I have a hunch what it may have been, but instead he whispers, "You look sexy as sin in my jersey."

"When I can, I'll wear only this jersey for you."

"Annie." My name is a warning and a promise at the same time. "I'll meet you in the dugout after the ceremony."

I nod and hurry to catch up to the group. Pulling up to the back, I overhear, "I wonder which modelling agency she works for. Somerset never has a real date, always some starlet or model. He doesn't keep them for long."

The brunette adds, "Although this one is wearing his jersey, unlike the others."

I glance at the group and note there are only a few other people wearing jerseys, and they aren't adults. Now, I'm certain they're talking about me.

"She'll be gone by breakfast." The busty blonde with a silver lamé top and black shorts barely covering her ass cheeks states.

That was the final straw. "I suggest you keep your comments to yourself. You don't know what you're talking about. I'm not some model or starlet and will certainly be around well past morning. Why don't you worry about yourselves?"

The women look back and forth between me and one other before pushing toward the front of the line.

When we reach the dugout, a petite brunette moves beside me. "Ignore them. If anything, it'll be them who aren't around by morning. I would bank on it, since I've never seen them before. Where are my manners? I'm Lacey Pierce, Hatton's girlfriend."

"Pleasure to meet you. I'm—"

"Julianne. Cal told me all about you last night over the delicious torte Marta made for him. I swear, that woman spoils him for nothing."

I laugh. "Colby too. Thank you for the rescue."

"You're welcome, but you didn't need one." Lacey is cute.

"I appreciate it anyway."

She nods tightly and climbs the stairs into the dugout.

I've been in dugouts before but never a major league one, especially not for this type of occasion.

"Isn't this fantastic?"

My gaze is pinned to the field off to the right where Colby is standing with the pitching staff. I see the joy, but the undercurrent of disappointment is still hovering beneath his gorgeous, smiling façade. Maybe Hatton can, but I highly doubt anyone else does.

"Julianne?"

"Huh? Sorry. I was—"

"Ogling your man like I was mine. I have a terrible habit of talking without looking at people."

"What did you ask?"

"Isn't this fantastic?"

Surreal is a more apt description. Dreaming about this moment for him and being in it are two extremes on the spectrum. "Yes, it is."

The public address announcer calls for attention, and the national anthem is played. As the familiar bars float through the air, my eyes find Colby's. I'm unsure how much time passes, but he doesn't break our connection until his name is called.

"Catcher Colby Somerset, who made…."

His name echoes around me and Lacey latches onto my arm and jumps up and down. It drowns out the rest of the accolades being shared. Colby walks to the plate, waves to the crowd, proceeds down the line, and high-fives or bro hugs his teammates. When the announcer completes the players with a few on the jumbotron, Mr. Wilson steps onto the field.

"Congrats on an epic win. Let's play ball!" He steps onto the mound, takes five steps forward, and throws the ceremonial first pitch to Bolton. He drops it.

My head whips to Colby, who is now staring at the turf. *Damn!* I know what he's thinking. Bolton has no respect for the sanctity of the game. He wasn't paying attention.

As I consider my options to get to him, the players start to disperse, and Colby walks straight toward me. "Lacey, it's great to see you again. If you could excuse us," he states. Without waiting for a response, he threads his fingers in mine and hurries into the clubhouse.

Outside the locker room doors, he stops.

"Breathe," I demand.

Colby inhales sharply and exhales slowly.

"All you need to focus on is that Bolton isn't you. You can't worry about him. Knocking your therapy down is your sole job right now."

"Despite everything, you still get to the heart of me. Rehab is... you're right."

"Do you want to go home?" I offer.

He scrubs his hand down his face. "Yes, but I shouldn't. I promised Hatton I would watch and see what he can improve on."

"Okay. Go change. Then we can sit in the bleachers like we used to when we were kids."

Colby pulls me closer and kisses the curve of my neck. "You'll be okay here?"

"Yes. I'll be fine."

We make our way to the nosebleed seats loaded down with snacks by the bottom of the first. I appreciate him sticking to his word about staying to watch Hatton. The next few innings were atrocious. Hatton is getting shelled. I saw at least three mistakes by Bolton. I'm sure there are more. By the middle of the fifth inning, Hatton gave up six runs, and his offense didn't provide him any. The opposing team threatens to score but leaves two stranded.

"After this half, we're going to head out. We need to go back up to the box level and then down the private elevator," Colby states.

I acknowledge his words. The anguish on his face is hard to watch. Colby is a stand-up guy and met his obligation to Hatton. The team doesn't score, and the inning is over quickly. As we climb down the stairs, a young fan asks Colby for his autograph, and he obliges. The sheer joy on his face perks Colby up the slightest bit.

Getting the autograph of Buster Posey and Brian McCann was one of the highlights of his life. He intends to make sure his fans feel exactly the same way he did. I only know about him meeting them because I was stalking his social media behind the scenes. The glee on his face—I've never seen anything like it except… when he looks at me.

The walk back to the players' lot is faster than the one to our seats. It isn't until he starts the engine of his Audi that the tension in his shoulders decreases. As much as I would like to talk about it, he isn't ready. I cover his hand with mine, and we ride home in silence.

CHAPTER TWENTY-ONE

COLBY

My blood is boiling, and there isn't a damn thing I can do about it. Bolton can't discern a fastball from a slider. Nor does he know when to call for one or the other. Hatton does, and when he threw what he wanted to throw instead of what Bolton called for, he missed, and the runners advanced more than once. This is my replacement. A catcher the team thinks will unseat me.

No. Bolton is not going to ruin this evening for me. For the rest of the day, I'm going to focus on the reason I'm here—to attend the gala with Annie and celebrate my first World Series victory. Resolved, I lift her hand to my lips and kiss the back.

My car alerts me to a text from Hatton.

"Can you push the read button, please?" I ask her because I'm not letting go of her hand. The mere feel of her skin against mine is calming me more than she could fathom right now.

"Please tell me you left and didn't witness that in real time. Hopefully, I'll see you tonight. The upside is Bolton wasn't invited." My car reads his words to me.

Annie twists in the seat, and a tempting glimpse of cleavage peeks out between the buttons of my jersey. "Feel like talking yet?"

"Don't plan on discussing it."

"You don't?"

"Nope. I'm good. I refuse to allow him to taint tonight for us. Like Hatton mentioned, Bolton won't be there. If anyone asks my opinion about today's game, I'll share. Otherwise, I'm letting it go."

"Are you sure?"

"Yes. Watching the game was a mixed bag. It was horrid witnessing Hatton struggle because Bolton is an idiot. However, being at a game with you was like old times, and I'm going to focus on those feelings instead."

"It was awesome especially the sticky concrete and smell of stale beer."

I laugh and pull into my garage. "To think we could've had shrimp, fresh beer, and a host of non-baseball snacks."

"Wouldn't have it any other way."

"Me either. Let's get moving, sweetheart. The glam squad will be here in thirty minutes for your hair and makeup."

She tilts her head in question. "The what?"

I smirk at her. "Lucia's sister, Madeleine's junior assistant, is a makeup artist and hairstylist." She's about to rebuff me, but I stop her. "I promised I would take care of everything, and I did. I want tonight to be stress free for you."

"Okay."

I'm shocked by her acquiescence, but I'll take it as a good sign. We snack on a few healthy items until they arrive. Lucia and her sister, Gianna, whisk Annie into the master bathroom. I grab my toiletries and shower in the guest bathroom to give them space, then throw on some clothes to wait until the last possible minute to put on my tux. To pass the time while they finish up, I prepare a snack for us.

An hour later, they emerge from the bathroom with huge smiles on their faces.

"Have a wonderful time, Mr. Somerset," Lucia states as they leave.

"Thank you," I reply, although I'm not confident they hear my response.

I gently knock on the door of the bathroom, and I'm met with one of Annie's signature laughs.

"It's your house, Two." She looks gorgeous, and she's wearing my bathrobe. Not surprising at all.

"Still gonna knock until you're used to me walking in on you at any moment."

"Noted. Those two are a hoot. How long do we have? Should I eat something before we leave?"

"Funny you should mention food; I made us a platter."

"Have I mentioned how amazing you are lately?" Annie asks.

"Hmmm. No, but I'm willing to listen if you want to share."

"Ha. How much time until we need to leave?"

"A little less than an hour." I take her extended hand and haul her into my arms. "I'm glad you're here."

"Me too."

Fifteen minutes, a shared glass of wine Jake would appreciate, and a charcuterie plate demolished, we dress for the gala. Annie disappears in the closet, and I don my tuxedo in the bedroom. The only logical reason is her gown is hanging there. That's a bald-faced lie. She's tempting, and we will be late if I get my hands on her and break my self-inflicted drought.

As I finish my last check, I note Annie hasn't left the closet. "Annie, you, okay?" I step over the threshold and lose my ability to breathe. Annie is standing before the floor-to-ceiling mirror. True, I've seen her in this dress, but with the hair, makeup, and the tailored fit, she's... "You're stunning."

She turns to face me, and my heart nearly stops. "Thank you. You look dashing."

I step closer. "Sean Connery or Daniel Craig as James Bond?"

"Connery, hands down," Annie replies with a laugh.

"Ready to walk the teal carpet with me?"

"Honestly?"

"Of course."

"I'm a tad nervous about that part but otherwise good."

"Nothing to worry about. It's the team's press office, not the sports media. They may ask who you're wearing, but that's about it."

"I feel much better then. Let's go celebrate you."

I love you. The words get caught in my throat. I'm confident we're on the same page in that respect, but we have some obstacles ahead of us. I knew restarting a relationship with Annie wouldn't be a cakewalk. Not true, the fact I never stopped loving her made rekindling our relationship easier. However, scaring her with my feelings too soon isn't the best plan. I offer her my arm and lead her to the car. The gala is being held at a bayside venue. The views compensate for the smaller ballroom. I pull up in front of the building. The valet opens Annie's door.

I set my hand on her thigh. "Please wait."

A smile tips up at the corner of her lips. I round the hood, hand the valet my keys, and take Annie's hand. Once she's secure on her sparkly shoes, she curls her hand around my arm, and I cover her hand with mine.

"Two?"

I turn and look at her. I'm the luckiest man on the planet, knowing she's mine. Screwing it up isn't an option this time. "Yes, beautiful?"

"In case I don't have the chance later. I'm crazy proud of you."

"Thanks, Bluebird."

Walking the teal carpet—teal for the team colors—was painless, considering Hatton and his girlfriend, Lacey arrived right after us. Unfortunately, the team press asked about the game earlier today. Hatton pushed them off with ease and hurried into the venue.

"Well done, Hatton," I offer.

"Thanks."

Lacey and Annie are gushing over their gowns and shoes. Inwardly, I smile for going with both pairs of shoes. The evening speeds up once we take our seats. Thankfully, we are seated with Hatton and other members of the pitching staff. Dinner service starts nearly immediately. Lacey and

Annie are chatting, but her hand rests atop my leg. As the decadent meal of porterhouse steak and savory seafood comes to an end, my nerves tick up. I start bouncing my leg on the plush carpet.

Annie leans closer and whispers, "Still bounce your leg when you're anxious?" She pulls back enough to see me close my eyes briefly and nod curtly. "No reason to be nervous. Walk up there when they call your name with your head held high and accept your ring. None of these guys would be getting one if it weren't for you. You called an amazing game and tagged Hausmann at great risk to your own physical well-being."

I press a kiss high on her cheek. "There are not enough words to thank you appropriately for how well you see me." Not true. There are three tiny words, but here isn't the right time. Mr. Wilson steps on stage with the coaching staff. The good news for me is they plan to bestow the rings in the same order as we take the field.

"Without further delay, I'm honored to bestow these rings on the World Series Champions beginning with the starting pitcher, Cal Hatton. Cal ended the game with…"

His words fade into the background as Cal circles to my side of the table, and we bro hug. "Wouldn't have pitched as well without you."

While I consider my response, he releases my hand and trots up the stage stairs. Cal and I made a great team. Not sure if we're going to get back to it again though. While my head swims with possibilities, Annie, slipping her hand in mine, grabs my attention.

I gaze at her wide smile when my name is called.

"Colby Somerset, starting catcher and…"

I tug Annie to her feet and kiss her deeply without a care for the sheer number of people in the room or making the rest of the team wait. The hoots and hollers have me pulling away. It wasn't that long. Then again, I lose all rational thought when Annie is in my arms.

"Go, Two. I'll be here when you get back."

I resist the urge to ask "Promise?" I button my jacket and walk toward Mr. Wilson.

"About time, Somerset." His words are meant to anger me. His intention is to rehash my choice to rehab with Jack instead of here. I refuse to allow him the satisfaction.

"Sorry, sir. I'm soaking this in. The chance I earn another one isn't very high."

He hands me the large ring box, and we pose for a picture before he mutters under his breath, "It certainly won't be here."

I bristle at his words and grit out a smile. I consider letting his sentiments roll off my back but decide I can't. "Now isn't the time or place to discuss my status with the team. However, if you believe Bolton is a better catcher than me after the game this morning, choose him. Mark my words though, you will regret it."

My gaze meets Annie's across the room. She knows me inside and out. Without a doubt, she sees the seething anger boiling beneath my custom tuxedo. It was inevitable for someone to replace me in the lineup. The problem I have with Bolton is… he isn't ready to be an everyday catcher in the major leagues. From a catching and experience standpoint, he needs more time behind the plate in the minors. His performance this morning highlights my observations from the stands today.

Mr. Wilson adds nothing further. I walk along the row and shake hands with the coaching staff and take my spot beside Hatton.

"Whatever he said, forget it for now," he suggests.

"Difficult to do when he hinted about letting me go."

"That sucks for both of us."

"Sorry, kid."

Hatton grumbles, "Me too."

"Probably best not to share publicly," I suggest.

"I won't."

I believe him. Then I look up and see Annie isn't at our table anymore. I scan the room and find her and Lacey off to our left, waiting for the presentation to end. When I refocus on the ceremony, the owner has started awarding rings to the bench and bullpen players.

My anger reduces to a simmer by the time the ceremony ends. Annie slides her hand into mine and leads me out the door into the courtyard overlooking the bay.

"What did he say to you?" Annie asks after wrapping her arms around me beneath the pergola with string lights.

She belongs here. With me. With me and my baseball family. With me at home and in Summit Creek. "It isn't important. Take a look at this." I attempt to deflect and open the ring box.

"No. Please share," she demands.

Begrudgingly, I divulge what he said.

"No, he can't do that! Can he? It doesn't matter. You won the title for him. I'm going to give him a piece of my—" She takes a step toward the ballroom.

I snatch her around the waist to stop her. "There's my feisty defender. As much as I would like to see you knock him down a few pegs, here isn't the time or place. Frankly, he shouldn't have mentioned it tonight."

"Exactly why he deserves—"

"It's fine, sweetheart. I'm fine. Did it sting? Yes. Did I know it was a possibility from the moment the orthopedic surgeon confirmed I needed reconstructive surgery? Of course I did."

"You didn't think they would do it though."

"No, I didn't. Now, Wilson has made his intention clear. Let's forget about him for a bit, and I'll reach out to Madeleine next week."

"I'm sorry he ruined your night."

"Not even a little. Would I have preferred to skip my conversation with him? Yes. However, tonight has been everything I dreamed because you're beside me as you should be." I don't add as she should've been my entire career, but bringing up my bonehead choice is something we agreed not to do again.

"Can I see it now?" Glee plasters on Annie's face.

I play coy briefly. "What?"

"Colby Carlton Somerset."

Not only is my birthday on opening day, but I also carry the name of one of the best catchers to ever play the game, Carlton Fisk. "Pulling out the full name, that's hot!"

Annie smirks and rolls her eyes at me.

I pluck the ring from the box and hand it to her.

"It's heavy!"

I chuckle and see in the admiration on her face. "I always wished you could've continued playing with us in high school."

"Me too." She takes my right hand in hers and pushes my ring on. "Perfect fit!"

"Fancy dessert and dancing?" I suggest.

"Only slow dancing."

"Still dance like the character from *The Wedding Planner*?"

Her smile widens despite the fact I'm picking on her. "Yes."

"It will pain me to hold you for the rest of the evening." I pull her closer and kiss her to the brink of inappropriate. Leading Annie inside, we stop at our table, and I set down the box and escort her to the dance floor. Whoever oversaw hiring the DJ for this event deserves a raise. He's mixing old standards like Frank Sinatra and Etta James with current ballads featuring Morgan Wallen and Taylor Swift seamlessly. Plus, it appears his instructions were to keep the rowdy club music to a minimum. Works for me. The less dance music, the longer I can have Annie flush against me in my arms. I don't need to study her here any longer. I want to work on a tactile map of her curves naked in my bed.

The notion of being with Annie again excites me and terrifies me at the same time.

"What are you thinking about?" she murmurs near my ear. The warmth of her breath sends pulses of desire down my spine.

"Later."

"Do tell?"

I shake my head. "I don't want to put too much pressure on us. Whatever happens or doesn't happen is fine."

Her head shaking is not the response I was expecting. "Nope."

I raise an eyebrow in question.

"We're going to tangle up your sheets until the wee hours of tomorrow. You're going to cook me breakfast, and then we're going to christen as many places in your house as possible. Work for you?"

I gulp hard, and I'm saved from responding when a fast-paced song flows from the speakers. We walk toward the table and indulge in the chocolate crème brûlèe at our seats. Rather than returning to the dance floor, we say our goodbyes. I purposely avoid speaking with Mr. Wilson again. Nothing good will come of it.

CHAPTER TWENTY-TWO

JULIANNE

I settle into the passenger seat and purposely allow the slit of my dress to leave my thigh exposed. I drag my hand along his thigh as he drives toward the house. However, he doesn't do the same. The closer we get to the house, the more nervous he becomes. He's gripping the steering wheel tighter to the point his knuckles are white. Colby's left leg is bouncing on the floorboard.

"What are you worried about? It's me."

"That is the scariest part. What if we mess this up?" He motions between the two of us.

"We can't. We've been through enough together and separately to weather anything. As I said when you shared your impressive drought, we figured it out the last time. We'll figure it out this time. Our chemistry leading up to now has been pretty amazing, right?"

"True."

"We're going to be fine." Not only am I excited, but scared at the same time.

He pulls into the garage and kills the engine. I thread our fingers together and lead him straight to the bedroom.

"Annie."

"It's going to be fine." After my words of reassurance, I invade his personal space, dip my hand beneath the shoulders of his jacket, and push it off. After laying it on the dressing bench, I lift his wrists one by one to remove his cufflinks. I set them beside the jacket. When I reach up to work the buttons, his hands cover mine.

Colby kisses each fingertip before dropping his lips to mine. Each skilled, eager touch makes me yearn to rush. Despite my desires to feel him deep inside me, I slow myself. Our pace picks up as far as disrobing. My dress falls to the floor in a silky heap at my feet. Taking my hand, he leads me around the bed with both of us only clad in our underwear.

I press an open-mouthed kiss to his chest near his heart and travel in a zigzag pattern over his washboard abs and down to the waistband of his boxer briefs. Slipping my hands beneath the elastic, I then push them to the floor. His erection springs forward and renews my desire to hurry. Lowering to my knees in front of him, I look up and see questions in his eyes.

"What are you doing?"

I wink. "Do we need to have a sex ed lesson?"

He laughs. "I thought…."

"Say it," I demand.

"I thought we were making love tonight for the first time in what feels like a lifetime."

"We are absolutely going to break your droughts. First, I'm going to make you come with my mouth."

"Why?"

"To help you last longer later when we're together later," I reply. "It's one of the reasons you're nervous, right?"

"You're a genius."

"Perhaps." Honestly, I'm nervous about being with Colby, and this will take the edge off for him even though my skills with this are limited. The way he touches me makes me believe once we come together again, I'll be ruined for any other man. It's a terrifying and wonderful place to be at once. "May I continue?"

He pauses a little too long for my liking. Then I recall, oral was his only choice. One I never saw coming but appreciate, despite my guilt for not choosing the same.

"Two." Using the endearment startles him in a good way. Reminds him it's me on my knees for him, not some random woman.

He nods tightly.

I may have read his mind. Without giving him another moment to get lost in his thoughts, I drag my tongue from the base of his penis to the top and swirl around the head. I lick the precum from the tip and guide him to the back of my throat.

The muscles of his abs and powerful legs constrict as he shudders from my mouth surrounding him. "Is everything better with you?" he mutters under his breath.

I smile. Colby reaches down and gathers my hair. His eyes are wild as we find our rhythm. As I stroke him with my hand and circle him with my tongue, I take him deeper than I thought possible. I hollow out my cheeks and suck hard.

"Fuck, Annie!"

Before I can respond, his hold on my hair tightens, his thighs flex, and he explodes down my throat. I swallow like I never have before. I haven't.

Panting, he pulls out of my mouth and hauls me to standing. Colby drags the pad of his thumb over my swollen lips before kissing me deeply. I anticipated Colby wanting time to recover, but I'm delighted to be wrong. Instead, he plans to rock my world.

I turn in a circle while he kisses along my jaw and down the curve of my neck. Colby wraps his arm around my waist and lowers me on the center of his massive bed. Being caged beneath his hard, muscled body is glorious. I can't believe we're here. I never thought we would have an actual chance again.

"Annie, look at me," he demands.

I open my eyes and find his gaze directly on me. Reading Colby has been a skill I have been particularly adept at since we were much younger. Despite the gap in time, it appears I still can. I see fear, anguish, and love mirrored back at me. His emotions and mine are exactly the same in this moment.

"Where did your mind go?"

"We're figuring this out differently than I thought. It's no problem."

He winks, kisses my forehead, and answers, "Good. I'm going to savor each inch of your body with my mouth and hands before I…."

Concern ripples through me. "What's wrong?"

"Nothing. We probably should've talked about birth control or at least purchased condoms."

I wrinkle my nose. "I have an IUD and was tested after I broke up with Patrick. The only thing getting me off since then is my vibrator."

He stifles a laugh. "I've never been with anyone bare, Annie, not even you."

"I'll happily accept that first too."

Without another word, Colby continues making good on his promise to savor me. Prickles of awareness course through me as he descends the valley between my breasts. With his left knee as an anchor, he circles my taut nipple with his tongue while kneading my other breast with his hand. The lower Colby travels, the more heat builds between my thighs. His mouth is dangerous to my well-being.

He drags his tongue from the curve of my hip bone down along my core without touching me. Shivers skitter over every inch of me.

"You like that, gorgeous?"

"Yes. Didn't know until you."

"I love hearing that. Let's see what other spots I can find to make you squirm."

I wrinkle my nose.

"You don't want me to find more spots on your gorgeous body, Annie?"

I shouldn't be surprised at him calling me out instantly. "I do."

"But?"

"I need to feel you move inside me more."

He blows out a jagged breath.

"Colby, it's me. If two naïve teenagers can figure it out, we can handle it as adults." To stop him from overthinking, I pull him against me and roll us. I shift and straddle him, my heated core hovering over him. His hardened length reaches toward me as his hands instinctively grip the flare of my hips.

Encircling his shaft, I stroke him twice and take him into my center with excruciatingly slow precision. The pressure and fullness of Colby buried to the hilt is miles better than I recall.

"Holy fuck, Annie! We feel incredible."

I smile down at him. "Wait. It will be unimaginable when I move."

"Do it, Bluebird."

After grinding my hips against his a few times to adjust, I lift and then lower down over him. Within a few moments, the friction between us grows, and an overwhelming sense of pleasure coils in my belly.

Colby pushes up to his elbows and bites lightly on my puckered nipple.

A moan falls from my lips, and he grins against me. In a brazen move, even considering I took control of our evening, I pitch forward and change the angle of my hips. Instantly, the pressure building at the base of my spine erupts. My inner walls tighten and pulse around him.

"Did we feel like this before?"

I shake my head and ride out the wave of my orgasm. "Not even close." Picking up my rhythm where I left off, Colby meets me thrust for thrust. Although his pace has increased to demanding and feverish.

"Don't stop!" I scream. A second wave of pleasure pushes me to delirium. Only he has ever made me feel this much.

His body is tight like the strings of a violin, and he shudders and bursts forward. The tips of his fingers dig into my skin. The moment he explodes inside me sends me careening over the edge of bliss. Collapsing on his chest, I'm sated and overjoyed. The sheer notion we found one another again and we're better than before inside and outside the bedroom is blissful. We may get our happily ever after... finally.

As we catch our breath, I memorize how we feel. It doesn't take much to know I'm radiating with ecstasy and can't wait to chase it again.

"Annie?"

"Hmmm."

"How much time do you need?"

I lift and see a devilish twinkle in his eye. "For?"

"Until we can make love again."

A laugh bubbles from deep in my soul. "We have all night, but—"

He frowns, and I giggle. "But?"

"I need some food first." I attempt to move, but Colby tightens his arms around me.

"Can I have a few more minutes to grasp the all-consuming emotions you just stirred up?"

All I can do is nod. I'm not able to come up with appropriate words. Not only have I accepted I'm still in love with Colby, but the pleasure he pulls from my body despite his inexperience is breathtaking.

Soon thereafter, we move into the bathroom and clean up a bit. I tug on his still buttoned dress shirt from the gala and nothing else. While I grab water from his drink refrigerator, Colby warms some food. A few bites into the leftovers, Colby is working the buttons of his shirt open. Within a minute, I'm laid out on his granite island like a feast.

CHAPTER TWENTY-THREE

COLBY

"Nice to see you, stranger," Jack chides. "You moving out of my guest room?" Honestly, I haven't been sleeping at their house since we returned nearly three weeks ago. Nor have I talked to Jack or Lorelei about our trip. Perhaps Annie did.

Aside from the drama of the game and ceremony, spending time with Annie in Florida was nothing short of perfect. It only felt like home because she was with me. It's exactly what I want for the rest of my life. Well, plus a mini-her and a mini-me or two. Waking up with Annie this morning in her bed was amazing despite her rushing around because I kept her there longer than I should have. I'm on my way to the office for my session with Jack. I sign in and make my way to his training room.

I shrug and get started on my exercises for the day. Truthfully, I feel amazing, but the regimen needs to be followed to the letter. I would appreciate being able to say I did my part before Wilson sends me packing.

"What went wrong with Jules on your trip?"

I frown. "Nothing. It was amazing. Wilson said some crappy things at the gala, and I'm worried about my job. Hence why I'm here and abiding by your rules."

"I won't speed up your treatment, Colby."

"Not asking you to. I'm frustrated with Bolton and how the gala went down. I need to be sure I can play without a setback. No shortcuts."

"Glad we agree. Finish your warmup, and we'll start today's work, which includes some baseball stuff."

"Funny, Jack. Very funny."

"Not kidding."

Glee washes over me. "On it." Once I finish warming up, I learn baseball stuff is running and controlled hopping. Better than nothing, I suppose. Arguably, all the squats he has me doing are the same as behind the plate.

After I clean up in the locker room, I head toward the school. Today we're going to play a simulated game at practice. I'm grateful Annie allows me to hang around the team. I love sharing my knowledge of the game with her players. I sling my bag over my shoulder and approach the main office where Reina is poised at her desk.

"Good afternoon, Coach. Miss Silva is in a meeting. She indicated you could wait here or the baseball office. Your choice."

"Afternoon, Reina. I'll stay here. Thank you." I take a seat on the sofa in her office and wait. Right before the end of the school day, she rushes into the room.

"Hi, sweetheart. Rough day?"

Instead of answering me, she leans forward and kisses me.

"What happened to no kissing at school?"

She pouts. "I said not in front of the players. My office is fair game."

I give her an unmistakable look.

"No, we aren't having sex in my office. Get that thought out of your head."

Now, I pout. "At least I know you were thinking it as well. What was your meeting about if you can share?"

"Broad strokes, it was about the fight before break and the increased upheaval I caused by doling out varied punishments. That was after a teleconference with the head of the board inquiring about my relationship with you. Apparently, our photo was on some sports website, and one of the trustees saw it."

"I'm sure you were on point. We were on vacation. Is it going to be a problem?"

"No."

"Good. It shouldn't be. Have you eaten?"

"Yes. As soon as the bell—" She drops her head at the chiming. "I need to change, and we can head to the field." She grabs her bag and steps into her private bath. I rise and follow her.

"You can watch, but no touching."

"Why not?"

"If you touch me, we will absolutely be late and provide a poor example for our athletes."

"Huh. Why is that?"

"Your hands on me, hell any part of you caressing me, sets my skin on fire, and I'm instantly turned on. Sometimes you don't even have to touch me," she replies, tossing her blouse on the sink. Wiggling out of her skirt, she tugs on shorts, a jersey, and a ball cap.

When we reach the field, the team is stretching under the guidance of Simonson and Fisher. Taking the lead is a great step toward solidifying a team dynamic.

"Well done, gentlemen. Let's get started. We are nearly halfway through the season and are tied for first in our division. Tomorrow's game will break the deadlock." Annie calls them in and puts them in our discussed starting lineup. "Tyler, take the mound. Warmup pitches only. We want you to be fresh tomorrow."

"Got it, Coach. Who is hitting?" Tyler asks.

"Me for a little bit and then your teammates will each take an at bat. By then though, I'll be pitching."

He nods and trots to the mound. It only takes a few swings before we're in the groove, and the practice passes quickly. After the boys leave, I gather my things and follow Annie home. Over dinner, we discuss potential changes.

"What is your opinion of swapping the center fielder and the left fielder?" she asks.

"The eight spot—the centerfielder—has great speed and a serviceable throw. The seven position has a stronger arm, but he's slow."

"Agreed. Just wondering if he can cover more ground from the left."

"You can always switch it if one of them gets beat," I offer.

"Good point."

After dinner, we sit on her patio before the bugs and a thunderstorm force us inside.

I sit against the arm of her couch with my leg outstretched against the back. Annie gingerly curls up against me. Is this what the last decade could have looked like at least during home games? I was an idiot to let her go. Being apart may have been tough, but if we still got to this point, it would've been worth it.

"What else can I do to assure victory tomorrow?" she wonders aloud.

"You can't do anything else, gorgeous. You're phenomenal with the team. After the rocky start, they respect you and listen to you. Plus, it shows on the field. Tomorrow is one away game in the middle of the season. We will play them again at the end at home."

"Thank you," she murmurs against my neck.

"You're welcome."

She continues kissing along my jaw toward my lips.

"Annie, if you don't stop, we're going to need to lock up and hurry upstairs," I warn.

With a sweet giggle, she tugs my lower lip between her teeth and bites down lightly. Without another thought, I bracket her waist with my hands and set her on the floor. She takes off toward the backdoor while I secure the front door and set her alarm.

I climb the stairs after her and collect her discarded articles of clothing along the way. "I've never seen this bra before." I reach the top of the staircase and lift a matching pair of lace panties from the newel. "Are you naked?"

"Yes. Catch up, Two."

I laugh heartily. Crossing the threshold, I find my dream woman waiting for me in bed. Without hesitation, I strip off my clothes and join her until morning.

We rush out of the house. Her to school and me to therapy. She's oddly calm when I reach her office for the game.

"Hi, sweetheart. You look happy and calm."

She smiles widely. "I'm excited about today."

I step into her space and greet her with a kiss. "As you should be." We make our way to the field and find the team ready to go. After three innings, the good vibes dissipate. Simonson is getting shelled. He's allowed up to eight hits and two runs. That isn't an issue. His offense has given him two in response.

"You going, or am I?"

"You go," Annie urges.

I walk out of the dugout. "Time." When I reach him, he extends the ball to me. "Not here to pull you from the game. Only Coach Silva can do that. Where is your head?"

"The pressure is a lot, and I'm buckling. Maybe you should take this ball from me."

"Pressure is a good thing. It will show you and your teammates what you're made of. Don't quit because you had a few rocky innings."

"I'm letting them down," he mumbles.

"Coach, wrap it up," the umpire warns me.

"No, you aren't." I grip his shoulders and turn him toward his teammates. They smack their gloves in a motion saying, "let's go."

"You have seven teammates behind you. Slow down your delivery a little and trust them to back you up. Baseball is a team sport."

"Thanks, Coach."

"You've got this, Tyler." We fist bump, and I walk back to my seat beside Annie.

She leans forward as he delivers his next pitch. It goes wide right. "Damn!"

"Don't worry, Annie. He's got this."

Tyler circles the mound, gazes at the stands, and pumps himself up. He throws his next pitch and never looks back. By the middle of the sixth, we lead by three runs. One half inning to go and we pull out the win. Then Telford takes a foul ball off his forearm.

"Time," the umpire shouts, and we rush to the plate.

"Coach, it hurts. I don't want to come out, but Carson might be better to handle the rest of the game."

I turn to the dugout and point to our backup catcher. He starts putting on his gear. We guide Telford to the bench and ice his arm.

While Annie tends to him, I chat with Carson. "Stick to what Tyler calls. He's been on point since we chatted."

"Got it."

I tap the top of his helmet, and he replaces Telford behind the plate. The remainder of the game passes uneventfully as far as gameplay. The team is now atop the division. However, later in the evening, we learn Telford's arm is broken, and he will miss the remainder of the season. I empathize with him. While our injuries are different, the inability to help your team succeed is difficult to accept.

CHAPTER TWENTY-FOUR

JULIANNE

I have been staring at the ceiling for more than the last hour. I shift to get a better look at Colby and find him staring at me.

"Morning, Annie."

"Morning."

"Why are you grumpy already? I mean, we woke up together on this dreary Saturday morning. It can't be that bad."

I purse my lips and frown. "My parents were supposed to visit this weekend."

He sits up and hauls me against his bare chest. "Want to call and see if he's willing for us to go there?"

"You would do that?"

"I'll do anything for you. If I need to stay in the car because your father is still upset about us, I will."

"No. I appreciate that, but no. I want you beside me if you don't mind."

He cages me beneath his rock-hard body. *How in the world did I get so lucky?* "I meant 'anything' Annie."

I lean up and kiss him deeply despite not having brushed my teeth yet. "You need to let me find out if they are open to company."

He winks at me. "Do I?"

"Funny, very funny. I'll bring up some coffee."

"Wow, coffee in bed. Can we make it our Saturday morning thing?"

"Sure, until it doesn't work with the schedule. Same goes for the crossword."

He tilts his head in question before asking, "When might that be?"

I shrug and walk out of the room without answering. I can think of a myriad of reasons: he isn't here because he's playing again, or we have a few kids who dislike sleep to name a few. Pushing away the worry, I start coffee. Yet my brain is still working on the reasons we won't be able to do this every weekend.

I'm ready to jump into the deep end, the forever with a ring with Colby. There are so many unknowns though. Will he be able to play this season? I can't leave here. I shake my head and dial.

"Morning," I say when my mom answers.

"Hi, Julianne. How are you?"

"I'm well. I know Dad wanted to stop his visits, but can we come there today even if it's short?"

"Your father is still sleeping and was quite clear he isn't interested in seeing Colby again."

"Mom, he's being unreasonable. This isn't about Colby at all. I'm not going to break up with him until... Dad's gone. Why? So, Dad can be happy with my romantic decisions. Frankly, I don't care if he doesn't want to see me. I want to see him."

I imagine my mother tsking. "My darling daughter, I saw the connection between the two of you at the hospital. Colby isn't going anywhere."

I heard the words she didn't say. *This time.* Perhaps I imagined them because of my father's opinion. "You didn't answer my question."

"Your father doesn't want you to see him in a deteriorated state. Please don't make the drive here. I will have him call you in the early afternoon."

"Not the response I needed to hear, Mom." Sadness filters through me. Doesn't she get it? Why is she siding with him?

"I understand. Nor do I agree with it. I'm in the middle of the two people I love most in the world. However, his wishes are what they are. He'll speak with you later."

"Mom…"

I feel him before he touches me. Colby slides his arms around me from behind and presses his lips to the back of my neck. I forgot how well he knew my body.

My mother continues, "I heard your objections and agree. However, I have to heed his requests at this time. He will call you."

"Fine." I press the button hard, knowing it isn't like slamming a receiver down on an old-school phone. Nor is it as effective in dispersing anger.

Colby turns me in his arms. "What can I do?"

I tighten my hold on him and will the tears forming not to fall. I fail in an epic fashion. Sobs wrack my body and soak Colby's shirt. Slowly, he walks me into the living room and settles me in his lap on the couch.

"What the hell am I supposed to do with his decision?"

"I—"

"My father decides, and I have to deal with it. What am I supposed to do? Start grieving now? Wait around until he chooses to call me?"

"Ann—"

"Half of me wants to say 'screw him,' get dressed, and drive there anyway. The other half is considering 'fine, have it your way' and give my father what he wants—to die his way."

"Ann—"

"I—"

"Nope. Julianne, please let me say something." He sets his index finger on my lips and tilts my gaze up to his.

I can only imagine how terrible I look with red splotchy cheeks, snot dripping from my nose, and puffy eyes. "Go ahead."

"One of the lesson I learned after walking away from us when we were young is owning my choices. Same thing when I saw you seemed happy with Brandon and Patrick."

"What does this have to do with my father choosing to die alone?" He isn't alone exactly, but I'm not invited.

"I'm getting there, sweetheart. Your father is trying to protect you. It's misguided, but it is how he sees the situation. Same way I did initially. The kicker is… only you will bear the consequences of his decision."

"That sucks! Why should my last in-person memory be of him questioning my life choices? Why don't I get to choose?"

"As cliché as it sounds, that's not how life works."

"Your words ring true, but I don't like hearing it," I mumble.

"In this instance, I don't relish being right. What do you say to a homemade brunch?"

"As long as you're willing to let me help and teach me Marta's recipes," I counter.

"Deal. I need coffee though."

We pad to the kitchen hand in hand and brew our first cups of the day.

"What is on the brunch menu?" I ask.

"Depends on what we have in the fridge?" He turns and surveys the ingredients we have on hand.

We. I want it to stay that way, but I know deep down it isn't possible. Is it?

"Bluebird, where did you go?" He's standing close enough to kiss me, but he isn't touching me. "Please share what is worrying you aside from your dad."

"You said 'we,' and I want a 'we,' but is it realistic?"

He sets the blueberries on the island before cupping my face and pressing a light kiss to my lips. "Yes. Will it be easy? No. Is it possible we'll be apart for long stretches of time? Yes. Will it be worth it? Unquestionably. I love you, Annie. I have loved you since I was six years old before I knew what loving a woman truly means. If you'll let me, I plan to love you for the rest of my life."

"I love you." I inhale sharply before asking the question that feels like acid in my throat. "Will it be enough this time?"

"Yes."

"How are you so sure?"

He kisses my forehead and adds a sliver of space between us. "I walked away from the love of my life when I was a teenager. It took two years for me to work up the courage to admit my poor decision. Three years later, my efforts were thwarted by an ugly ring on your finger." I laugh at his description. "Now is our second chance. It's time for us to launch our moonshot over the short porch in left field. I refuse to lose you again." Without giving me a chance to respond, he kisses me deeply. We hurry upstairs, dropping our clothes along the way despite the fact we should eat.

After we tangle up our sheets, we return to the kitchen for a late brunch. I suppose it could be termed lunch at this point. Either way we prepare brunch foods including Shakshuka, which is a spicy egg dish with peppers and Indian flavors. To balance out the spice, Colby prepares berries with limoncello and basil. Boozy berries before talking with my father. Yes, please. Lastly, I make the single dish Jill and Jordan taught me. Tomato and cheddar tartlets are deceptively easy to make and tasty. Once our creations are done, we sit side by side at the island and eat.

My phone rings as soon as we finish our meal. Despite wanting to ignore it out of spite, I take my father's call.

"Hi, Julianne."

"Dad." There's an edge to my voice I fail to hide. Not sure I care, frankly.

"I can hear the anger in your tone." He calls me out.

"Good. You don't agree with my choices, and I don't with yours. We're even." Am I acting like a pouty child? Perhaps, but I don't care. Him thwarting my attempts to spend more time with him while he's dying is unfair.

"I'm trying to save you some heartache," he responds, then coughs deeply.

"With all due respect, it isn't your place to decide what I can and can't handle. Our decisions are in direct conflict with one another. I will heed your request. I don't like it, but I'll do it."

"Thank you. How is coaching baseball?"

I don't recall sharing that with them, but.... "It's going well. After some initial bristling, the boys are fine with a female coach. They lead the division right now with two weeks left in the season."

"Good for you. Thank you for taking my call despite your feelings about visiting. I need to rest now. Bye, Julianne."

"Bye," I respond to dead air. My father's choice to prohibit my visits makes me feel hollow… as if he's already gone in a way.

Colby curls his arm around my waist and tugs me closer. "Want to talk or stew?"

"Stew."

"Okay if I stay with you?"

"I would like that."

He kisses the top of my head. "Me too."

For the next hour, we sit in silence like we did when we were young. I vividly recall after I was told I couldn't play baseball in high school, I locked myself in my room for an entire weekend. I refused to let anyone into my space. I ignored my mother's pleas for me to eat. The only person I allowed in was Colby. Unbeknownst to my parents, he climbed the trellis and slipped into my room.

In the present, it's nice to know he's here for me again and plans to stay. I'm skeptical about how it will work out, but I'm with him—all in.

CHAPTER TWENTY-FIVE

COLBY

We spent yesterday like I hope we spend the rest of our Sundays going forward. We opted to do the crossword together on her patio with breakfast and coffee. The puzzle this week only took forty minutes, and we didn't use the dictionary to complete it. Annie hurried out of here early this morning for a meeting with her new athletic director.

I park in front of Jack's office and wander inside. It only took five months, but his staff ignores me now.

"Morning, Jack. What's on your exercise list for this session?"

Jack turns and points to the table. "None today. We need to do an assessment for the team."

I tilt my head. "Why didn't you tell me sooner?"

"I didn't want you to worry or focus on it."

"You're worried though?"

"Yes and no. You will pass, and I must report it to the team."

"Isn't progress a good thing?"

"Yes, but—"

"You're concerned they will try to pull something again?"

He drops his head. "The thought crossed my mind."

"Jack, let's get the test done. You share the results. I won't go back until you clear me. You're worried our personal relationship will affect your analysis of the results."

He shrugs.

Then it dawns on me. I'm roughly at the point where the team said I would be able to play again. "I chose your timeline. Don't worry about theirs. To be honest, I feel great. I'm fine with the progress of my rehabilitation. However, I'm not in shape to catch Hatton's fastball yet. To even have a chance is a credit to you."

He extends his hand to me, and we bro hug. Then he completes the assessment. Thirty minutes later after repeated measurements and notes, he looks up at me.

"Well?"

"Your range of motion puts you ahead of the curve by about ten percent."

"Okay. Report the truth, and then we go forward from there. What does that mean for my therapy?"

He shakes his head.

"What aren't you telling me?" A sliver of trepidation settles in my chest.

"Nothing. Concerned is all."

"I chose you to torture me, Jack. It isn't going to change midway because the team learns you're a stellar physical therapist and I was right to choose you."

"Thanks. It means you can start running... slowly. Then we will ice your knee and add in agility movements."

"Nice." True to his word, Jack instructs me to stretch and follows me to one of the treadmills. It's unlike one I've ever seen before. He catches my reaction.

"This treadmill is anti-gravity. It will carry some of your body weight, at least initially."

"Cool."

"It will be goofy at the beginning, but it will decrease the stress on your joints and tissues."

"Let's do this," I add. After some basic instruction and limits on how long I can run, I start running. It feels amazing, but I heed Jack's words to keep perspective.

I clean up, grab lunch for me and Annie, and drive to school. We have three more games in the season and then the playoffs. When I arrive, Reina informs me Annie is in a meeting with a reporter who arrived without an appointment.

I nod and take a seat in the conference room. At the conclusion, she joins me.

She kisses me lightly without checking our surroundings, and I'm ecstatic. "Hi, sorry about that. The paper wanted a quote for today's game."

"No problem, Coach. I'm proud of you."

"Thanks."

She takes a seat, and we eat in comfortable silence. Being proud of her progress with the team is one thing. The pride I feel for my own team is more difficult to quantify. They are three months into the season, and their record is abysmal. Through sixty games, they have twenty-one wins and thirty-nine losses. Yes, they have a losing record with fifteen more games until the all-star break. The World Series Champions are in the cellar of the division and likely have no chance of making the playoffs this year.

I would like to say expediting my rehabilitation would help, but with the roster changes the team ownership made, I'm not confident it would matter in the slightest. As if their record wasn't bad enough, there are only two ways the front office could handle it: spend an exorbitant amount of money at the trade deadline, which is at the end of July, or purge the remaining high value contracts the team is carrying. Considering my status in baseball purgatory, I fit into the latter category. Based on this new information, choosing Jack may not... no, I'm not ready to be behind the plate now. I highly doubt I would be with their physician either.

Swimming in my thoughts, it takes Annie setting her delicate hand on my forearm to get my attention. "Are you okay?"

"Yeah. Lost in my head for a bit."

"Feel like sharing? I'm an excellent listener as well." She winks at me.

"I passed my assessment this morning with flying colors," I offer.

She purses her lips briefly. Then plants a kiss on my cheek. "Why didn't you tell me you were having one today?"

I shake my head. "I didn't know, which Jack did on purpose."

"Probably. Why are you worried?"

"I don't trust ownership. More accurately, I don't trust Sanford Wilson."

She pauses with her iced tea near her plump lips. Lowering the drink, she adds, "Not a great place to be mentally."

"Nope, it isn't." I take in my gorgeous woman, who listens to every word, hoping to hear a way to fix the issue. Both of us know full well that she can't. "I want to keep you here as long as possible. I would prefer to be beside you—literally—for the rest of your days. However, you're an exceptional principal and coach among other things. I'm sure you have work to do before the game."

"Thank you. I do, but you need an ear more."

"Much appreciated, but I'll be fine until we get home. Go, sweetheart. I'll join you in your office to walk to the field."

She leans over and kisses me lightly. "I love you, Two."

Her endearment for me amplifies the ache in my chest more. What if I never catch again? "I love you."

Annie disappears from the conference room, leaving me with my thoughts. Before I think better of it, I call Madeleine's office.

"Good afternoon. How may I direct your call?" Simon is an exceptional gatekeeper for my agent. Since the moment we met, I picture him perfectly coifed behind his desk outside Madeleine's office. He's ready to tackle anything she needs as long as it doesn't rumple his clothing.

"Hello, Simon. It's Colby Somerset."

"Nice to hear from you. I saw some photos from the gala. Your date looked stunning."

My heart warms. "I'll be sure to share your sentiments with her."

"Is she the reason you agreed to Madi's setups?"

"Yes."

"Glad it worked out in the end."

Me too.

"How can I help you?"

"Can you schedule a call or meeting with Madeleine for me?"

"Of course. Do you have a preference?"

"Whatever is easier for her is fine." For the most part, I'm a low-maintenance client. Although since my injury, I appreciate her extra attention to me. Things likely wouldn't have gone my way in my initial meeting with the team regarding my rehabilitation regimen or timeline for that matter.

"She has space for a call tomorrow at eleven. Does that work?"

"Perfect. Thank you, Simon."

"Have a nice evening."

"You as well." I end the call feeling slightly relieved. As much as I would like to talk to Annie about my contract, Madeleine is the one with her ear to the ground. She will know about any rumblings, possible destinations, and my contractual options. I push my predicament out of my mind when Annie rejoins me in the conference room.

"Ready to beat Valley Crest?" she asks with a huge smile on her face.

"Yes. Are you?"

"They're prepared. We could clinch the regular-season divisional title today."

"I know. Let's go cheer our team to victory." Coaching with Annie has been a welcome addition to my rehabilitation with Jack. I can't wait to coach our kids when the time comes. We walk side by side down the wide corridor. As we pass one of the stairwells, I glance both ways and hurriedly guide her beneath the stairs.

"Two." Her voice wavers but is laced with lust. "There are cameras in the halls."

"Are we out of range here?"

Instead of answering, she melds her lips to mine and kisses me deeply. I comply and kiss her. Before things get out of control given our location and schedule, Annie pulls back slightly but sets her forehead against mine. "The last time you kissed me beneath high school stairs has nothing on today."

"No, it doesn't. Let's go guide our team to winning a championship banner, sweetheart." With a sweet peck on my lips, we hustle the rest of the way to the field. Seven innings later, the team is celebrating a victory with two games to round out the season and the tournament up next.

Celebrating a victory as a coach isn't much different than a player, at least it isn't when we're a couple. Annie and I dance our way into the house, leaving a trail of clothing in our wake as soon as we get home.

Breathless but sated, we amble to the kitchen for a late dinner of Thai takeout.

After therapy the next morning, I'm on edge waiting to talk to Madeleine. I'm confident Jack sent his report to her as well as the team. The question is how the team handles it. I answer Madeleine's call while I drive toward the school.

"Good morning, Colby."

"Hi, Madeleine. Thank you for squeezing me in."

She laughs. "I'm sure Simon made you think that. I'm headed to a short getaway with Christoph in a few hours."

"I appreciate it even more then. My issue can wait until you get back."

"Nonsense. Please share. Christoph excels at keeping me in vacation mode." Inwardly, I smile. Madeleine and her husband are a perfect match. From the outside looking in, one may not think so, but they balance each other out. "I gather you're calling about your progress assessment. It was stellar. Mr. Harlow has done an exceptional job. What are you worried about?"

I swallow hard. "As I'm sure you know, my team is at the bottom of the division, and it isn't looking good for them. I don't want to return to a decimated team next season. Ownership can either spend a ton of money bringing players in, including a catcher because Bolton isn't a fair replacement for me. Or they can purge the roster and start to rebuild. Additionally, Wilson made a few comments at the gala before handing me my ring."

"Understood. I'll review your contract. If I recall correctly, you have a no-trade clause. We may be able to use it as leverage. Do you have any parameters?" she asks.

Leverage—you can dump the last year of my huge contract on another team. Probably not a likely scenario, but I'll retire before I rebuild at the end of my career. I share my ideal landing spots with her and my intention to retire earlier than planned if a deal can't be done. "Thank you, Madeleine."

"You're welcome. Will I see you at the Devereaux wedding?"

I laugh. "Annie has mentioned it numerous times but hasn't officially invited me."

"When you have a teal-carpet debut as a couple, it follows you're each other's plus one going forward. Right?"

"Yes. I'll be there."

"Lovely. Don't worry, Colby. We will find the perfect landing spot for you."

I can't stop the smile on my face. I end the call as I park in the Point Academy lot. I expect today's session to be light. Instead of practicing on the field, the team, along with Annie and I, muddle through an active recovery workout. It's mostly stretching and yoga.

"Did you check with Jack first?" I whisper.

"I did. He said as long as you're comfortable, then you'll be fine."

"Thanks, sweetheart." Without thinking, I plant a kiss on her cheek.

Annie's eyes widen, and the boys snicker and tease.

"Sorry, Bluebird."

She shakes her head and instructs the boys on the first stretch. At the conclusion of practice, we head home like we have been since I arrived for my rehabilitation.

The rest of the week passes in a whirlwind. I've made progress as far as time and distance with my running and agility. Our team won their last two games and earned a first-round bye for the tournament. If our boys win next Wednesday, they will hang a regular season banner in the gymnasium.

It isn't until now that I've had the ability to rehash my concerns about returning to Florida and Madeleine's assurances. The last thing I want is to spend the end of my career on a team at the bottom of the league. Ideally, Madeleine will be able to find a soft-landing spot for me near Summit Creek.

CHAPTER TWENTY-SIX

JULIANNE

Waking up to a slew of notifications for numerous players on Colby's team, including Hatton, as potential trade candidates would not have been my choice, especially not on the day of the championship game for my players. Colby's name on the list spikes my adrenaline as well. My nerves are off the charts, and I'm not playing. Somehow this one has me more edgy than the regular season title. I consider it more and realize the reason. Defeating the same team three times in one season is statistically difficult.

"Stop worrying, Bluebird. The guys will be fine," Colby states from across the island. He either dislikes wearing clothes at home, or he's tempting me by walking around clad in only his boxer briefs for breakfast this morning. It's likely the former and the latter is a bonus.

"Not worried about my team."

"Me? I feel great, sweetheart." He circles the island between us and draws me close.

"Remember I mentioned I had bots which scour the internet for stories about you while we were apart?"

He frowns. "Yeah, I recall. Why?"

"Well, I had a bunch of notifications this morning with your name and others on the trading block."

"It's part of the game. Plus, I wouldn't mind a new place to call home if my team is broken up before the deadline. I don't want to rebuild in the last year of my contract."

"Makes sense."

"I'm sure you can easily deduce who is looking for a veteran catcher, even one with a bum knee."

I shrug. He's right. A few teams in the northeast could use his leadership and skills behind the plate, assuming he can play. The problem is… both organizations in California could use his skill set as well. "You're right."

"Love hearing those words first thing in the morning. I'll see you at the field. I have a few errands to run before I come to the game," Colby informs me.

I raise my eyebrow in question and with the hope of more information.

"Nope, not sharing. It's a surprise."

"For me or the guys?"

"You'll see. Also, when is the actual graduation ceremony?"

"In a week. Why?"

"I mean specifically when. I want to be there. Do I need to take a day off from therapy?"

"Oh. Maybe, it starts at noon."

"I'll work it out with Jack. Use my SUV. I want to ride back with you after the game." After a quick kiss, he urges me out the door with his keys.

I don't have time to overthink it. I slide into the buttery leather seats and hustle to school. On the way, I chat with Lorelei.

"Morning. How are you?"

"I'm well. You?"

"Nervous for the team and frazzled this school year is coming to an end."

She laughs. "You know I'm asking about Colby."

"I do. It's kind of perfect and terrifying. Today's sports news doesn't help my fears. I trust his word. We will figure this out together."

"I'm excited for you."

Me too. "Thanks, lovely. What about you? Any progress on the next step of your life plan?"

Lorelei and Jack have been trying to have a baby for the last year or so. "Mayyyybe."

"Shut up! Seriously? I was messing around."

"I'm waiting for my second trimester to share. Please don't tell anyone. Plus, I didn't want to add to everything you've got going on right now."

"Does Jack know?"

She giggles. "Of course he does." It takes me an extra second to realize Colby is aware as well. "You can talk to Colby, but that's all. I'm sure Jack swore him to secrecy."

"You're the best. I'm crazy excited for you. Please don't withhold stuff from me. We have been chatting at least once a week." Honestly, I'm a little bummed for myself. I shove my self-pity back and revel in my bestie's amazing news. Our timeline is different now. "How are you feeling?"

"Better. The nausea has lessened."

"Glad to hear it. Coffee on the patio?"

"I'll be there with my cup of decaf. Good luck this afternoon."

"Perfect. Bye, Lor." I end the call and push through my day of last-minute graduation details and a year-end pep rally for the baseball team. Luckly, Kate is handling the specifics. She has taken to her role as athletic director with gusto. Hiring her was a coup in my book.

As the clock ticks toward lunch, I start to worry. Then I recall Colby is meeting me at the game. When the day ends, I change into my coach's uniform, perhaps for the last time, and make my way to the field. I didn't think I would love coaching, but I do. I'm considering withdrawing the job requisition. I'm the second person to arrive.

Colby checks our surroundings and kisses me deeply. "Hi, gorgeous."

"What's with the tent?" A large white tent has been erected just outside the right field fence.

"Post-game preparations is all."

"Uh-huh."

"Everything inside the tent is appropriate." He leans forward to kiss me again, but his attempt is thwarted by the players rushing onto the field.

I wait for the stragglers and call the team together. "Many of you were skeptical about having me as your coach at the beginning of the season. I appreciate this opportunity more than you could possibly know. We need twenty-one outs, and you will be tourney champions. Win or lose, you've had an incredible year. Most importantly, Coach Somerset and I are proud of you and your progress as a team. Hands in. Falcons on three. One. Two. Three."

"Falcons." The guys break the huddle and warm up on the field.

"Nice speech, Coach," Colby offers.

"Thanks."

"Do I need to distract you with dirty words since I can't kiss you right now?"

As much as I want to roll my eyes at his statement, he's correct. "No. You can kiss me instead."

"Are you sure?"

"Yes."

Thinking quickly, Colby grabs my hand and leads me behind the dugout. Could we be seen? Yes. Do I care? Not anymore. I melt into his kiss and allow the pleasure to wash over me.

"I told you they were a thing."

Colby pulls back and notes who made the comment. Simonson, Telford, and Fisher are standing in a row. Simonson is the one who called us out. "She's amazing. Get back to warmups. We'll be right there."

They laugh and walk around the dugout but not before singing, "Coach and Coach sitting in a tree. K-I-S-S—"

"Let's refocus on the game, guys!" I shout before burying my head against Colby's chest briefly. "That went well."

"The kiss was epic. Come on. We have a game to manage."

After the national anthem has been sung and the starting lineups are called, the players take the field. My love for the game as a player may equal being a coach. Watching the guys succeed has been fulfilling for me. Coaching with Colby has been more than I dreamed of. At the end of the fourth inning, there was still no score. Fisher, our ace from last season, is on the mound. As much as I would've liked to give Simonson the start in his senior year. I didn't feel it was fair to change the rotation. Also, Simonson has been accepted and committed to play baseball at a southern powerhouse next spring. Fisher is still weighing his options.

During the top of the fifth, our opponent's clean-up hitter lines a shot straight back at Fisher. The most vulnerable player on the baseball diamond is the pitcher after delivering the ball to the plate. He crumples to the ground on his right side and is screaming in pain. The crowd falls eerily silent. My chest tightens with concern.

Colby and I rush to the mound, and the opposing team's coach is consoling the batter. The trainer joins us soon thereafter.

"Hey, Fisher. What hurts?"

He stares up at Colby and answers, "The ball clipped the side of my head above my ear."

"Will you move your glove so I can take a look?" the trainer asks upon hearing Fisher's response.

He has a bloody gash on the side of his head about three inches long.

The trainer pulls a gauze pad from the bag and holds it against Fisher's head and offers instructions. "Sit up slowly. Use the coach's arm to stabilize yourself. I'm going to support your back. Slowly."

Fisher complies. The crowd claps as he sits up. I notice Simonson and Stricker are warming up off to the side.

The trainer completes a concussion test. Fisher has a borderline result. "Can you stand?"

"Yes," Fisher replies.

"Use me and Coach Somerset for support."

Colby and the trainer assist Fisher to his feet. The crowd claps, and they take measured steps toward the dugout where his parents are anxiously waiting for information.

"Who are you thinking?" Colby asks.

"Not sure. It should be Simonson as he's next in the rotation. However, Stricker has a better record against the upcoming batters."

"Tyler will understand your logic," Colby offers.

I nod, squeeze Fisher's arm in support, and retreat to the opposite side of the dugout. Simonson and Stricker approach.

"We thought we should warm up," Stricker offers.

"Good job. I'm going to stick with the normal rotation. Simonson, head out to the mound and take your practice throws."

"Got it, coach." He glances at Fisher and nods tightly, seemingly indicating "I've got this," before he heads to the mound.

"Coaches," the umpire calls. We meet off to the left of home plate. "Are your players prepared to continue the game, Coach?"

His question is directed at me. "Yes, we are."

"What about your team?" The umpire asks the opposing coach.

"The batter is shaken, but we're ready to play otherwise. What are the rules? Can I pinch hit for my batter mid at-bat?"

The umpire shakes his head.

"Understood. Simonson inherits the batter with the same count, correct?"

The umpire replies, "Yes. The batter has two balls and one strike count. There are no outs, and the bases are clear."

With the assistance of the trainer and Colby, Fisher walks slowly toward the warmup circle on the opposing side of the field. He and the batter exchanged a few words and a bro hug.

As he walks back in my direction, Fisher stops with Colby beside him. He extends his hand to me. I take it, and he returns to his parents, who walk him to their car. I'm glad he came around this season and I was the coach to make it happen.

When the umpire shouts, "Play ball," I turn my attention to the field.

In all my years around the game of baseball, I've never seen a team pull together so quickly or so well. Simonson shut out the side and then our bats came alive in the bottom of the sixth. We scored three runs and allowed no runs in the top of the seventh inning to secure the championship.

"Congratulations, Annie!" Colby throws his arms around me and kisses me lightly.

"Thanks. I couldn't have done it without your help and support."

"You could have, but I'm glad I was beside you."

As the team is celebrating, Simonson pulls me aside. "Coach, is there any way we can take this celebration to Fisher?"

I swell with pride and reply, "Let me see what I can do." After a few calls and promises to bring the school van back in one piece, we travel to the hospital. The caravan stretches about twenty cars deep with the players' parents following us as well.

When we arrive, the staff is extremely helpful. I'm sure allowing a huge group of champions to take over their staff lounge for a post-game celebration is a unique situation. I'm confident one of the trustees, who happens to be a surgeon here, played a key role in pulling this off as well. Within fifteen minutes of our arrival, the lounge is set up with the contents of Colby's SUV, which the guys helped repack, and Fisher joins us with his parents in tow.

"Thanks, Coach. I appreciate the effort to move everyone here," Fisher offers as he slowly walks into the room.

"Honestly, I can't take credit. Simonson suggested the visit."

Simonson, who was within earshot, and Fisher bro hug before Fisher sits at the table beside him.

I address the team with Colby beside me. "As I mentioned before the game, you pulled together and did the hard work. Now, you're champions! Aside from thanking you for trusting me, I offer my sincerest congratulations."

The team hoots and hollers, and a chorus of congratulatory and joyful cheers fill the room.

"Before I get too mushy, I'm going to turn this over to Coach Somerset, who would like to share his thoughts."

Colby hugs me close and whispers, "You were meant to be their coach, Annie. I love you."

"Thanks. I love you."

He kisses my cheek and turns toward the team. "Once you accepted Coach Silva could handle the job, you flourished under her leadership. Both of us are proud of your progress and success. Annie, the guys and I got you a gift." Colby hands me a bag, and the guys cheer.

"Thank you."

Chants of "Open it" surround me. Shaking my head, I slip my hand between the layers of tissue paper and pull out a plaque shaped like home plate. Inside, with a maroon background, is a baseball embossed with each player's name. Fighting the tears is harder than I anticipated. I swipe my cheek. "Thank you, guys. I love this!"

Colby leans in and whispers, "You were born to coach, Annie. I'm glad you allowed me to assist." He kisses my cheek and turns his attention to the team. "If you will get into a line in the order of your numbers, we have gifts for you as well."

The guys scramble to their feet. As the players approach, Colby hands them a bag and congratulates them on their amazing season. Inside each bag is a personalized hoodie, a Point Academy hat with their number embroidered on the back panel, a pair of sweats, and a keychain made from baseball leather embossed with their number as well. Simonson and Telford are walking with Fisher as if they have been tasked as his bodyguards. More accurately, they've grown as teammates this season.

Addressing me, Simonson states, "Coach, I wouldn't have made it through this season without your guidance and support. Thank you."

"You're welcome. Good luck next season."

"I couldn't have done it without you." Simonson hugs me and then Colby.

After the remainder of the players accept their gifts, the guys demolish the cupcakes, water, and snacks we brought as well. Slowly, the team leaves. Fisher and his parents approach us on their way out.

Fisher extends his hand to me and then Colby. "Thank you for giving me a chance. I didn't deserve it, considering how I treated you at the beginning of the season."

"You came around," I offer. "Take it easy and heal. I'll see you at graduation." The last few players finish their goodbyes and head out, leaving only Colby and me.

Colby pulls me into his arms. "Are you ready to celebrate?" He glances around the room to make sure we're alone. Something he should've done before now. "Privately?"

Heat floods my body. "Yes!" Then I frown. "I have to return the van first."

"Well, let's get to it then." Colby and I clear the remaining debris from the team and hurry back to the school.

Once we drop off the van, I hop into Colby's SUV and a flood of well wishes from my family come through.

Reese: Congrats on the big win, Auntie! I'm proud of you. Love you.

Me: Thanks, sweetie. Love you too.

My siblings and their better halves, as well as Jake and Norah, offer congratulatory words.

"Your smile is huge, gorgeous. Please share," Colby says while I finish the final reply to Callie.

"Never once when I was a child did I yearn for a family. I had my parents. Having my extended family reach out after the game makes me wonder what I truly want for us."

"What do you mean? A houseful of kids, no?"

I laugh softly. "I do… did. No, I want a family, but it was always our biological children. Now, I'm considering adding adopted children as well."

"Why were you afraid to share your desire with me?"

"Not afraid exactly. Just not the right time."

"I'm fine with adding to our family with children in need, but I want to see you pregnant with my child as well," he answers.

"Me too."

He pulls into the garage, and we're both naked by the time we make it to the bedroom. I lose count with the number of orgasms we achieve. Thankfully, we can sleep in tomorrow morning.

CHAPTER TWENTY-SEVEN

JULIANNE

Almost immediately after the graduation ceremony, Colby and I flew to Florida. We're going to be here for a little more than a week before returning for Jordan's wedding. Initially, we were going to stay in Summit Creek, but both of us wanted to get away. With the progress of Colby's therapy, he can do most of the workouts on his own.

For the last three days, he has been exercising in the morning and spending the afternoons with me. Sometimes we leave the house. However, often, we lounge around either reading, watching movies, or defiling every possible surface we can find, including the pantry and the chaise on the patio. Making up for lost time has been beyond my expectations.

It hasn't been all roses though. I've attempted to talk to my father a few times, and my mother has pushed me off with promises of a call later in the day. A call that never comes. It's hard, but I'm honoring his wishes despite the premature pain it's causing me.

After breakfast, we stroll down the street to the beach and people watch. I purposely left my phone to disconnect for a bit.

"Keeping with our newfound reversed roles, I planned a date for tonight," Colby shares when we're on our way back to the house.

"You did? I love when I merely have to show up."

"Me too," I reply and loop my arm through his. The calm of the beach and our phone-free walk crashes to the ground the moment we check our messages.

"Damn, I have a few missed calls from Scala," Colby states.

"I have two as well, my mom and Lorelei, but not in that order. I'll go outside and return Lor's." I press my lips to his cheek and step outside.

"Hey, Lor. Colby and I were taking a walk."

"Have you talked to your mom?" she asks.

"Not today, but I have a missed call from her." Then it hits me. My mother doesn't call me. I call her. I have been wrapped up in happiness and chasing a life with Colby, so I didn't...

"Jules, are you still there?"

"Yeah." I muster the courage to ask, "Is he gone?"

"Yes. She took him to the emergency room last night at eight. He died a few hours later," Lorelei replies.

Anger floods my body. Why didn't my mother tell me immediately? She waited until the next day. She shared with Lorelei first? Why? I answer my own question. My mother thinks I'm in Summit Creek. I didn't get to say... I attempt to grab the arm of the chair, miss, and crumple to the ground.

"Jules, what was that noise?" I hear the concern in her voice. "Where's Colby?"

"I fell. He's inside talking to Madeleine."

"Ohmigod! Are you okay?"

"I'm physically fine. I need to make some arrangements to come home. Talk soon."

"Love you."

"Love you back, Lor."

I sit on the patio floor for a few minutes, grasping the fact my father has succumbed to his cancer. Tears roll over my cheeks as I curl into a tight ball. Time passes, I regain my composure—as best I can anyway—and push to my feet.

I walk into his office. He's currently leaning on the credenza beneath the window. "Will you call my mom with me?"

He wrinkles his brows. "How do you know—" I hope he misses the fact my face is tear-streaked and puffy.

He doesn't. Colby rounds the desk and lifts my chin until our gazes meet. The words aren't necessary. The last time I spoke with my father after the game was short. I could tell the call was difficult for him. I rest my head on Colby's chest and clasp my arms around him. "I'm sorry," he whispers.

My shoulders drop more. "I had two notifications—one from Lorelei and one from Mom. I was already dialing Lor when I realized the news wasn't good." Silently, I take his place behind his desk, and he sidles beside me. His arm possessively around my waist for comfort and support.

"Julianne, I left you a message hours ago," my mother admonishes me instantly.

"Really? I don't want to argue about semantics with you. I was taking a walk without my phone. Besides, he passed away late last night and yet you called Lorelei first."

"I—"

Shaking my head, I cut her off without hesitation. "No. I don't want to hear excuses. Where are you holding the services?"

"I'm heading to the funeral home with Aunt Pam as soon as she gets here."

"Where?" I ask, knowing the answer may break my heart. Deep down, the choice to leave our hometown was my father's decision. My mother simply went along with it.

"Summit Creek," she replies.

"We'll be back as soon as possible," I state and look to Colby for confirmation.

He nods.

"I'll call you when I have the final details," my mother adds. I end the call and collapse into Colby's arms. Once I settle my emotions a bit, we leave the office and prepare to travel back to Summit Creek for my father's funeral.

My mother decided on a simple service at the funeral home with a repast at a local establishment. We stand hip to hip at the edge of the room with Colby beside me. Whether purposeful or not, there are six chairs set up. Perhaps my mother was honest about accepting Colby this time around. The services begin with local friends and my Aunt Pam and Uncle Tom, as well as Jack and Lorelei.

Midway through the calling hours, a throng of large, well-dressed men and gorgeous women file through the door. Caroline Silva never had a passable poker face. She murmurs, "You shouldn't have invited them."

Through gritted teeth, I reply, "I didn't. Along with you and dad, they're my family." With Jordan and Jill at the head of the line, they introduce themselves.

My brother extends his hand to my mother. "Mrs. Silva, please accept our condolences. I'm Jordan, and this is my fiancée, Alejandra. We would've preferred to meet under different circumstances."

"Your eyes are the same as my daughter's" are the only words my mother can muster.

"Yes, ma'am." My brother answers before he and Alex slide to the right and hug me tightly.

"How are you holding up?" he asks.

"I'm doing. Thank you for coming. With all the planning for your wedding, I'm sure you have plenty of other things to do."

"You're my sister. We may not have known one another our entire lives, but we're family. Family shows up." Jordan hugs me, and I introduce him to Colby. "Jordan, please meet my… Colby."

"Pleasure."

Colby looks between Jordan and me and shakes his head. "Nice to meet you as well. You two could be twins."

Jordan smiles, and Alex laughs softly.

Jill is next, and my mother is awestruck. Aside from the height difference, it's unmistakable Jill and I are related.

"The three of you… wow!"

"Mom, this is my sister, Jill."

"Thank you for coming," she manages. I introduce Jill and Colby before continuing with the rest of the family. Jake, Connor, Norah, and Maia round out the group.

None of us were prepared for the sheer number of people who showed up to honor my father. Truly, they came for me.

As we drive to the repast, Colby's phone vibrates repeatedly.

"Do you need to talk to Madeleine?"

"Not now. Nothing is more important than you right now."

I shift to face him in the back of the town car. "Was today fun? Not at all. However, with you by my side, I can handle anything."

"The only person I'm focused on is you. Everyone else can wait a few more hours, including Madeleine."

The repast is small and includes Mom, us, and about ten other people. The meal passes quickly with a few anecdotes of my father and questions about my relationship with Colby. I eloquently pushed them away as inappropriate.

The onslaught of messages continues while we eat. By the time we arrive home, the sheer number is astronomical. We strip off our clothes and get comfortable to filter the messages.

"You should wear that on our next date night," he suggests. "The restraint required to refrain from tossing you onto the bed is utterly insane. Your revealing black lace lingerie is wholly inappropriate for the occasion."

"Perhaps. I'll join you in a few minutes." I turn toward the bathroom. Before I take a step, Colby encircles my wrist and tugs gently before collapsing his arms around me. "Are you stewing or...."

"I'm dealing. My father died, and he did it his way. I would have preferred to have an honest conversation about our relationship with him and why I decided to give you a second chance, but it wasn't meant to be. Frankly, that hurts more than the fact he's gone. The notion he didn't allow to explain why you're the one for me despite the pain from our teenage years."

"I will never hurt you again," Colby adds emphatically.

"I know. Go start your messages and calls. I'll be down soon."

CHAPTER TWENTY-EIGHT

COLBY

"Are you ready, Annie? Alex is expecting you by one," I state from the threshold of her master bathroom. After Mr. Silva's services, we decided to stay in Summit Creek until the wedding. Alex is her future sister-in-law. My gorgeous woman is fussing with her dress. It's sleeveless and royal blue with a cinched waist. The fabric feels decadent beneath my fingers. Keeping my hands to myself during her brother, Jordan's, wedding today is going to be difficult.

"Almost. Which shoes? Sparkly or not?" She has one shoe on each foot.

"Both make your legs look a mile long and are sexy as hell. If I must choose, sparkly."

She nods tightly. "Okay. Let's go."

She sets her shoes on the floorboard, slides into the passenger seat, and inputs the address. Her plan was to introduce me to her family before the wedding, but with therapy, coaching, and her dad's death, there hasn't been time for us to visit. True, they came to the services, but aside from a cursory explanation in the receiving line, I didn't get to meet them. Also, I need to make time to speak with Madeleine today about my options. She left a message earlier today.

I pull down the gravel path. Honestly, I'm not positive we're in the right place. "Are you sure about this address?" A gorgeous modern colonial is at the end of the long driveway.

"Yes. The ceremony is at the Michelson's house. Alex wanted to get married at a spot important to them."

I nod as if I know the story behind her statement. I don't but also don't press her to share. Parking along the side of the driveway, Annie pulls on her shoes, and we enter the house. It's a large modern colonial with a wraparound porch and a treehouse in the backyard possibly from when Connor was a child.

"Julianne, it's lovely to see you again." An older woman greets her.

"You as well, Connie."

She fills in the relationships while they hug. Connie is Jordan and Jill's social worker and Connor's mother. Connor owns Blackthorne and was Alex's boss.

Annie continues, "Connie, this is Colby."

"Pleasure to meet you." She throws her arms around me and hugs me as well. Despite the way her parents are treating her at this moment, I'm glad her biological family is welcoming to her and especially to me.

"You too."

Connie adds, "Reese will be back momentarily to escort you to Alex." Her words are in Annie's direction. Turning to me, she says, "The guys are in the family room. The stairs are the first door on the left down the hall."

"Perfect. Thank you," I offer.

Connie leaves as Reese bounds through the French doors. "Auntie, you're here! Hi, who are you?"

Annie laughs. "Reese, this is my... Colby." Jordan and Alex decided not to bring Reese to Mr. Silva's services. She stayed with Callie and the babies.

"Is he the guy who gave you the pretty ring a long time ago?" Reese asks without hesitation.

A fierce blush blooms on Annie's face. "Yes, he is."

Flustered Annie is new. It's hot as hell.

Reese turns and looks me squarely in the face. "Don't mess up your second chance. Auntie is awesome!"

"Never. Pleasure to meet you, Reese." I bump her fist with mine.

"You too. Are you ready, Auntie?"

Annie turns to me and kisses me lightly. "I'll find you after I talk to Alex."

"Okay."

Reese loops her arm around Annie's and leads her down a hallway to my right. I turn left and join the guys. Luckily, Christoph is here and introduces me around. Now I have officially met Annie's new extended family and their better halves, as well as my nieces and nephews. Well, it'll be official eventually. Once that's out of the way and my head is spinning with connections and relationships, I grab a bottled water and wait for the ceremony to begin. Less than an hour later, we walk to the riverbank where a pergola has been set up with about fifty white chairs with bows adorning the back.

When I begin to get antsy sitting alone, Annie slips into the chair beside me and threads her fingers with mine.

"Hi, beautiful."

"Hey. How was your more in-depth introduction?"

I laugh quietly. "Christoph was a pro."

"Good. I can connect more—" Annie's words are cut off by soft music playing.

Jordan takes his place under the pergola along with Tyson Beck and Cameron Beau. Not only were they teammates in college but now in the professional league as well. Then Alex and her brother, Miguel, whom I met earlier, pause arm in arm at the end of the aisle.

The sheer emotion on the bride's and groom's faces is palpable and impossible to miss. Frankly, I see the look with every man in this group from Jake to Cruz to Christoph. I have no doubt the same grin is on my face when I look at Annie. Less than fifteen minutes later, time I spent staring at Annie instead of the bride and groom, Jordan and Alex kiss and walk to the awaiting SUV.

The rest of us scatter to our vehicles and drive to their house. While we make our way to the reception, which is about a fifteen-minute ride, Annie is contemplative.

"Care to share, Bluebird?"

"It isn't new. I'm happy for them but angry at my dad as well."

"About?" I realize this question is open-ended, but she could simply be upset he won't be here for her—our—wedding, or the display of familial love surrounding us today makes her sad.

"All of it. I'm ecstatic they found one another. Overjoyed Reese has been officially adopted by Alex. Attending a huge family event with you is amazing." Annie's shoulders drop, and she shifts in her seat.

"What else? Feeling sad or mad is okay too."

"I love how well you know me, Two."

"Same. Keep going," I urge her.

Abruptly, Annie shakes her head. "Nope, not ruining this afternoon. I'm going to focus on things I can control."

"Who are you, and what have you done with my Annie?"

She laughs softly and leans over the console to kiss my cheek. We turn down their street and are stopped at the gate. I give the guard our names, and we proceed to their driveway.

The stereotype surrounding professional athletes, especially successful ones, is we spend tons of money on frivolous things like houses, cars, and vacations. While some most certainly fall into that category, it appears Jordan doesn't, much like me. A person who desires to have a home may see it as extravagant. It isn't. His is about the same size as mine. Modest given our salaries.

Annie leads me through the house to the backyard. There is a lighted pathway to a large tent set near the edge of the lawn. We follow the path and locate our table. The bride and groom have us sitting with family, which I'm sure Annie appreciates. After another round of more thorough introductions including her sister Jill, sister-in-law Norah, and Callie, we stand and watch the bride and groom enter for the first time.

Jordan and Alex have their first dance, and dinner service begins. The food is delicious, and I have no doubt from the information Annie shared, Jill or Jordan himself had a hand in preparing it. Once the main entrée is served, the dance floor begins to fill up. The tempo is too fast for Annie's liking. We stay seated with Christoph and Madeleine. Madeleine shifts to a chair next to me.

"Mind if we talk now, or would you prefer to wait until tomorrow?" Madeleine asks.

"Now is fine."

"As I'm sure you know, both teams on the West Coast have expressed interest. However, neither meet your parameters."

I nod tightly.

Madeleine continues, "Mr. Wilson is not willing to let you go easily. Even if it means dumping the huge payment in the last year of your contract on another team."

"Why?" I answer my own question. "He has his heart set on Bolton."

"Between you and me, Wilson may be high on Bolton, but those in the clubhouse aren't. Specifically, Coach feels Bolton is a hothead as well as the fact he is performing below the standard they would like."

"Well, he isn't me."

Annie covers my hand with hers.

"No, he isn't, but I refuse to allow you to retire when you can still play at a high level," Madeleine adds.

Annie stiffens beside me and releases my hand.

Fuck!

Before I can speak, Annie pushes to her feet, says, "Excuse me," and walks away on her red-soled sparkly heels.

How could Annie not realize that? Did I tell her specifically? No, but... I would never choose a life without her again even if it means not catching again.

"I assumed you told her," Madeleine states with a look of concern and dismay in her eyes. "Despite your injury and inability to play baseball, you've never been happier than you are with her."

"I did," I drop my head. *I did, didn't I?* Given her reaction, I'm not so sure.

"Colby, I won't give up until the teams are exhausted. Even with your permission, retiring truly isn't an option, is it?"

"For her, I will retire." There is no waver in my words.

Recognition of my conviction crosses her face, and Madeleine replies, "I understand," and shoos me away to find Annie.

It takes me a little bit, but I find her in a guest suite near the front of the house. "Annie."

She turns away from the window to face me. Her face is tight with hurt, which doesn't make sense.

"Why would you tell your agent you're willing to retire if you can't secure a trade within certain parameters?"

I eliminate the space between us and take her hands in mine. "I learned my lesson the first time. I refuse to walk away from us again. I need you, not baseball. Our relationship is more important than any game."

Tears cascade down her cheeks. "You can't give up your career for me."

"I can, and I will if Madeleine can't secure a spot for me on a team with a chance to contend. I don't need to get back to the World Series, but I don't want to be in the cellar of the league at the end of my current contract either."

Annie tilts her head to the side as if she's processing my words. She probably is. Parsing out the teams that would meet my requirements. Given her knowledge of the league, I'm confident she would come up with the same list I gave Madeleine. "Baseball is in your bones."

I swipe my thumb along her cheekbone. "True, but... you are my marrow." I cup her face and kiss her deeply. Our kiss isn't long, but it's laced with yearning and hope for our future. I add space between us and meet her gaze.

"Colby—"

A breathless Reese pushes open the door. "There you are. Dad is looking for you. Something about a sibling dance."

"I forgot. I'll be right there, sweetie."

Reese casts a serious look in my direction but doesn't call me out. I'm grateful. I have a strong feeling she would fight for Annie to the death now that they've become acquainted.

"We can talk about this more on our flight to Florida in a few hours," I suggest.

Annie grabs a tissue and blots her cheeks. "I don't think we need to discuss it more."

Surprised, I ask, "We don't?"

"No. Would I have preferred to be with you all these years? Without question. However, no one knows me better than you. I likely would've quit school and followed you around. Your motives were altruistic, even if they hurt like hell. We're together now, and I refuse to give you up again. If we're supremely lucky, one of the teams you approved will see the benefit of having you on their roster next season."

"Okay...."

"I only ask one thing.... Please don't make any life-altering decisions on your own."

"You have a deal. Let's go before Jordan comes looking for you himself." I already made a second life-altering decision, but she's going to have to understand it was necessary to ensure the occasion is perfect.

The rest of the evening passes in a blur. Annie and Jill both have a sibling dance with Jordan in place of a traditional mother-son dance. I'm able to hold Annie close and enjoy the reception despite the guest list which includes her huge extended family. Many of whom are celebrities.

Near midnight after a lengthy goodbye, which included more hugs than I'm used to, I close the passenger door after Annie takes her seat. We park in the long-term area of the lot and make our way to the private terminal and are immediately ushered onto the plane.

"Colby. Julianne. Nice to see you again," Cash Morgan greets us.

"You as well," I reply. "I thought you only flew sparingly?"

Cash smiles. "I do. However, your assigned pilot is about to become a father."

"Appreciate the accommodation," I answer.

"You're welcome. Please take a seat."

Johnny drops us off at my house after we land. Without further thought, we fall into my huge bed until morning.

CHAPTER TWENTY-NINE

JULIANNE

It has been two weeks since we arrived in Florida. Each morning Colby gets up before me and works out with Jack over video chat. Is it necessary for Jack to be watching? Probably not, but he will keep Colby from overdoing it even from afar. Colby's progress has been remarkable. He's nearing six months in his rehab and is ahead of the curve.

I pad into the kitchen and pour myself a cup of coffee to enjoy by the pool. As I pass, I peek in on Colby finishing his session with Jack. It's peaceful here. I'm sure the fact I'm on summer break impacts the ambiance as well.

"Morning, gorgeous," Colby states, approaching from the house. He's shirtless with each dip, ridge, and curve on delicious display.

Damn! He's hot! "Morning. How was your session?"

"Good. The team reached out to Jack. They're requesting an assessment."

My eyes widen with concern. "For trade purposes?"

"Probably."

"It would make sense."

"Why?" he asks.

"News of the potential three-team blockbuster trade broke this morning." I inform him.

"Oh. Haven't deleted the bots yet, huh?"

I smile. "No. Do you want the details or…?"

"Nah. I'll wait to hear from Madeleine."

"Has Madeleine made any progress?"

"The last time I talked to her, she was in discussion with Kansas City and New York."

"Okay." I try to hide the edge to my response, but I fail.

"Kansas City isn't a viable option, Annie."

"I know." The best part is two of the three teams in his trade are on his list. Ideally, he will be close next season. "Despite your intentions, I don't want you to retire for me. We can make it a year apart, can't we?"

Colby sits beside me. "We can, but I don't want to. If I play baseball again, I need to wake up with you when I have a home game. I want you in the stands wearing a jersey with my name on the back."

"Okay. Do we still have a date tonight?"

"Yes. I have the entire evening planned."

"Are we actually going out this time?"

He winks at me. "Maybe."

"Colby, the last time I got all dolled up. I ended up naked on the hood of your McClaren in the garage."

"Are you complaining?" He tilts his head as he asks.

"No. Hell no. Sex with you is mind-blowing. I would prefer to skip the getting dressed up part."

"Happy to hear it. Although, there is something about you in a short dress that drives me to insanity. Your sexy toned legs may be my kryptonite, much like me wearing a backward hat is for you."

"You remember that?"

He hauls me into his arms. "Yes, every single detail both good and bad. There are still a few spots we need to christen before we go back home."

"I'm absolutely on board."

He leans in and kisses my temple. "Eggs work for breakfast?"

"Sure. I really love that Marta taught you to fend for yourself."

"She could share her knowledge with you as well."

I lift my shoulder. "Perhaps."

We shuffle inside. After eating breakfast near the pool, we split up. He heads to his office and checks his messages while I do the same in the library. After clearing my work inbox, despite it being summer vacation, and my personal one that I let fill up for the last few weeks, I call my mom.

"Morning," I offer when she answers.

"Hello, Julianne."

"How are you doing?"

My mother sighs heavily. "I'm taking one day at a time. While we didn't always agree, your father and I were a great team. Deciding things for myself is exhilarating but sad as well. I'm sure that doesn't make sense."

"Maybe a little. It's similar to figuring out how to be in a relationship with Colby effectively this time. Instead of choosing alone, we need to talk about them."

"I suppose you're right. I wanted to ask you more about your siblings and large extended family."

Instantly, I'm defensive. "What about them?"

"It isn't bad. I would like to send cards to them, but there are so many. Can you give me an address list for each household?"

"Of course. I appreciate your receptiveness to them regardless of the occasion."

"Except for Jill's height, the three of you might as well be triplets."

I laugh softly. "Meeting them and seeing my eyes staring back at me was eerie initially."

"I would like to get to know them better."

Warmth and disappointment cascades through me. Deep down, I was confident only my father wasn't interested in meeting my biological family.

"You're welcome to join me at my next visit."

"Thank you. What is the status of Colby returning to Florida? Are the trade rumors true?"

I smile. "Actually, he's on a call with his agent as we speak. The only details I'm aware of are what was in the press. Three teams are working on a trade."

"Okay, then I will stay put for now."

I frown. "What do you mean?"

"I'm considering moving to New York near Pam and Tom."

Oh! "Oh, good for you. I figured you would come back to Summit Creek."

"Summit Creek and with Pam are my two options." Silence passes over the phone line for a solid minute before my mother ends our call. "Thank you for the addresses. I'll talk to you soon. Love you, sweetheart."

"Love you too, Mom." Disheartened by our call, I take a minute to push away the conflicting emotions. Then I follow the sound of his voice to the office.

"Are you serious?" he says.

Madeleine replies, "Completely. It's contingent on you passing the assessment again with their doctor and agreeing to play for the last year of your contract plus at least two more."

He scribbles the time frame on a piece of paper and shows it to me. I drop my head in agreement. I don't know which team, but it's clearly one on his list. Plus, after our discussions, I trust him to make the best choice for us. My pulse races and my mind is spinning. For the first time, we may both be able to chase our dreams and be together.

"Colby, did I lose you?" Madeleine's voice bounces off the walls as he turns on speakerphone.

"No, I'm here. Please iron out this deal with Philly. Can you have Simon or Lucia send me more details as they become available?"

"Of course."

"Thank you, Madeleine. I would be retiring or miserable on the West Coast without you and your team."

"You're welcome. I'll be in touch soon with more details and firm numbers for the added two years." She ends the call.

"Philly, huh?"

A huge, glee-filled smile grows on his face. I don't begrudge him the happiness of the moment. He deserves it. "Yeah. The timing isn't ideal, but I may need to report within a few days of the agreement being signed."

"Okay," I mumble. His life is about to get hectic, and I'm excited to be a part of it this time.

It seems as if we're meant to stay in Summit Creek. Whenever we travel to Florida, there's a reason to turn around and come home. At least this time, it's a good one. We fly home and skip his meticulously planned date. We arrive midmorning. Colby decides to read beside me in bed while I catch a few more hours of sleep. I'm not pleasant without a decent amount of shut-eye each night. When I wake, I find Colby's side of the bed empty. After I make my way downstairs, I hear laughter from outside.

"Easy, dude. I'm not one of your teammates." Jack is shaking his hand, presumably from Colby's throw.

Colby's sexy laugh warms me. I slip my feet into my flip-flops near the back door and join them.

"Hey, Jules."

"Jack."

Colby turns and walks in my direction. Without a second thought, he kisses me deeply.

I pull back and ask, "When do you plan to have your last assessment? We have time now unless you're too tired from traveling."

"I'm waiting for the go-ahead from Madeleine. My new team wants their own physician to complete the tests."

"Ouch!" Jack adds.

"You're coming with me," Colby states plainly.

"I am?"

"Yes. I need you beside me to make sure it goes well. Plus, I know you will speak up if it isn't."

"I'll be there," Jack replies and tosses the ball to Colby, who is crouched down as if he's catching.

"It feels good to crouch, doesn't it?"

A sexy glint appears in his eyes. "Yeah. I miss playing, but I wouldn't trade games for the time reconnecting with you."

"I know. I understand your love of baseball better than anyone. Hell, I miss playing too, and it's been significantly longer for me. Is there stuff we should be doing?"

"Like?" Colby asks.

"Finding a place to live in the area, for starters."

My gorgeous man, who is about to make moves for his career, shakes his head furiously. "I'm staying here."

"No."

Colby's head snaps up as if I slapped him. "Yes."

"No. It's too far. Ninety minutes each way is a lot. I can stay there during the season. Jack will watch the house, right?"

Jack meets my gaze when he hears his name. Clearly, he was attempting not to listen to our conversation which strayed toward personal. "I will what?"

"Look after the house while we're in Philly."

"Of course," he replies instantly.

"Annie, this is your dream home," Colby counters.

"It was never about the four walls, Two. It was about sharing it with you and a backyard with our best friends. I will be where you are."

"I'm gonna…." Jack turns and walks toward his house.

Colby scrubs his hand down his face. "Are you sure?"

"Completely. I want to wake up with you. The commute to Point Academy is about the same from Philly distance-wise anyway. We can figure out times to visit your cars in Florida too."

Colby draws me closer and kisses my temple. "I love you, Bluebird."

"I love you, Two."

I grab the ball from his hand and run to the spot where Jack was standing. After about twenty throws, we run inside and search for a temporary place to live in his new team's city. Although it isn't official yet, I don't foresee any issues with the results of his tests. It's going to be a change for both of us. The most convenient places to live near the stadium are townhouses, which is fine with me. The only amenities I would like are a garage and an outdoor patio.

We narrow down the list to three choices before Colby suggests. "What do you say to an old-fashioned movie night?"

"Without chaperones?" My voice drops when I realize only one remains.

Without missing another beat, Colby says, "I'm sorry, Bluebird. I wasn't thinking."

"No, it's fine. I'm sad he's gone but glad he isn't suffering. You know?"

"Yeah."

"Pizza from the Tipsy Tomato and a double feature with you sounds perfect."

We throw on some clothes acceptable for outside of the house, place our order, and then hop into his SUV. We set up our takeout on the ottoman when we return home. Our behavior is excellent until the first movie is halfway over. *Bull Durham* is a classic. One we've both seen numerous times. It starts small with me draping my legs in his lap. Unconsciously, he drags his fingers along the top of my legs, sending tingles straight to my now-wet core. Before I overthink it, I grip his shirt and haul him over me. Within a few minutes, we're both nearly naked and lost in each other. It's easy to forget our surroundings. His mouth and hands sliding along my skin and lips make me yearn for more. Regaining the time isn't possible, but it sure is deliciously fun to try.

"Hey, hey! Where are you?" Lorelei calls from the back door.

"Lor! Stop walking!"

"What?" she replies.

"Lor, stop walking! We need a few minutes."

Immediately, she starts chuckling and says, "I'll be on the patio. Let me in when you're ready." Laughter follows her out the door. We take a few minutes to dress before letting Lorelei inside.

She's trying her best not to burst into hysterics again.

"Did you just get home?" I ask.

"Yeah. I had a late session with a client in crisis. I wanted to come over and congratulate Colby personally. I'll text first next time."

My cheeks heat up. "We will do the same."

She turns toward him and says, "Congratulations, Colby."

"Thanks, Lor. I couldn't have done it without Jack."

"You could've, but it wouldn't have been as thorough in both your baseball and personal life."

"True. How are you feeling?" I ask her.

"Tired now but overall better. In fact, I'm going to go home and collapse into my bed after a long shower. You two can go back to doing whatever... Nope! Not going to picture it. Love you both." Lorelei hugs us, and we turn in as well.

CHAPTER THIRTY

COLBY

Hand in hand with Annie, I walk through the doors to the medical complex.

We're greeted by an overly cheerful brunette. "Good morning, Mr. Somerset."

"Morning."

"Dr. Bushka will be with you in a few moments. Unfortunately, your entourage will need to stay in the waiting room." Her gaze is pinned on Annie and Jack.

"Both will be accompanying me as I previously requested."

The brunette bristles and leads the three of us into a large training room. Soon after she closes the door, a burly man enters the room.

"Mr. Somerset, I'm here to take you for your MRI."

"Please follow me."

I kiss Annie, shake Jack's hand, and follow him to the MRI. I meet Dr. Bushka and the radiologist. "Mr. Somerset, pleasure to make your acquaintance."

"You as well." I return thirty minutes later.

Dr. Bushka breezes into the room with my results. I assume he has discussed the results with his radiologist. He greets Jack first. "Mr.

Harlow, pleasure to meet a colleague in person. I've reviewed your rehabilitation notes and regime thoroughly. It's impressive."

"Thank you," Jack replies.

"Good morning, Miss?"

"Silva."

Not for much longer, if I can help it. I refocus on this test and not worry about the engagement ring in my bag rather than on Annie's finger.

"Please hop up on the exam table, and we'll get started. From the notes, I will perform the same tests Mr. Harlow has previously used during your rehabilitation."

Dr. Bushka has me extend both legs out on the table, and he examines both my surgically repaired left knee and my right knee. Then he performs the valgus stress test at full extension and then at thirty degrees. The second portion is the Swain test, which measures stability and rotation by flexing my knee to ninety degrees and externally rotating my shin.

Once he completes the test, he asks, "May I speak freely?"

"Yes," I answer.

"Your IKDC, Tegner, and Lysholm scores indicate stellar progress since your injury. Your responses to the questionnaire mirror those statements. The preliminary results of your MRI are promising as well."

Pride and glee filter through me. I've heard the names of the outcome measure test from Jack before. "Great! Thank you for fitting me into your busy schedule."

"You're welcome. I'm sure your former teammate will be happy to have his battery mate back." The battery is a baseball term for the pitcher and catcher.

Hatton was traded to Philly too? Fantastic! Having Hatton there will decrease the time it takes me to get up to speed with at least one pitcher on staff. "I would be." I stand and shake his hand.

"Mr. Harlow, your work with the patient is remarkable. I would be interested in speaking with you about joining my practice."

Jack is floored and unable to speak.

"He would be happy to hear your proposal, Doctor," I supply.

"Yes, thank you," Jack manages.

The door clicks closed. I haul Annie close and pull Jack into our hug as well.

"You did it!" Jack exclaims.

"No, we did. I couldn't have pulled this off without you. Would you consider working here?"

"I'm shocked by the offer, but I would certainly discuss it with Lorelei."

"As you should. Let's grab a quick lunch and head back." After securing food at Reading Terminal Market, which offers plenty of options for all of us in one huge place, we eat quickly. We pull onto the interstate and return home. As I park in the driveway, my phone vibrates a few times.

Jack escapes to his house through the backyard.

"I need to check these messages."

"Okay. I should probably do the same. I'll be in the office in a few minutes. I want to change first."

I smile, kiss her lightly, and watch her as she walks away. As I pass through the kitchen, I grab bottled water. Opening my laptop, I start filtering my emails. Two messages from Scala surge to the top of the list. Without more thought, I call.

"Scala Talent and Sports Management. Simon Dumont speaking."

"Hello, Simon. Colby Somerset returning Madeleine's call."

"Please hold one moment."

While the soft jazz plays through the speakerphone, I delete a few emails and pause when I see Edmund Silva's name in my inbox. As my finger hovers to click, Madeleine greets me.

"Hello, Colby. How is Jules holding up?" While Madeleine was unable to attend the services, Christoph was there with Jake and Connor.

"Better than expected. I'm waiting for her to fall apart."

"And you?"

"I'm fine. Thank you for asking."

"I'm sorry the timing is terrible for this."

"Not your fault. What do you need from me?"

"The team is offering to absorb the last year of your current contract and add two years at three million each with incentives, depending on how many games you play."

"All of them starting next season," I reply with gusto.

Madeleine laughs. "My thoughts exactly. Dr. Bushka will forward the results of your assessment to the other parties. When the team is satisfied, based on the preliminary details, I'll meet you to sign your new contract. Also, they want you in the clubhouse even if you don't play this season."

"This is above and beyond, and I'm grateful."

"Stavros taught me well."

"Pretty sure he saw your tenacity when you piped Carys's music into his car and office until he caved," I suggest. Hearing her sing at Jordan's wedding was a delightful experience.

"Perhaps. I'll see you soon."

Ending the call, I wonder about the email from Annie's father. Not long after Caroline's injury, I reached out to him, imploring him to reconsider his position on my relationship with Annie. He refused.

Instead of mulling over what I did, I scroll down and open the message. I find a recording attached. The body of the email includes a short note from Caroline.

Colby,

I have not listened to this. I felt it would be an invasion of his privacy. Laughable now, I know. Whatever Edmund wanted to say, he didn't share with me. He requested I send his messages to you and Julianne when I was able.

Best, Caroline

I brace myself and press play.

The voice I hear isn't his. It sounds as if it's text to voice. "I owe you an apology. As much as I preached people could change, I didn't allow you room to do it. For that, I'm sorry. Even though you were in Philadelphia because Caroline was injured, Julianne never looked happier. Deep in my heart, I realized it is because of you. I wasn't ready to see it. You have dutifully reached out to me at least twice a week. I have rebuffed you each time, much like I did before you left to play baseball all those years ago. It was callous and thoughtless on my part. You are taking the traditional path, which I know my daughter would appreciate if she knew. My daughter loves you. I'm sure she has since she was a young girl covered in red clay from the Little League field. Colby, you have my blessing to marry my daughter. I expect compliance with this request as I won't be here to see it personally. Love Julianne and take care of her for the rest of your days."

It isn't until the message ends do I realize I've been staring out the window, and I'm no longer alone.

"You got one too?"

I turn to the whispered sound of her voice.

"Yes. What did yours say?"

Annie takes a step closer, but stops. "It doesn't matter."

"Not true."

She wraps her arms around herself and shares. "Not really. He didn't give me what I wanted to hear and that sucks. I wanted to hear he was wrong for stealing my time with him. He didn't bother to apologize. My father was only apologetic about his opinion regarding my siblings. He said nothing else. He didn't mention his treatment of you at all." She moves closer to me, turns the chair, and curls into my lap. "You asked my dad for permission to marry me? When?"

"It doesn't matter."

"It does to me."

"The last thing I want to do is cause you more pain."

"Now you have to tell me."

"Annie, I don't want to tarnish your memory of your father any further."

"Colby, tell me, please," she implores.

"The first time I sought permission to marry you was…" I lean forward and cup her face in my hands. "I asked three weeks before graduation—our high school graduation."

"He said 'No' then."

I close my eyes and nod tightly.

"And now? When did you ask more recently?"

"The first time I reached out was after your mom's injury. Unlike over a decade ago, I didn't give up. For the last two months, I have been reaching out to your dad to seek his permission to give you my last name permanently. He rebuffed me each and every time, much like he did you when you attempted to visit him more frequently or share the good news in your life over the phone. I reached out at least twice a week. I planned to propose in Florida but couldn't."

"When? Our date... before my dad died?"

"Yeah."

"Ask me now," she demands.

"I want it to be perfect."

"Life isn't perfect, Colby. Although together we are."

"You're serious?"

"Yes, I am."

I press my lips to hers and kiss her deeply. Bracketing her hips with my hands, I lift and set her on the hardwood floor. "I'll be right back." Stepping out of the office, I ascend the stairs and secure the old mine cushion cut ring from my garment bag. I was confident Annie wouldn't need to look in there and accidentally find her ring.

I steel myself and return to her side before taking her hands in mine. "I planned to wear a suit, and you would be wearing a sexy-as-fuck dress."

A shy but genuine smile appears on her face. To this day, it baffles me that Annie doesn't see what I see when I look at her. "Yoga pants and a V-neck for me and athletic shorts and a shirt for you is fine too. Both outfits are us."

"Too many years ago, I gave you a ring. One that symbolizes our relationship. Despite the turbulence of the last decade, we found our way back to each other. Frankly, I'm not sure either of us ever truly gave up hope."

"Colby."

"I'm willing to forgo the clothes, a roomful of peonies, and the fancy dinner, but please let me do this part right."

Annie pulls her lower lip between her teeth to prevent herself from talking.

I continue, "There's a portion of a movie I've watched repeatedly, which nicely dovetails with the description in your ring and my tattoo. Anthony Hopkins in *Meet Joe Black* says this to his daughter, 'Love is passion, obsession, someone you can't live without. I say, fall head over heels. Find someone you can love like crazy who will love you the same way back. How do you find him? Well, forget your head and listen to your heart… there's no sense in living your life without this. To make the journey and not fall deeply in love, well, you haven't lived life at all.'" I lower to one knee in front of her and open the ring box.

Her hand covers her mouth.

"I knew when you showed up with your bat and pink glove to a boy's baseball game determined to play on the team, you would change my life. I thought baseball was my passion. I was wrong. It's you and building a life with you. You are my passion and obsession, Julianne. Annie, will you be my moonshot?"

"Yes. If you promise to be mine in return."

"Absolutely." I twist my original ring off her finger and replace it with an engagement ring. Rising to my feet, I then lift her into my arms and kiss her deeply. We kiss our way to the back door, lock it, and set the alarm before hustling upstairs to our bed. We tangle our sheets twice before succumbing to the pull of sleep.

CHAPTER THIRTY-ONE

JULIANNE

"Bluebird, are you ready to go?" Colby asks, hovering near the kitchen island.

"Yes. I'm so excited for you."

"I am too."

We're meeting Madeleine in Philly to sign his new contract and look at two places with immediate availability this afternoon. Thankfully, the team is on a road trip. Colby will be joining them for their last fifty games of the season and the playoffs in a few days. I'll be heading back to the school building soon as well. Sadly, the new school year starts in a little over two weeks.

The drive to the complex is smooth. We arrive about twenty minutes early.

"Good morning. How may I direct you?" the gate attendant asks.

"Morning, Steve. I'm here to join the team," Colby answers.

"Welcome, Mr. Somerset. Follow the red line around the stadium to the office entrance. There's ample, secure parking."

"Thank you." As instructed, Colby follows the path and parks. He rounds the car with a stupidly gorgeous smile on his face and opens my door. Moments later, a large, black SUV pulls in a few spots over.

After Madeleine's driver opens her door, she slides to the ground. "Morning, Colby." She turns her attention to me. "Julianne, nice to see you again."

"You as well." I take her extended hand.

The three of us enter the building and are ushered into a conference room. A few minutes later, an older gentleman and a young man who could be his doppelganger join us. "Mr. Somerset, welcome to the team." The older man greets him. My cursory research leads me to believe he's the owner.

"Dad, he hasn't signed anything yet," the younger one adds.

"Always meticulous, Ash. Executing his contract is the reason he's here. Well, that and we need his help behind the plate." He looks toward us. "Please take a seat."

As we sit, the owner greets me and Madeleine while Colby reaches for a pen. With our hands linked beneath the table, Colby signs where Madeleine indicates. After what seems like one hundred pages, he reaches the final one in the stack and scribbles his name.

"Welcome to the organization."

"Thank you, Mr. Lyons. Happy to be here," Colby replies.

"Would you like a tour of your new home?" he offers.

"Yes," he replies, attempting to disguise his glee. I hear it. Madeleine might as well. However, no one else will. Over the next hour, Mr. Lyons leads us through the clubhouse and the training areas. Silence falls over Colby when he steps onto the field.

I pause at the top of the dugout steps to give him a moment alone. He insists I join him at the plate.

"Is this real?" he whispers.

I squeeze his hand tighter. "Yes."

"I owe you an apology."

I frown. "You don't. What do you think you need to apologize for?"

"It took me too long to get us right."

Setting my finger on his lips to quiet him. "No. We got here eventually. I'm crazy proud of you. I love you, Two."

"I love you, almost Julianne Somerset." He kisses me lightly.

"Who said I was changing my name?" I scoff.

"You aren't?"

Containing my laughter is impossible. "Of course I am! I signed my name with yours as far back as sixth grade."

"Phew! Can we get married soon?" he murmurs near my ear. He knows exactly what he's doing to me without a question in my mind.

"As soon as we can get the entire family together is fine with me."

"Does Jordan's bye week work?"

"Yes." It can be as soon as six weeks from now. Can I pull it together that fast?

"Forget the thought in your mind. Whatever it costs to make it happen quickly it costs."

"That will take some time to get used to."

"Perhaps. You can start this afternoon when we look at places to call home for as long as I'm here."

I nod as Madeleine joins us at home plate. "Ready? You have more appointments later today."

Colby acknowledges her.

I glance at the scoreboard and note Colby is listed as the starting catcher with Hatton on the mound in four days. I guide him to look at his name in lights.

"Wow!" Eloquent, babe.

"Yeah. Let's go find a place to live for the next few years."

As we walk out, Madeleine states, "The team will be back later today. You should report tomorrow morning."

"I'll be here, bright and early. There aren't enough words to adequately thank you."

She laughs. "I love this job the most when my clients are in a place to thrive and be happy. I'll see you in a few days."

"See you then." Colby shakes her hand, and she leaves after briefly hugging me.

We grab a snack and hustle to the first townhouse. Our realtor, who was recommended by my brother-in-law, Jake, gave us the lockbox code. Otherwise, we wouldn't be able to tour this one today. The property has three bedrooms and two bathrooms. The floors gleam, and the kitchen is modern. Perfect for Colby. It meets all our requested requirements, including the private patio and off-street parking.

"What do you think?"

"It's nice." It is, but I've never lived in a city before. Even when I worked here for my first job, I commuted to Summit Creek.

"We can live at your house if you hate it," Colby offers.

"I don't. It's a change is all. Let's go see the second one."

Colby takes my hand and leads me to the car.

The second option is closer to the facility and has better highway access for me. It's furnished, which is a huge plus. The kitchen is equal to the first option, but the rooftop patio is exponentially better. There is a fire pit and comfortable furniture. A slice of home in the big city.

Colby wanders down the hall to check out the rest of the room. "Annie." His voice beckons.

I follow the sound down the hall and find him in a library. *Sold!*

"Should we buy this one?"

I smile and jump into his arms. "It pales in comparison to mine. Yes. Let's buy this one."

In a few hours, I learn what it means to have his level of wealth. We have a home in the city with an indemnity agreement and a little finagling. After signing the papers, we pick up a rental until Colby's Range Rover is transported here from Florida. We also shop for some clothes. During the first away series, I'll pack up my necessary items from the house and move them here.

It feels like morning, but it's pitch black in the master bedroom. Also, Colby isn't in bed anymore. Then I recall the blackout blinds built into the windows. I check the clock and note it's slightly before six. It appears after our whirlwind day of buying a home, shopping, and arranging a rental, we collapsed in bed. Shuffling to the kitchen, I find him bare-chested, retrieving a bag from a delivery person.

"Thank you," I overhear and wait for him to join me.

"Coffee?" My voice sounds as if I'm begging for a fix like a fiend.

"Breakfast," he replies after kissing me.

I scowl despite the kiss.

He winks. "Fine, it's both."

"You're the best ever!"

"Don't you forget it, sweetheart." He takes the stool beside me and digs into the goodies from the bag. "Could you get groceries sometime today?"

"Sure. I only plan to be at school for half a day. Anything special you need?"

"You."

I resist rolling my eyes. "You have me, silly. I mean foodwise."

He kisses my temple. "Basics for now, Bluebird. When I need specific ingredients for one of Marta's recipes, we will get it. I'm sure Hatton will ask for a torte. Then I will have to attempt to make it for him. Jack is bringing my supplements and shakes to the game, and I ordered some to be delivered here."

"Okay." We finish the delicious baked goods and dress for work. "Have a great day, Colby."

He smiles and kisses me breathless. "You too, sweetheart. I love you."

"Love you."

After a productive morning and a trip to the grocery store, I return home around three. Once everything is put away, I set out chicken for dinner as my phone chimes with a text.

Two: I'll be home around five.

Me: Perfect. I'll cook. Can't wait to hear about your first day.

Two: Love you.

Me: Love you.

Before I decide against it, I call my mom. There's no answer, so I leave a message. It isn't lost on me that I haven't seen her since Dad died. She claims she isn't ready to visit. Nothing I can do about it. Ironically, she's probably a fifteen-minute drive away now.

"Honey, I'm home." Colby's voice interrupts my thoughts.

I laugh softly and meet him in the foyer. "Hi. How was it?"

Rather than answering me, he hauls me close and kisses me deeply. "Sorry, I've always wanted to do that."

"Do what?"

"Come home from the stadium to you."

"Awww, sweet talker."

"Only for you."

I kiss him again and add, "Dinner will be done in about ten minutes. Please tell me about your day."

A wide, child-like smile graces his gorgeous face. "It was great! My knee feels better than ever. Hatton is on fire. Not sure why Wilson traded him."

I know the details of the trade from a discussion with Colby after he singed his new contract but didn't fully parse them out. My focus was Colby's happiness and continued ability to play. Nothing else. "What's Hatton's take?"

"He asked to be sent here with me," Colby shares.

"Surprising."

Colby shakes his head. "Not really. His agent, Brandon Manheim, is good friends with Madeleine. They worked their magic together. I gather Hatton requested a trade early in the season because he and Bolton couldn't seem to get on the same page."

"Nice. Is Lacey coming up too?"

Colby frowns. "No. They broke up. She can't leave her patients and wasn't willing to do long distance."

"How sad. They were cute together."

"I guess. How can I help with dinner?" he asks.

"It's done and edible," I assure him.

His hearty laughter surrounds me. "How can you be sure?"

"I made your childhood favorite."

He raises an eyebrow. "You made macaroni and cheese and dino nuggies?"

I giggle. "Kind of. I made a grown-up version."

"Sounds perfect! Let's eat," he urges.

"Still always hungry?"

"Pretty much."

After dinner, we settle outside on the patio. I can't see as many stars as at my house, but it's lovely up here.

"Can I ask you a strange question?"

"I'm intrigued, Bluebird. Go ahead."

I wrinkle my nose. "Do you have any pregame rituals I need to know about?"

Colby grins. "None of my rituals will impact you."

"Good," I reply.

"Why?"

"We need to put our mark on this home."

He purses his lips. "I see." Then he climbs over me and devours me for the rest of the night.

CHAPTER THIRTY-TWO

COLBY

With a huge smile on my face, I tiptoe out of our bedroom. Today is so much more than my first game in Philly. It's the first time Annie will be in the stands to see me play. *Little League and high school don't count. At least they don't to me.*

After preparing breakfast and coffee, I change and return with a huge box in hand.

"You need to leave already?"

"Yeah. I feel like it's our first game for the Summit Creek Blue Bandits."

Annie smiles and rubs her eyes. When she sits up, the sheet falls to her waist, reminding me of last night's horizontal adventures. It takes monumental restraint not to reach out and take her again. If she realizes it, she doesn't cover up. I appreciate that immensely.

"A car will pick you up at eleven and bring you to the field. I left a pass to the luxury box on the island and box seats on the first base line tickets as well. You can ride home with me. It'll be a bit longer but worth it."

"Okay. I'm probably going to sit with Jack and Lorelei instead of in the luxury box. I'm crazy proud of you, Two. Have a great game. Love you."

"I figured as much. I'll see you later. I love you." I kiss her, on the brink of my control breaking, and leave the bedroom. A few steps down the hall, I turn back. "Oh, yeah. There's a gift for you on the dressing bench too." I wink and trot out the door. Obtaining gear and a jersey for Annie was a feat. Annie isn't an everyday fan. What I mean is she's my biggest fan and needs a jersey from this team, not my old one, for this game. Not surprisingly, there are a sparse number of cars in the player's lot when I arrive.

I stop at my locker and drag my hand across my name with red letters and head straight to the field. When I reach the dugout, I find Hatton sitting on the bench.

"Morning, old man," he says with amusement.

I laugh, and we fist bump. "You asked to have the 'old man' back, and I'll never forget it."

He shakes his head. "You aren't allowed to retire until I say so."

"You're funny, very funny." I will play as long as my body holds out, and Annie doesn't object to me hanging around her baseball team. Annie has decided to stay on as the baseball coach at Point Academy. Madeleine included a clause in my contract allowing me to help as long as it doesn't interfere with my responsibilities to my team. "I'll meet you in the bullpen in a bit."

Hatton nods and retreats into the clubhouse. I step onto the field and absorb the quiet. The same peace I channel when I'm behind the plate. The irony isn't lost on me. My last game resulted in a significant knee injury and a championship with Hatton on the mound. Tonight will be different. The team is in second place in the division with an outside shot of making it to the playoffs. Returning with Hatton for my first game is great. However, the fact Annie will be here in the stands makes it... perfection.

I trot down the tunnel back to the locker room and find a host of my teammates milling around. There is still a solid hour before we are required to report. Sitting in front of my locker, I sift through my bag and find a small gift box inside.

When did she slip this in here? Intrigued, I tear into the red paper and find a small velvet box from a jewelry store. Before opening it, I note a card as well.

Two,

   I know you wear the mask charm I gave you in high school like I wore my ring. I wanted to add to it today. I love you, Annie.

Inside the box rests a charm of my number, which has been the same since Annie and I were teammates and hers. I add the number eight, for her, and the number two for me. Although I don't do it often, I pull out my phone and text her.

Me: When did you get these?

Bluebird: As soon as I knew you would be playing again this season.

Me: I love them and you. See you later.

Bluebird: Have a great game! I love you.

I tug on my gear and head to the bullpen with Hatton. "Ready for this?"

He grins at me and retorts, "Are you?" He takes his warmup throws and is on point today. Before we join the team for the national anthem, we rehash our pitch strategy for the heart of the order. As the song plays, I search for Annie in the stands. I find Jack, but the seats beside him are empty. As with every game, I thank my teammates and coaches in my head. Today, I add two more people, Jack and Annie. Without Jack, I wouldn't be here, able to catch. Without Annie, I would be pining for the woman of my dreams instead of building a life with her.

Hatton and I bump gloves, and I take my spot behind the plate. Another glance at the stands and I smile when I find Annie beside yet another surprise. My parents and my sister are beside her in the remaining box seats. It has been too long since my family has been to a game, notwithstanding my injury. I'm grateful and shocked they agreed to come. Usually, they insist I don't spend my earnings to get them to my games despite my desire for them to attend more than they do. My parents come when my games are in their state but not any others. Part of me wonders how Annie pulled it off. I ignore the thought and focus on this moment.

I mouth, "Thank you."

Annie smiles and mouths, "I love you."

I reply in kind, kiss the charms on my necklace, and crouch behind the plate. A surreal feeling as well as a twinge of fear passes over me until Hatton delivers his first pitch.

Ball one.

Followed closely by a second. I pump my hands to calm him down and give him the sign for a fastball.

Hatton nods tightly and delivers the first strike of the at bat. He settles in and retires the batter and the next two. We hustle to the dugout and sit on the bench.

"Somerset." The team manager approaches. "Good job calming Hatton down quickly. Both of you are an excellent addition to the team. I have you in the clean-up slot in the batting order today instead of Smolley."

"Okay." I'm intrigued. Smolley has been in a slump lately, but I'm not sure it will sit well with me taking his slot in the order. Can't worry about it right now. While I stew in my head, the leadoff and second batters have reached base. I tug off my gear and wait until I can step into the on-deck circle.

My teammate, Lewis, lines out to the shortstop for the first out of the inning. As he passes, he mutters, "Don't make Coach look like a fool for putting you in Smolley's spot."

Well damn! "I won't." My confidence isn't exactly at the level I portrayed, but I always give every at bat and every pitch my all. Always have. As I walk to the plate, I find Annie again in the stands. When we were younger and teammates, we would fly through our secret handshake before each plate appearance for both of us. Today, I come up with a plan on the fly. With our gazes locked, she places her right fist over her heart while I do the same with my left. We may not be able to make it through the entire handshake, but we would end up with our arms in these positions at the end.

I step into the batter's box and take a pitch.

Ball one.

The second pitch follows closely thereafter.

Ball two.

The hitter in me screams to take the next pitch regardless of where it's placed. However, the veteran catcher in me who knows a fast ball is coming, urges me to swing big.

The pitcher winds up and throws a fastball. Before I can stop myself, I swing for the fences. I run as the ball sails over the short porch in right field. I run along the bases and catch Annie jumping for joy as I cross home plate. My teammates are waiting for me, and we celebrate back to the dugout.

The rest of the game pales in comparison to the bottom of the first inning, but we won, and I'm elated. When I exit the locker room, Madeleine and Cruz are chatting with Annie and the rest of my family.

Annie breaks away from them when she sees me and launches herself into my arms. "In-person is beyond my expectations! Great game!"

"Thanks, Bluebird. Having you here is beyond what I imagined." I walk with Annie wrapped around me toward the group. Setting her down, I shake my father's hand, hug my mother and sister, and greet Jack and Lorelei before I can speak to Madeleine. "Thanks for coming, Madeleine. Hey, Cruz."

"No place I would rather be. While I have clients who are in the entertainment business, I prefer my athlete clients because honestly, their games are much more fun."

"Noted. Where are my manners? Madeleine, these are my parents and sister. You've met Jack. This is his wife, Lorelei. Guys, this is my agent." They exchange pleasantries and chat until Madeleine leaves. Turning to my family, I say, "I can't believe you're here."

"She's quite persuasive," Violet offers and then nudges Annie. My sister continues, "Truly, she called and invited us, and we were free this weekend."

I accept the fact they're here, and Annie made it happen. It appears she will do anything for me, as I will for her.

We linger in the hallway a little longer before exiting the stadium. My arm is curled around Annie's waist as we walk to the car.

"Are you up for dinner?" I ask everyone.

A chorus of "I'm starving" surrounds me.

"Perfect." I pull out my phone and make a reservation at the restaurant Annie and I weren't able to visit when we were here earlier this year.

The remainder of the season passes in a blur. Annie attends every home game she can. It makes for some late evenings for her, but I'm ecstatic having her in the stands. Our record over the remaining fifty games was astounding. We only lost fourteen times. In a unique twist from the baseball gods, Hatton and I are headed to the World Series again.

I have a few requirements this time. Tucker and his mom, the boy I met at the hospital, are sitting in the stands and attended batting practice before the game. Annie will be here to witness a huge win for my new team without me sustaining an injury. She will be here cheering for me as it should've been all along.

EPILOGUE

JULIANNE

FOUR MONTHS LATER

Turning over, I notice Colby has already gotten up for the day. My husband has always been an early bird. We got married on our Little League field a week after their World Series victory and the boisterous celebrations. Our guest list was exactly as we wanted—our families, including the entirety of my extended family. My mother spent our reception, which we held in our backyard, chatting with Jordan, Jill, and their significant others. She decided to split her time at the townhouse in Philly and Summit Creek. Keeping the townhouse allows her to attend home games with me. When Colby retires, she plans to move home permanently. Colby and I wasted no time and tried to grow our family immediately. Based on Jack and Lorelei's experience, we got lucky. Our little bean has increased my need for sleep. It was high before. Now, it's astronomical.

"Bluebird," he whispers when he reenters the room.

"I'm awake, Two." I shift on the bed and sit against the upholstered headboard.

"What is your poison this morning? Decaf or orange juice?" Smells were an issue during my first trimester. He's still cautious despite the sensitivity mostly dissipating. He's flying to Florida to report for spring training. The good news is he can stay in his house, and the commute to the team facility is only forty minutes.

"Both, please."

He sets them on the bedside table and sits beside me. "Lorelei and the baby will be here to spend time with you. Jack is joining us in Florida for spring training."

"Okay."

"Please don't do anything you aren't supposed to do. I need to know you and our little pitcher are safe while I'm away."

"I won't. Colby Jr. will be fine."

My better half laughs heartily. "I already told you, no junior. We need a good strong baseball name for him."

I wave him off. "Fine. I'll think on it some more. Perhaps Colby as a middle name then?"

"I'll consider it. I'll call you as much as I can. I love you." He leans in and kisses me deeply.

"I love you. Make sure you kick Hatton's butt into shape. A repeat World Series victory is waiting."

"From your lips, my love." He kisses my forehead, places his hand on my abdomen, and walks out the door. As I alternate between my coffee and juice, I imagine how the season and our future will pan out.

Colby and Hatton will be All-Stars as his career continues as if he were never injured. I will serve as the baseball coach for Point Academy. I hire an assistant for my second season to support me when our little one arrives. However, my team will fall short in the championship this year without Simonson and Fisher on the rubber.

I smile and set my feet onto the floor and prepare for the day. I smile knowing without question, Colby and I can achieve whatever we set our minds to as long as we're together.

Thank you so much for reading *Moonshot*!

Ready for a new Blackthorne HEA? Is Sawyer next?

Did you love *Moonshot*?

Thank you for taking the time to read it. I hope you loved it!
If you liked this book or another one of my books, please consider posting a review.
A short line or Two will be perfect! It helps indie authors like me get noticed. I appreciate your support and feedback.

COMING SOON

A Blackthorne Security Novel

Protecting Home

MY BOOKS

Protecting Us

Hers to Protect

Protecting Our Family

MATCHMAKERS' BOOK CLUB

For Love & Coffee

For Love & Basketball

For Love & Cookies

All my books in one place: www.nicolevidal.com/books